REBEL BRIDE

CHICAGO PLAYERS

KATE MEADER

PROLOGUE
JUNE

Hatch

"WELCOME ABOARD, HATCHLING!"

I grinned at my dad, thankful that for once he hadn't used his other nickname for me, Dino Boy. Better that people thought less about my conception origin story and more about the aggression I was bringing to the ice.

"Thanks, Dad."

"Eh, it's 'captain' now." My little brother Conor lifted his Diet Coke and brought the straw to his lips. "The guy's not just dad, now he's your freakin' boss."

"True, true." Theo Kershaw—Dad, team captain of the Chicago Rebels, and one of the most legendary defensemen in hockey—nodded sagely before breaking out that smile he had gifted the entire family. That would be me, the eldest, my sister Adeline, twins Conor and Landon, and our baby sister Tilly.

I had recently signed a contract with the Chicago Rebels. While Dad and I had faced off against each other during my time as a power forward with Denver, it was his dream to play professionally on the same team as his son. To be honest, I had resisted efforts by the Rebels to bring me on board. It might be my hometown team, but Chicago was the last place I wanted to be. However, this would probably be *the* Theo Kershaw's last year in the league, and who wouldn't want to be part of that legacy?

My uncle Jason, a defenseman with the Boston Cougars, set another IPA before me.

"J, I haven't even drunk the first one yet."

"Call yourself a hockey player." He pointed at Conor who was eying the three, now four, bottles lined up in front of me at the Empty Net bar in downtown Riverbrook. Located about thirty miles north of Chicago, this was the team's and fans' usual watering hole. "Don't even think it, Connie."

"Me? Why, I've never touched a drop in my life."

That set Jason and me off. Dad was too busy chatting with his co-defenseman on the Rebels, Lars Nyquist, but would probably have found Conor's profession of sobriety just as amusing. A few months shy of drinking age, the kid was a rising senior at the University of Michigan, my alma mater. I knew what college was like, and Conor was no saint. But he was also aware that our family had a certain rep to maintain. Underage drinking in the Net was liable to get him splashed over the pages of that tabloid rag, *Hot Goss.*

Instead he indulged in another vice by turning to the cute blonde at his elbow who had been making eyes with him all night. This gave Jason a chance to lean into me and murmur under his breath, "You okay?"

We'd had this conversation before. "Fine."

"Yeah, but"—he lowered his voice even further—"I know this isn't exactly what you wanted."

Unfortunately, I'd shared that confidence with my uncle after a few too many of those IPAs a while back. I had a good reason for not wanting to join the Rebels, but I had set it aside because this was my dad's dream. Time was running out and I couldn't deny him.

"It'll be fine. If anything, I just need to ignore the media who think I'm getting a spot on the team handed to me on a silver platter." Never mind that I was drafted in the first round to Denver four years ago. Or that my stats the last couple of years with that same team had been as solid as they came. The sports media loved to scream "nepo baby" whenever my name came up. Playing with my dad would be a unique type of pressure cooker, but I could handle it.

As for the real reason this trade wasn't my favorite thing, I would ignore it. I would have to.

"I better hit the head before I make a dent in these." I pointed at the pretty row of IPAs. "Conor, hands off."

My brother grinned and gestured with a nod to the girl beside him. "Got my hands full here, H."

Yep, that kid was going to knock up some chick before he could legally drink.

My journey to the restrooms was like a wade through Chicago streets after a Winter blizzard as I was forced to stop every couple of seconds to accept backslaps and congratulations from fans and future teammates. Near the jukebox, Rebels forward Peyton Bell, aka Dingaling, shoved a shot of bourbon in my hand.

"Dude, you must be psyched to finally be on a good team! Drink up!"

So the Rebels had made it further than Denver in the

playoffs this past season, but that level of shade was, well, shady. Such was the lot of a pro hockey player, though. Chirping was our love language.

I knocked back the shot and got whoops of approval from players Cody "Jakey" Jacobs and Noah "NoBo" Boden. I'd hung with these guys at holiday parties and cookouts, on visits to the practice rink and to locker rooms. They were my dad's crew, and now they were mine. Together, we would make or break Theo Kershaw's final season, and I would be on hand to bear witness. To be a part of history.

The bourbon was warming my stomach and softening my edges. This year would be fucking awesome.

"Kershaw Junior!" Dash Carter shoved Jakey aside and threw his arm around my shoulder. "You here to steal my spot?"

Carter had been three years ahead of me at Michigan, senior to my freshman, so we played together briefly back in the day, sometimes vying for the same position. A trust funder who didn't need to play hockey, he was a decent left-winger yet acted like he could happily give it up any day if he chose. That attitude was only one of the things about him that pissed me off.

"We'll see how Coach wants to play it." Seemed I could throw some shade of my own.

"So you are gunning for me!"

What was I supposed to say? *Don't worry, man, we're not in competition every time that roster is posted?*

"Better watch your back, Carter," Jakey said with a wink at me.

"I'll leave now," I said, "and you guys can bitch about me when I'm gone."

"Starting the text thread now. '*KJ puts C-Dog on notice.*' That's Kershaw Junior."

NoBo shook his phone with a laugh but sent me a look of approval as I walked away. I got the impression Carter wasn't a locker room fave, which pleased me more than it should have. He certainly wasn't a favorite of mine, and it wasn't only because of his smack-talkin' attitude.

Finally, I made it to the hallway where the restrooms were located, but before I could enter, my phone buzzed with a text from Rosie.

> Congrats, friend! Finally where you belong.

That made me smile. Rosie and I had grown up together and were inseparable as kids. I'd pulled her pigtails, she'd kicked me in the nuts, that kind of thing. She and my sister were best friends, currently on a round-the-world trip and lapping up the rays on some Greek island. I kind of wished I was there with them.

> ME
>
> It's a good move.

> ROSIE
>
> It is. This is going to be a great year for the Rebels.

I hoped so. That moment with Carter reminded me that I would have to put my head down, ignore everything happening off the rink, and focus on my game. Nothing else mattered. Not the press, not my imaginary competition with Carter.

Not the woman coming toward me now.

For someone so petite, it constantly surprised me that Summer Landry would have such an outsize impact. After all, she was just another WAG, so I shouldn't have cared that all five foot three inches of girl-next-door, violet-eyed blonde seemed to light up every room or that the sight of her changed the air around me.

Assistant to Rebels GM, Ryder Calloway, she was one of those sunny girls who was friends with everyone. That was probably why I hadn't warmed up to her: she was far too nice for someone like Carter, who treated her like a trophy. And because of that—because I could see her taking the shit he shoveled with a perky smile and an indulgent "oh, Dash!"—I assumed she was your standard gold-digging puck bunny. She met players every day, could get anyone she wanted, so why else would she choose that dick? It certainly wasn't his personality.

Today she wore a peach-pink sundress with thin straps that revealed perfectly rounded shoulders and a hint of cleavage. I had at least a foot on her, and this close, I felt like I was looming over her like a fairytale ogre.

I made to move around her, but she stopped right in the center of the corridor, forcing me to pull up short. In the dim light, she shone like a beacon, and I hated that for this one brief moment, I loved the feeling of being bathed in her glorious, fucking glow.

"Hatch! I haven't had a chance to congratulate you. Welcome to the Rebels!"

"Thanks," I muttered. *Please carry on.*

"You must be psyched to play with your dad. We love him so much. If we could clone him, we would, so maybe you're the next best thing!" She laughed at this incredibly funny joke she'd made.

"I'm not my dad."

Her face fell, thinking she'd offended me. Had she? Not really, but I didn't mind letting her think so. Anything to get away from her.

She grasped my arm. "I'm sorry. I didn't mean that how it came out. I just wanted to—well, you know ..."

"Sure." I inched forward, clueing her in that I needed to pass. Her hand was still on my arm, her fingertips searing my skin, her floral scent curling into my lungs. I had a sudden urge to lift her against the wall and shut her well-meaning mouth with my own.

She dropped her hand.

The madness passed.

"Okay, you take care now," she said as I walked by. The words came out twangy, almost irreverent. Interesting, that. I wouldn't have thought she had that kind of snark in her.

A couple of minutes later, I headed back into the bar, determined to start putting away those IPAs.

I was just in time for the main event. The player group I had passed on my way to the restroom was standing in a circle, wider than before, and as NoBo leaned to one side, I saw why.

Carter was on one knee.

"Babe," he was saying, his dark head turned up, his hand outstretched with the Tiffany-blue box open to reveal a rock the size of a puck. "Will you marry me?"

Jakey's broad back blocked Summer, so I shuffled an inch to my left and fixed my gaze on her face. Two spots of color flagged her cheeks, and she pressed a hand to her chest.

"Dash, I-I can't believe this." She blinked quickly and snatched a breath. It was quite the act.

"C'mon, babe. Just say yes." He pushed the ring toward her, dangling it like a leash, an owner encouraging his puppy to go walkies.

My heart thundered. Maybe she'd have the common

sense to turn him down. Surely, she saw what I did. What everyone did.

He's not good enough for you.

You need a guy who knows your worth. Who will worship the ground beneath your feet and the air above your head.

"Okay, uh, yes?" She let out a nervy tinkle and blinked again.

The crowd roared its approval like Carter had just found the net. The circle around them tightened as the team rushed in to offer the happy couple their congratulations. They were completely surrounded but I caught a fleeting glimpse of Summer's face, her eyes all a-glitter now that she'd won her prize.

Pulse rocketing, I turned away and headed for the bar where the beer bottles celebrating my acquisition were lined up like a row of accusing judges.

As elder statesman and team captain, my father had already moved in to give Carter his best. No sign of Conor, which meant someone was getting lucky. That left my uncle Jason at the bar, watching my approach with a concerned frown.

"You okay?"

"Just fine."

His green eyes, same as my dad's, same as mine, searched my face.

"Seriously, J, it's all good." I eyed the bottles on the bar. I wasn't sure they would be enough, or that there was sufficient alcohol on the planet to blot out what I'd just witnessed. "I'm going to head out."

Jason gripped my shoulder. "Your dad's thrilled you're on the team, Hatch. You've done a good thing."

"I know."

He wanted more, but I didn't have it in me to give it. As I left the bar, a champagne cork pop and a celebratory cheer mocked my exit.

This next year was going to suck.

Summer

"IS THAT ... *A TATTOO?*"

Arabella Carter's shriek pierced my ear drums, but to be fair, my hearing had become attuned to the decibel levels. For the last week, my future mother-in-law had criticized every aspect of the wedding preparation in the highest volume possible.

Nothing I did passed muster. My wedding dress showed too much leg (*who wears a high-low hem beyond the age of six?*), the rehearsal dinner had too many guests (*I'm sure half of these people were not on the list*), the wedding favors of hockey puck Christmas ornaments were too tacky (*in July? And adding a diamond to the center is trying a smidge too hard, isn't it?*), the reception table centerpieces had far too much lilac (*a trashy flower choice*). Even the church was too liberal (*was that a rainbow flag I saw outside?*).

I could go on and on, but then I might sound like Mrs. C.

I longed to shout at her that this was what she was getting. A daughter-in-law from the backwoods of Mississippi, who up until a few years ago had only seen centerpieces in waiting room magazines. If the woman had the slightest inkling such dubious blood was about to contaminate her family tree, she would choke on her Van Cleef double string of pearls.

The Carters had certain expectations about the woman their son would marry. She should be elegant, pleasant, attractive, but most of all, malleable. She should be good at fitting in and not too flirty with his teammates. She should be the perfect wife to a hockey superstar. Not that Dash has reached superstar status with the Chicago Rebels. He was good, with the potential to be great, but I always suspected his non-hockey wealth gave him an excuse not to work as hard as everyone else.

Dash Carter's wife should not be a shack-dwelling swamp child who had lied her way into every good thing she had.

"Summer, you can't show that on your wedding day!"

Mrs. Carter's hand hovered over my bare shoulder, not touching, yet I still felt her disdain dripping on me like the creature's acid saliva in the *Alien* movies. Though she'd never said so aloud, she didn't like my name, which sounded like a snake's hiss on her lips. As if, in trying to speak it, she sensed the truth about me.

Such a liar, Summer. Ain't no one gonna take you for a society princess.

Oh, shut it, Shelby Mae.

My inner voice had become noisier the closer we got to the big day.

In the mirror Mrs. Carter spoke to my reflection, locking her steely gaze with my decidedly less steely one.

"A butterfly?"

A souvenir of my rebellion from Rusty's Tattoo Parlor in Biloxi, inked when I was fifteen, the first time I'd run away. I thought I'd escaped for good, that I wouldn't have to marry Jem Boudreaux. The butterfly was my reward, the symbol of my rebirth.

They found me but I still had the tattoo.

"Her dress will cover it." Rosie Burnett-Moretti was one of my bridesmaids, though not my maid of honor because Dash's mother had insisted that exalted position be taken by Dinah, Dash's sister. Along with Adeline Kershaw, Rosie was the only person I knew in the wedding party. The rest, all cousins of Dash that I had met a couple of days ago for the first time, were chosen by Mrs. Carter.

The old battleaxe sent a disparaging look Rosie's way, evidently concluding that my bridesmaid's full sleeve of colorful ink disqualified her from commenting on the appropriateness of my tiny shoulder tattoo. I didn't think it was the end of the world if it peeked through the gossamer silk bodice, but then I had never been part of a high-society wedding before.

Right now, I wore only the undergarment bustier, panties, and a well-placed towel across my lap. My collarbones poked from my skin like antlers through a tarp. I hated how I looked. Thin, gaunt. Panicked. One of the bridesmaids, Dash's cousin Genevieve—or maybe Geneva— had spilt champagne on the dress, so I had removed it to clean it up. Now it hung a few feet away, almost daring me to daub it with lipstick. Ruin it before it ruined me.

Mrs. Carter tutted. "I'll go see if that make-up girl has concealer."

My unsuspecting cosmetic artist would be seated in the church along with the rest of the four hundred guests. I had wanted something small, but Dash let his mother control the invite list, a concession I made so we could marry in Chicago. (*This should be happening at Stately Wayne Manor!* Joke. The Carters called their ten-bedroom mansion on Cape Cod The Arbor, which made it sound like a retirement home.)

"If we're not doing it on the Cape, at least let her have this, babe," he had reasoned.

So I did. Because I was pliant and malleable, the good girl who did as she was told after years of scratching my way through the dirt.

Things would be better once we were married.

This had been my mantra since we got engaged over a year ago. I'd dated Dash for almost four years prior to the proposal, and up until he asked me to marry him, I had considered our relationship fun and rather unserious. We didn't live together, hadn't even stashed extra toothbrushes or claimed a dresser drawer. Dating a hockey player for that long might look like a monumental commitment, but not for me. Only when I started taking an interest in my career did Dash start taking an interest in me.

Babe, it's time we got down to brass tacks. Marriage, the whole nine yards. You're twenty-five and my mother thinks we should be three years in with a couple of kids by now.

Not the most romantic of viewpoints, but Dash tended to see things in black and white. I still held out hope that he wanted this independently of whatever his family believed. That he wanted us.

At least I had until this morning when I'd come across a printout of his vows. I couldn't resist a peek. Positively lovely, they made my heart go boom and assured me that maybe this could work after all.

Then I re-read them and realized he had left the AI prompt in. *Write my wedding vows with some love shit.*

Love shit, indeed.

With Mrs. Carter gone, I lay my forehead on my arms and took a breather on the vanity. Peeking up, I caught Rosie's concerned gaze in the mirror. "I know, I know."

"Didn't say a word." She placed her warm hands on my shoulders. "Now what can I get you? Tequila? Nunchucks? An Uber ride?"

All of the above ...

I offered a pinned-on smile. "What happened to Adeline?"

"Oh, she's on the phone to Lars, asking him to bring her favorite guitar pick."

Adeline would be singing during the ceremony, a choice not approved by Dash or his mother. I'd insisted on it, a way for me to add a personal stamp to the proceedings.

The rest of the wedding party had left to flirt with the single hockey players, the society princesses going wild with the jocks for the evening. Unlike me, a swamp girl finally nabbing her prince.

I looked at my dress, and the sight of it filled me with a peculiar dread.

"I should probably put it back on?"

Rosie frowned. "Only if you want to."

I hadn't meant that to sound like a question. Of course I wanted to don my dress. How else would I get married?

Sure, wear the dress, Summer. What's one more lie to all these nice people?

Zip it, Shelby Mae!

Rosie squeezed my shoulder. "You know, it's just one

day. Once it's over, you'll be back to normal. Chinese food in sweats, binging Netflix, hanging with the girls. All the stuff you did before you were married."

Not all. There was the honeymoon to get through first in St. Bart's, though it would be less honeymoon and more family vacation. As we would be staying at one of the Carters' many homes, Arabella—sorry, Mrs. Carter—saw it as a perfect opportunity to get to know each other better. Then I would return to life in Chicago, except not to my "low-paying administrative job" as assistant to the general manager at my husband's place of work.

How would it look, the wife of a billionaire hockey star filing folders and doing coffee runs for my franchise? There was also this gem: *I earn millions, babe, and even if I got injured tomorrow, it wouldn't matter because … trust fund!*

Adeline came in, her green gaze troubled.

"Is everything okay?"

"Of course. I just hated having to make Lars turn around with Mabel in the back seat. But he's getting it now."

Mabel was Lars's adorable toddler. "We can wait for him. No one will mind if I'm late."

"He won't be long." Her expression cleared. "So, I saw Dash's mom, giving off Mrs. Danvers energy."

"She's searching out concealer for this monstrosity." Rosie grinned and gestured to my tattoo. "We're just about to put the dress back on."

Time to make this real. Accept my fate.

The girls helped me into the Sadie Yates A-line wedding dress with a tight-fitting V-shaped bodice, sleeveless but with wide enough straps that my tattoo was concealed. (*See, Mrs. C?*) Crafted from silk satin, the skirt featured delicate pleats and an asymmetrical cut that showed off my legs. I thought it charming and modern.

As for Mrs. Carter ... well, she had sent numerous photos of princess gowns with voluminous fabric and multiple tiers, had even wanted Vera Wang to custom design a dress because off-the-rack was for "the rudely aspiring middle class." I had insisted on a dress by Sadie. The funky designer was married to Gunnar Bond, a former Rebels player, and her playful fifties-era and rockabilly style spoke to me.

"Oh, wow!" Adeline touched her collarbones and looked a little weepy, even though she'd seen me in the dress once today. "You look so beautiful, Summer."

I blinked at my reflection. The dress was lovely, the make-up on point, my blonde hair perfectly styled and flowing down my back.

"Now, the veil." Rosie pinned it in place. Suddenly conscious of a need to get this over with, I stepped into the Jimmy Choo satin pumps. It was almost showtime and I couldn't delay any longer.

And why on earth would you want to—

Not now, Shelby Mae!

"Absolutely gorgeous." Rosie stood back to let me fill the mirror's entire reflection. It was me and it wasn't. The girl I was and the woman I was trying to become. Successful, accepted, important.

I gave up my job.

Working as assistant to Ryder Calloway, the Chicago Rebels general manager, I had been learning the ins and outs of the franchise. It wasn't all filing and coffee runs. But Dash was right. It was one thing for the girlfriend of a player to support herself this way, but keeping the position once married was just greedy. There were plenty of women who needed a job like that, who harbored ambitions to learn the business of high-stakes professional hockey. I might have been one of them once, but not anymore.

I would be Dash Carter's wife.

I shook myself back to my new reality.

"I think I'll call Lars again," Adeline said. "See how close he is."

With a nervous smile, she stepped outside, leaving me with Rosie, who regarded me with a curious expression.

"Sure you're okay?"

"Just jitters. Normal, right?"

"Definitely. But ..."

"But what?"

She shrugged. "You've gone awfully quiet. The closer we get to lift-off, the quieter you've become."

I gave up my job.

After today, I would spend two weeks with Dash's family on an inescapable island, then I would return to a life I wasn't prepared for. Society princess. Player wife. Stay at home—*don't even think it.* Not yet.

"I-I'm fine. Just think I should potty one more time." I probably should have thought of that before I put the dress on.

"Okay, need help in there? I could probably stand to the side and hold the skirt, as awkward as that sounds."

"Oh, I'm fine!" I picked up my phone and placed it in the hidden pocket Sadie had sewn into the gown. The heels felt a little wobbly but nothing I couldn't handle.

Inside the restroom, my fingers went instinctively to the rectangle of plastic wrapped in paper, secreted inside my bustier. My momma's words came back to me, both counsel and warning.

You ain't got boobs big enough for a comfy bra, hun. But

there's always room for a GOOD-lite. Make sure you got one, no matter the situation.

Pretty much the only decent advice she ever gave me.

A streak of sunlight from the window above the trash can lit up my GOOD-lite as I took it out. A one-hundred-dollar bill wrapped around my driver's license and my ATM card. Most people had more practical necessities for the equivalent of a go bag: a first-aid kit, a multi-tool knife, a decent supply of cash, even a passport. From the age of sixteen, I carried my survival kit, minimalist as it was, on me at all times.

<u>G</u>et <u>O</u>ut <u>O</u>f <u>D</u>odge. GOOD-lite.

So much for spine and gumption, earned from my scrappy journey to this point. I gave up my job. I caved to Dash's demand without much of a fight. I could have managed the rest—Dash's family, his occasional self-centeredness, even the lies I had to tell to get here, but my job? Anger rose, swift and sharp. That job meant the world to me, maybe more than my fiancé. He hadn't even questioned when I said my family was dead and I wanted no one from my childhood at the wedding.

He didn't want to know, and I didn't want to tell him. Now here we were, setting sail on a new life with nothing but secrets and resentment to steer us.

I can't do this.

Time to GOOD the hell out of here.

CHAPTER TWO

The Chicago Rebels bosses are keeping the roster plans for the upcoming season on the down low, though sources tell us that the franchise has definitely offered legendary defenseman Theo Kershaw a one-year contract renewal after he indicated he might be willing to forego his planned retirement for another season. Kershaw had hoped to go out on a high but was denied in a Game 7 Finals heartbreaker last month. Does the Rebels lynchpin have the legs and will to stick around for one more year? And will the franchise keep Hatch Kershaw on its books after his, frankly, disappointing maiden season with his father's team? The novelty and popularity of a father-and-son duo on the Rebels roster might have to give way to reality.
- @RebelsInsider

Hatch

. . .

GROOMSMAN BY DEFAULT wasn't a very promising start to a marriage.

Not that my "friendship" with the groom said anything substantial about his impending nuptials, but it did say something about him. Dash Carter and I had not become particularly close in the last year. I didn't even want to be in his wedding party, but he'd pissed off someone and a spot opened.

It would've been churlish to refuse. The guy was a teammate, and professional hockey franchises tended to operate better when the players got along. No one wanted a repeat of the drama of last season when my dad and his partner on the defensive line demonstrated that there were limits to team friendships.

Nyquist's nose wasn't the only thing fractured.

They made up, but games were lost in the process. The team dynamic was upended and all because of what? A woman. Worse, my sister. These days Nyquist and Adeline were sickeningly in love, he and my dad were pals again, and the Rebels had made it to the Finals. Winning the whole shebang would have been the perfect send-off for my father, but alas, it wasn't meant to be.

Sometimes I wondered how much his blow-up with Nyquist contributed to our failure at the last hurdle. By the time the Finals rolled around, they were back to being the Defense Dream Team, but had that breakdown in the earlier part of the season taken its toll? I'd rather think that than reckon with my own mistakes. How I flubbed the shot that could have won Game 7.

I checked my phone. Ten minutes to go. Groomsmen were supposed to dawdle at the church entrance, handing out programs and directing people to their seats. I'd told my teammate and fellow wedding party member, Peyton Bell, that I needed to slip away for a moment, so here I was, back against the wall below the church's gable as I scrolled through the hockey news. The muggy July air was making my underarms damp, or maybe it was the post-playoffs sports gossip. More of the same flashed from the screen, some sports journo making digs at me because I was Theo Kershaw's son, and how I'd only made the team because the legend wanted to play with me before he retired.

This summer my dad would consider whether he wanted to stay with the Rebels.

While I would consider how best to leave them.

"What are you doing skulking out here?"

I lifted my gaze to our tender, Noah Boden.

"The church is still filling up. Figured I'd get some air before the show starts."

NoBo smirked. "Kind of weird that Carter put you in."

"That's what happens when you fuck off one too many people, and your mom demands you have an even number on both sides."

"Yeah, he's kind of a momma's boy, that's for sure." Words you rarely heard uttered about a hockey player. "Thought you were going to crack his head at the bachelor party."

"I said I'd be a groomsman. Didn't think I had to attend the groom's bridal shower."

But NoBo wasn't referring to my reluctant attendance. I had no problem hanging with the guys in social situations, getting into rowdy messes, and waking up with killer hangovers. I just didn't enjoy the forced camaraderie of a bachelor party—and I didn't need to bear witness to the groom's bad behavior as he slobbered all over the hired stripper. Just seeing him play the asshole I knew him to be had me itching to beat him to a pulp.

NoBo laughed. "I don't think I've ever thrown up so much. Carter's looking a little green around the gills in there, though it was two nights ago. But he drank a ton at the rehearsal dinner, too. Poor Summer won't have much of a wedding night."

Yeah, poor Summer.

The thought of standing there, watching her slow-walk down the aisle, was starting to piss me off, so I changed the subject, which I usually did whenever Carter's fiancée was mentioned.

"You bring a date or are all the strippers taking naps around about now?"

We chitchatted for a while, but eventually NoBo looked at his Rolex.

"You coming?"

"Soon. See you in there."

I checked my phone. Five minutes to lift off, so I really should head inside. Pin on a smile and show the world I'm a good teammate. I took a step toward the front courtyard, but didn't get far as my attention was snagged by a noise behind me.

Someone was opening a window.

A shoe emerged above the frame. A white high-heeled shoe with tiny pearls dotting the strap. Inside the shoe was a tiny foot with a shapely ankle giving way to the pale curve of a calf. If I hadn't been standing there, I didn't think I'd have believed what came next.

The sight gave new meaning to "Here Comes the Bride."

She straddled the sill, her veiled head bent so she could clear the top of the frame. With each jerked movement, my pulse rate notched a few beats higher. She seemed completely unaware of my presence, or of the fact she was a good six feet off the ground.

She recognized both problems in the same instant, and two seconds later, the fact that one of those problems could be solved by the other.

"A little help here?"

I looked up.

She looked down.

"The church is the other way," I said.

"Well, I know that, don't I?" She sounded different, more … country. Of course, she barely spoke to me, and I usually avoided her like the plague, so I probably hadn't picked up on that before.

This should have been my cue to ask her why she was choosing to leave the church by a side window instead of through a door like a normal person. Either way, she appeared to be hightailing it out of her wedding.

I wasn't the hero of this tale, so I made no move to help her.

At which point she jumped.

Summer Landry, all five foot three inches and 110 pounds even with a shit-ton of bridal fabric, landed on my chest, a hard-core check that took me down.

"Oh God, Hatch, are you okay?"

She stared down at me with those violet-blue eyes, her blonde hair falling like a wispy waterfall over my face. Splashes of color washed her cheeks, blushing through her bridal make-up. Her rouged lips parted in concern.

But not so much that she thought to climb off me. No, she remained where she was, her dress ridden up as she straddled me. All I could feel was the heat of her against my stomach. That, and the pain in my hip where it had hit the ground as I collapsed to break her fall.

"Maybe get off me so I can see."

"Oh, right!" She clambered to her feet, pulling her dress down but not before I caught sight of her thigh, gift-wrapped with a garter. The bodice of the dress had slipped a little, giving hints of tempting cleavage while the floral garland holding the veil had been knocked askew.

She offered her hand. I ignored it and scrambled to a stand, mentally checking my body for injury. Other than what would likely be a bruise to my hip, I was in good shape.

My mind, however, was still reeling from what had just occurred.

A million questions duked it out, and the winner was, "Are you hurt?" I might have taken the brunt of that fall, but it didn't mean she hadn't sustained an injury.

"No, I-I'm fine." She chewed on her lip, stepped forward, and looked around for the shoe she'd lost in her unorthodox exit.

Spotting it a few feet off, I moved to retrieve it. Before I could hand it off, she closed the gap and grasped my arm.

"I need your help."

"I've got your shoe right here." Though I knew that wasn't what she meant.

"Hatch, I'm not getting married today."

CHAPTER THREE

HATCH KERSHAW WAS the last person I expected to see as I made my great escape.

With one foot over the window sill, I'd asked for his help, and he ignored me. Just stood there, hands fisted on hips, looking every inch the hockey god in his tux. He didn't like me—never had—but he was Theo Kershaw's son, and I suspected a vein of decency within him that wouldn't allow me to fall without some attempt to catch me.

His dark, wavy hair caught glints of sunlight, giving it copper tones. Perfectly bladed cheekbones angled down to meet full lips, almost too sensuous for a man. But his eyes were the real stars of the show. Like his sister Adeline, his were a jewel green with dark gold glints. Unlike her, those eyes had always held nothing but contempt for me, where the not-so-secret message was "I hate you, Summer Landry, and you'll never know why."

He held my shoe in one hand, and something about his demeanor told me I might have to bargain for it. Finally, he spoke. "What did you say?"

"I'm not getting married today."

His dark brows slammed together, not, I suspected, in confusion, but in annoyance. Of course, the last thing he wanted to deal with was a bride who had changed her mind. I considered how far I'd have to walk to catch a taxi. I could call an Uber, but even then, I'd need to wait somewhere inconspicuous—namely, far from this church.

In a day of wild notions, I felt another one taking root. Hatch Kershaw despised me. Time to see how much.

"Could you give me a ride?"

"You're actually leaving Carter?" The full import of what I was doing had finally reached his puck-battered brain.

"Like I said, I'm not getting married today." I spoke a little slower and enunciated each word.

His eyes narrowed, that gorgeous green gaze darkening in suspicion. "What's going on here?"

Good grief, did he think I was pranking him? How many brides had he seen make their escape through a church bathroom window?

"What are you not getting? I need to leave." I looked over his shoulder, expecting Mrs. Carter to appear any moment in a plume of Sulphur-accented smoke. "I told them I needed a moment in the bathroom, and now that moment has stretched from wedding day jitters to bride's prerogative to holy-shit-this-ain't-happenin'.'"

Hatch glowered, and I was reminded that (a) my accent had slipped there, which inevitably occurred when I was stressed, and (b) this man was the worst person I could have landed on when I scrambled out that window.

"Oh, never mind!" I took a step around him, which was enough to remind me that I was toting one heel, a wedding dress, and an ever-increasing sense of dread about what I had just done. Maybe it wasn't too late to change my mind. I would need a hike up and back through the window or I could call Rosie to meet me at a side door. All the reasons I had for going a little mad could be dealt with. AI vows ... the worst in-laws on the planet ... I gave up my job ...

Sure, go back in there and lie your pretty little head off, Summer.

Screw you, Shelby Mae.

I turned back and gestured for the shoe he was still holding hostage. But instead of that, he delivered something unexpected.

His hand.

He wrapped it around mine, gave a gentle tug, and said, "Let's go."

IF THIS WAS a fairytale or a rom-com, I would have bundled myself and my wedding dress into the front seat of a convertible and driven out of that parking lot to the tune of George Michael's "Freedom." My veil would have been whipped off my head by the wind, the perfect symbol to my new-found liberation. No more Mrs. Carter and her micro-management of everything, no more snooty, snarky comments from Dash's awful family, and no more playing the little woman to my superstar fiancé.

But this wasn't a fairytale. This was my life, and I'd just fucked it up.

They would come looking for me. The wedding cost a fortune, more money than I'd ever dreamed possible for a girl's big day, and I had not upheld my end of the bargain. Dash would be pissed, and then he would be persuasive. After all, I'd cozied my cold feet against his warm ones several times over the last year and he'd always managed to allay my doubts.

It's just nerves, babe.

You know this is meant to be.

Four years together. That's a long time.

Hearing Dash talk about the "sunk costs" of our relationship had assured me he was right. I was an investment, both Dash in me, and me in myself. I had emerged from my sorry background, pulled up my knee-highs, and found a man worthy of the new me. I had a job I loved (once), friends I enjoyed (who knew zilch about me), a life I'd built from nothing (through blood, sweat, and lies), and this wedding was supposed to be the topper on that delicious cake I'd baked.

Turned out I'd used too much salt.

"Where to?"

Hatch had released my hand to open the passenger side door of his SUV, and now he stood with his hand on the open door, looking down on me. Familiar, that look. Still didn't like me, though I was hard-pressed to know why. I suspected he saw right through me. Knew me for the impostor I was.

"I-I'm not sure."

"Changed your mind, have you?"

Those sensuous lips curled in a sneer. It was hard to believe he was the son of the beloved captain of the Chicago Rebels. He looked like him, but in temperament they were so different. Where Theo was cheerful and sunny, Hatch was broody and closed off. Or maybe that was just with me.

Something about his attitude rankled. He didn't like me,

but he wasn't a fan of Dash either. I thought Hatch would have liked if I returned to that church, leaving behind this fossilized evidence of my bad behavior, information he could lord over me.

"Can we just leave?"

"Fine."

He slammed the door, catching my dress in it, but I didn't care. It was so representative of my life right now. I unpocketed my phone and sent a text to Dash:

> Please forgive me. I can't do this.

Then I switched it off. Once in the car, Hatch turned, dipped his gaze quickly to the phone, then back to me.

"You sure?"

"I am."

With a curt nod, he peeled out of the parking lot space and headed for the street. In the rearview mirror, I spied Peyton Bell, one of Dash's groomsmen, at the church entrance. Had he seen me? Would he recognize Hatch's car? Did people already know what I'd done?

So much for fearlessly embracing my new path. Coward that I was, I ducked my head.

CHAPTER FOUR

Hatch

EVEN IN DISTRESS, the bride looked beautiful.

Brides always looked beautiful though, right? I couldn't recall an ugly bride, so my conclusion about Summer's appearance wasn't really all that startling. Or maybe I liked that she looked upset. She should be after what she'd done.

None of which explained why I was helping her.

This woman had just jilted a teammate, and I assumed she had not done it to his face, judging by her scrambled exit from a church's side window. My initial instinct to help a woman in need was now giving way to annoyance that she'd placed me in this position. My team should always come first, and even if Carter was a jerk, he didn't deserve to be humiliated like this on his wedding day.

"I'll drop you at home."

Her gaze snapped to mine, and she bit her lip, which accounted for that bruised fruit look.

"No. Dash will find me there."

"Right now, he's being comforted by his friends and family and is probably halfway to getting hammered. He's not likely to be chasing you down."

"And you're sure of this?"

"It's what I'd do if the woman I was about to marry lost her nerve and jilted me at the altar."

"I didn't lose my nerve."

"Ah, so you *planned* the poor guy's destruction on his wedding day."

I took the corner into downtown Riverbrook where Dash and Summer lived.

"It wasn't planned! I just knew I couldn't do it. I couldn't—"

"Yep, you said. You more than said. You actually did it. Left the guy in front of everyone he knows."

She glared at me. "Stop the car."

"We're almost there."

"Stop the car!"

I pulled over, just past the gates to Founders' Park. She yanked at the passenger door handle. It took her a couple of tries to get it open.

"Seriously?"

She held up a hand. "Thank you kindly for the ride. I'll make my own way from here."

Thank you kindly? "We're just a couple of blocks—"

She slammed the door. Through the window, I watched her lean on the hood of the car while she adjusted the strap of her shoe, dipping her body so the dark valley between her breasts was exposed. Then she smoothed the dress and without a glance in my direction, headed back the way we'd come. Was she planning to return to the church?

While I did not approve of her actions today, I could not

in any shape or form condone *that*. No way in hell was she going back to him after what she'd done. Giving everyone whiplash because she couldn't make up her mind.

I exited the car and caught up with her. "Where are you going?"

"None of your business."

"Back to Carter?"

She stopped. Turned. Delivered a look of such pure hatred I felt my balls shrivel.

"You really think the worst of me, don't you?"

Her lipstick had smudged, her mascara made her look like a miserable panda, and the bodice had slipped again, revealing another sliver of creamy skin.

"I don't think anything."

"Liar."

Guess I wasn't winning any acting awards.

She lifted her dress, though it was one of those that was short at the front and long at the back and didn't touch the ground or need lifting. Instead of walking straight down the street, she hooked a left into the park.

I gave her a short head start, then followed until she took a seat on one of the benches facing the pond. It was peaceful here. A few people strolled the path on the other side while over here a couple of ducks playfully skirted the edge of the water near the rushes.

I approached. "Mind if I sit?"

"It's a free country."

I took a seat at the end of the bench. "If you can't go to your apartment then where were you planning to go?"

"I-I don't know. I just need to get out of here. Out of the city. I need time to think without all *that*." She waved at some point behind her, then slid a look my way. "You've never made a bad decision in your life, have you?"

"Everyone's made bad decisions. You don't have a monopoly on that."

"Okay, tell me one."

"A bad decision?"

"Yes. Tell me something you've done that you regret."

"I screwed up a pass to Cody Jacobs my first time out on the Rebels and the Motors scored a goal." I'd rather recall that than the game-losing error I'd made in the last game of the Finals.

Her expression was withering. "A game mistake? That's the worst you can think of?"

The worst thing I could think of was not for her ears.

"So what's *your* worst decision? Backing out of marrying Carter?"

She scoffed. "Backing *into* marrying him. That's what it felt like. Being backed into a corner. Trapped into this life I thought I wanted. My reward for working so hard."

Even gold diggers felt like they worked their way to the top. Carter always treated her like a trophy, and she had put up with it. It was the price she was willing to pay to be married to a dick and now she was experiencing buyer's remorse. Was I supposed to feel sorry for her?

"So you're out of it. It sucks but you can move on."

"Like that's possible. I don't even have my job!"

"Why not?"

"It doesn't matter," she said sullenly. It was kind of fascinating to see a bad-tempered Summer. She was usually all glitter and unicorns, a total Miss Sunshine, not that I'd ever bought it.

My guess was that Carter encouraged her to quit. He made a tidy sum playing hockey, but the family billions were the true jackpot. No way would the heir to the Dominion Hotel Group want his wife working in the front office for his team. He probably expected her to stay home, nesting and keeping house.

If I had billions, would I expect my wife to play Susie Homemaker and prep for the passel of kids I'd fill her with? I like to think I'd be open-minded enough to let any wife of mine choose her own path. But the partner of a hockey player often had their life circumscribed in ways partners of civilians did not. The threat of trade was ever present, and a trade upended a family. It was hard for a spouse to build a career that was location-dependent when their husband's took precedence. That might have sounded harsh, but it was the reality of a pro-hockey athlete's life.

"Seems like the least of your worries. You're going to have to talk to Carter sometime."

"Not now." She stood, grasping her skirt, and headed over to the edge of the pond. For a second I thought she might hurl herself into the water, but then she pulled out something from a hidden pocket at the side of her dress. A moment later, the pond's surface was dotted with pieces of cracker. Momma Duck and her two babies attacked.

I moved forward to stand beside her. "You just happened to have crackers?"

"Rosie gave them to me because I barely ate anything for breakfast. Told me to nibble on them, but I think these little guys need them more."

Something shifted in my chest. Rosie was one of my closest friends and she'd already texted asking me where I was. My absence from the church had been noted.

What *I* had noted was that Summer was thin. Too thin. Like she needed those crackers. Maybe it was a bride thing, losing weight to fit in your dress, but I suspected more. Over the last few months while we skated our asses off to get to the Finals, Summer had always looked drawn and tired, even during the post-game celebrations.

I might not like her much, but I hadn't enjoyed seeing that. She was supposed to be happy and healthy, gearing up for her big day and thrilled at her man making it so far in the playoffs.

"What do you want to do, Summer?"

She startled at my gentler tone. "That's the first time you've said my name to my face. Not just today, but ever."

I doubted that was true, but I was in no mood to argue with her.

"Next steps?"

"I just want to get away from here. I can't face them. Any of them."

"What about your family?" Come to think of it, I hadn't seen anyone from the bride's family at the rehearsal dinner.

She shook her head, her eyes welling with tears. If I were a gentleman, I would have taken her in my arms, folded her skinny frame up tight, and comforted her as best I could.

But I wasn't a gentleman, not where Summer Landry was concerned.

Instead, I said the dumbest thing I could think of:

"I've got somewhere you can hole up for a while."

CHAPTER FIVE

Dash Carter in "Jilted at the Altar" Shocker!

In a stunning turn, guests at the wedding of Chicago Rebels forward, Dash Carter, the Dominion Hotel Group heir, were shocked to learn that the nuptials were cancelled—and the bride, Summer Landry, was nowhere to be found. Dash's best man, Saxon Carter the Third, made the announcement to the congregation of four hundred at St. Martin's Episcopal Church in Riverbrook, just a few miles north of Chicago.

"Apparently she left without a word, not even to Dash," Zara Jacobs, wife of Rebels center, Cody Jacobs, observed. "No one saw it coming." Peyton Bell, Rebels forward and one of the groomsmen, reported that the couple had always seemed very happy, though they had broken up several times in the early days of their courtship. "But each time, they found their way back to each other. They were

perfect together." One guest, who asked to remain anonymous, commented, "No one would ever have thought Summer capable of this. She always seemed like such a nice girl."

It looks like there's more to the runaway bride than meets the eye. Get ready for a "summer" of Rebels drama, or as we like to call it in the Hot Goss bullpen, R-Drama. We'll be bringing you the tea as it's poured!
-@HotGoss

Summer

I AWOKE with a jolt to find we were still driving. Time had passed, though I couldn't tell how much. The sky looked different, more muted, signifying that it was later in the afternoon. On one side of the road were pretty ranch-style houses, on the other a large body of sparkling water.

Up ahead a yellow road sign came into view, splashed with an artists' paint palette in the upper-right corner.

Welcome to Saugatuck, Michigan
Birthplace of NHL Legend, Theo Kershaw

"Saugatuck?"

I turned to find Hatch staring straight ahead, and the movement made me realize that not only had I curled in on myself like a snail but that I was covered with a jacket.

His jacket.

When had he done that? Had we stopped already, and I slept through this small act of kindness?

More likely, he'd covered me up because my wedding dress was too stark a reminder of my crime.

He hadn't answered, so I repeated to his stone-faced profile, "Saugatuck, Michigan?"

"The very one. The perfect summer vacation spot."

There was no missing that sarcastic tone. *Exactly what I needed*, he was saying in his uniquely passive-aggressive manner. *A summer vacation.*

He had promised me a safe house. I had assumed he meant his condo in Riverbrook. Instead he had driven a couple of hours out of the city.

Maybe I should have asked more questions, but the moment he said he had a place to bring me, I had jumped at the idea. For all my panic at my life being taken over by Dash and his family, at my decisions being no longer my own, in that moment I craved someone else to take control. I'd handed it over without a care because strangely I trusted Hatch to keep me safe. If I went back to Dash's place, I would never feel safe again.

Away from the city, I could catch my breath, figure out next steps. Maybe even call Dash and explain my actions.

Oh, sweet Summer, you can't possibly be that stupid, can you?

Shelby Mae, butt out!

I had hurt Dash, that was a certainty, but he had hurt me first. Three nights ago, I'd overheard him talking to his momma.

"She's not the most polished of girls, darling. I swear she had no idea which was the salad fork."

Dash sighed. "Mom, who cares which fork she uses for

the Waldorf? It's disgusting anyway. I hate celery and walnuts."

My heart had cheered his defense of his bride, albeit through the language of salad, until his next words chilled me to the bone.

"You'll hardly ever see her anyway. She'll be too busy once I get her pregnant."

Oddly enough, Dash made fun of my supposed baby fever. It didn't exist, but whenever I'd showed interest in any baby, such as Lars Nyquist's daughter Mabel, Dash acted like I was dying to have one. I had said I'd prefer to wait, and he'd rolled his eyes and murmured, "sure, babe." Now I questioned his strategy—was it just a ruse to pretend disinterest, so I would let my guard down?

"I'll get Rosa on retainer," Mrs. Carter said. "We'll want to make sure any offspring has the right nanny. If we can't control half the nature, we can control one hundred percent of the nurture."

Rosa was Dash's nanny up until he turned fourteen, though why he needed a nanny for that long, I had no idea. These people were already planning the childcare for my unborn children.

I'd brushed it off, resolving to discuss it with Dash later. But we never got the chance. Wedding preparation kicked into high gear, and we were too exhausted from socializing and entertaining his family to have a single moment alone. And what would I say? I'd already capitulated to the Carter Grand Plan when I gave up my job.

I pulled myself back to the present where Hatch was driving us through the postcard-pretty town of Saugatuck, filled with galleries, fudge shops, ice-cream parlors, and high-end boutiques. I half-expected him to wave to Leslie Knope heading into the Pawnee diner for a waffle brunch or salute Lorelai grabbing a coffee in Stars Hollow. But then I realized he wouldn't want anyone to know about the shameful package he was smuggling in. I caught my hollow-eyed look in the mirror—I was still wearing my veil. I grasped it, tearing it away from my head with such vehemence it stung my scalp.

Hatch remained silent throughout my Tony-worthy performance.

Five minutes after driving through the town, we turned into a graveled driveway and stopped outside a large Crafts-man-style house, painted alabaster white and slate blue.

"Is this your place?"

"My family's. Well, Aurora, my great-grandmother, but she signed it over to me and my siblings. We own it jointly."

"And I can stay the night here?"

He frowned. "It sounded like you needed to get away from everything. No one will know you're here unless you want them to."

What a relief. I handed his jacket back to him. "Trying to cover up the evidence?"

"You were shivering. I didn't even have the AC on."

I tended to get cold easily. Dash hated that I was forced to bundle up, even in summer. He wanted to see my skin because it was an expectation of being a hockey player's girlfriend, I supposed.

"Thank you."

"Sure." He stepped out of the car with his jacket. He didn't put it back on, and I got a glimpse of his strong back muscles straining against the crisp white shirt. The one he wore because he was part of my fiancé's wedding party.

What had I done?

Shelby Mae, for once, was silent.

I slipped on my shoes and exited the car. Hatch was

already at the front door, opening it with a key he found under a stone frog. Such a cliché, but then everything about the Kershaw family was cozily cliché, from their perfect family dynamics to their media-friendly story. They weren't as wealthy as Dash's family, but they were rich in vibes.

Hatch looked over his shoulder to see me hesitating on the threshold, a vampire, waiting to be invited inside. That's what I had been doing my entire life, and each new situation hurtled me back to that worldview. I had to reset, recalibrate, reinvent myself at every turn.

Here I was again, starting over. No job, no fiancé, no clue about what came next. Just trashy little Shelby Mae looking for a toehold on the rock face.

Hatch stared, his gaze dipping over my body. Probably wondering why he'd made this damn fool decision.

"You coming in?"

I nodded. "Lead the way."

THE INSIDE WAS AS BLESSED in appearance as the outside. A large, but not too large, great room with cozy furniture in a combination of navies and creams. An inviting stone fireplace, the mantel covered in family photos. This was a well-loved and lived in home, and I was instantly charmed.

Tiredness hit me like a Zamboni crashing into the plexi. I wanted to sit in one of the gingham-checked armchairs or lie flat on the velvet-tufted sectional, but I was still in my wedding dress, still wearing my clown make-up, still trussed up like a bridal turkey.

"You want to freshen up?"

Every time I thought of an obstacle, Hatch anticipated my need. It was one of his great strengths on the ice, how he knew what the opposition was about to do. It was almost eerie how often a player would move one way and find Hatch already bearing down, ready to steal the puck off his blade.

Now he was doing it again. Good thing I had nothing worth stealing, not even my pride.

"If you don't mind."

"There's a bathroom on this floor but maybe you want to shower and change in the bigger one upstairs?"

At my nod, he led the way. I followed, feeling weary, but not so much I didn't notice how good his ass looked in those tuxedo suit pants. The guys always rocked Euro supermodel in their game day suits but my eyes had never strayed to any ass other than my future husband's.

One jilted groom later, and you're already lookin'? I guess blood will out.

Oh, she's back!

"This is Aurora's room and en suite." He gestured to what looked like a master bedroom. "There should be towels and everything you need in there."

"Thank you. You didn't have to do this."

He looked like he wanted to say something but bit back the words.

I took a breath. "I know I've been asking nothing but favors from you, but I have one more."

Still silent.

I turned my back and peeked over my shoulder. "I need help undoing my bustier. It has a ton of little hooks I can't reach."

He didn't move. Just stood there like a statue or a particularly gloomy gargoyle. For a second, I worried he hadn't heard me, but just as I was about to repeat my request, he moved forward.

His fingers brushed my skin above the zipper.

I shivered.

He didn't apologize for cold hands, probably because they weren't cold. We both knew why I shivered as that electricity zinged through me. The scrape of the dress's zipper sounded foreign. Forbidden. This would have been my husband's privilege, yet here I was asking a stranger to undress me on what should have been my wedding night.

With the back of my bustier revealed, I insisted that this was a necessary evil. How else could I get undressed?

His breath felt hot against my neck.

"You just need to—"

"I know what to do." His voice sounded strained. God, he really did not like me.

There had to be about twenty hooks, and each one took an eternity. But with each successive unfastening, I felt a corresponding shift in my chest. Liberation. Freedom from the past five years.

With the last hook undone, I pressed the loose undergarment to my chest and turned to thank him. His expression was pained, the awfulness of this experience plain to see.

"I'm-I'm sorry I had to ask you to do that."

His troubled gaze clouded over, immediately replaced with familiar contempt.

"Anything else?" He may as well have tacked on, "your highness."

"No, that's it. Thank you."

He left the room, closing the door behind him and leaving me disheveled and doubt ridden. As each piece of the wedding get-up dropped to the floor, I tried to see it as a positive. A fresh start. But a dress in a puddle didn't look fresh. It looked soiled. Finally, I removed my engagement ring, an oval cut diamond in a nested jeweled setting. I'd always thought it ostentatious, but Dash said he wanted everyone to know I belonged to him.

In the bathroom, I stripped quickly from my underwear. I unpinned my hair, stepped into the shower, and scrubbed until my skin turned raw and the water ran cold.

Drying myself, I studied my reflection in the mirror. I had lost so much weight this past six months, initially because I wanted to look good on my wedding day. But I realized now that a lot of it was worry about the commitment I was about to make. Wrapping my skin-and-bone frame in a fluffy towel, I opened the door to the bedroom. My wedding dress still lay in a heap but now there were spare clothes on the bed.

Hatch Kershaw anticipating my needs once again.

CHAPTER SIX

Hatch

I MUST HAVE BEEN out of my mind.

What was I thinking taking Summer here of all places? So I'd planned to head here after the ceremony, even had a suitcase in the trunk. Probably poor form not to attend the reception but I would have done my duty. I was looking forward to a little alone time, a chance to decompress after the season.

But just the sight of her, bedraggled, thin, scared, but doing everything in her power to hold it together, had me jumping in to play the savior. Completely absurd because that wasn't me.

That was my dad. He was the kind of guy who rescued people. When he knocked up my mom—with me—he stepped up to the plate immediately. He never had doubts about what should happen next, and that certainty played a big part in how he wooed my mom. She needed that, someone to take the reins. If the stories my great-gran told me were to be believed, my mom resisted big time. But that push-pull eventually settled into the balance they had now.

We were alike in looks, my dad and me, but not so much in temperament. I suffered a lot of comparisons to him, mostly about our game, but sometimes about our personality differences. Where my dad was easygoing, I was less likely to let things slide.

None of this really explained my behavior. I didn't usually jump in and take over. I was typically more cautious than that. But today—no. Very little thinking and a whole lot of acting on instinct.

When she asked me to help her out of her wedding underwear, I almost walked out of there. Touching her was so wrong and completely unfair to Carter, who must be feeling so low right now. Yet here I was playing his part, undressing the man's bride. The pearls of her spine bulging so prominently, her skin red raw from the tightness of the underwear, that butterfly tattoo—all had combined to make my heart beat madly.

This whole thing was mad.

During the journey down, I'd left my phone off, and now I checked it, bracing myself for drama and accusation. Plenty of messages from family and friends, but I focused on the wedding party group thread, absurdly named "Carter's Cool Crew," like we were in middle school. Created by his best man and cousin, Saxon Carter the Third, it fortunately did not include the groom, which gave leave for everyone to gossip away to their hearts' content.

Peyton Bell, aka Dingaling, got the ball rolling.

D's freaking me out.

NOBO

Man, he must be crushed.

JAKEY

Yeah, I can't imagine getting dumped like
that. Pretty hard core when your girl would
rather escape out of a bathroom window
than marry you.

DINGALING

No, that's just it. He's kind of okay with it?
Like this is just a hitch in an otherwise
regular run of events.

I tried to understand Carter's thinking here. Why the
hell would he think of this as a "hitch"?

NOBO

So he's gonna talk to her? Change her
mind?

DINGALING

Maybe? He said something about how
she's flighty and indecisive. He thinks his
mom scared her off and that she just needs
time to think it through.

JAKEY

Not sure I'd be that understanding.

NOBO

Not sure it sounds like Carter.

CARTER GOON 1

C-Man rules!

CARTER GOON 2

Fuck that bitch!

The inestimable contribution of a couple of Carter's
douchey cousins, whose names I never bothered to learn.
They'd obviously decided the champagne shouldn't go to

waste.

NOBO

KJ's being awfully quiet. You still with us, man?

KJ was me: Kershaw Junior. A few more texts followed, mostly speculation on what Summer was thinking and why she'd handled it that way. The thread had been quiet for the last thirty minutes, so my contribution was due.

Sorry, guys, I was driving and had my phone off. Figured I'd hit the road as soon as I saw it was a bust.

NOBO

You missed Carter's mom turning into the Wicked Witch of the West. She flew out of the church on her broomstick.

JAKEY

Can you blame her? She spent a lot of money on that shindig.

DINGALING

Drop in the bucket for the Carter dynasty. Not sure screaming at the bridesmaids was justified. Rosie had to be restrained from throwing a punch!

I smiled. That sounded like my friend.

CARTER GOON 1

Auntie Arabella is pissed!

CARTER GOON 2

Not as pissed as you, fuckhead. You ruined my tux!

ME

So did they hold the reception anyway?

NOBO

Yep. Food was great! No dancing, though,
because, obvs.

Good old NoBo. Always had his priorities straight.

My phone rang with a call from my agent. I wasn't really in the mood, but she was currently working on some business stuff that was time sensitive.

"Hey, what's up?"

Lauren Yates—or Special Agent Lauren as I'd nicknamed her—was the sister-in-law of Gunnar Bond, one of my dad's old teammates on the Rebels roster. Formerly an excellent professional hockey player, she had retired and moved into agenting with The Mallinson Group. I had signed with her last year a few months after I was acquired by the Rebels. Previously, I was with my dad's agent, Tommy Gordon, but I always felt like I was in his stable more as a favor to the old man. As soon as I switched to Lauren, I got an endorsement with Sunshine Granola and just missed out on the Holy Grail of deals, an underwear branding.

"Just checking in on one of my favorite clients."

"More like thirsting for a steaming hot mug o' tea."

She laughed. "Oh yeah, baby! Give it to me."

I filled her in without mentioning my part in it and Summer's current location.

"That *is* wild. I hope Summer's okay. She's always come across as such a nice person."

So everyone said. Did nice people jilt the man they supposedly loved?

"You heard from the Fenton people?" She was talking to the hockey equipment business, trying to cut me a deal.

"Not yet, but I have heard from Tampa."

"And?"

"Very interested. I've been trying to convince them you're undervalued. That the deal getting you onto the Rebels wasn't as good for you as it should have been."

Only now my brand was tarnished. In the last year, I hadn't played up to my potential with the Rebels and part of the reason was because I felt pressure as Theo Kershaw's son. We didn't play the same position—he was a D-man, I played right wing offense—but that didn't stop the comparisons. To start, the press and the franchise had loved it, but when I wasn't always dressed for a game or above the third line, there were the inevitable digs at the fact I would never be as good as him. Playing on the Rebels for my dad's final year was one thing. But if he continued, I wasn't sure I wanted to live in his shadow.

First world hockey player problems, for sure.

"That's good, I suppose."

"Thought that's what you wanted. Are you worried your dad will take it badly?"

Yes, but I hoped he'd understand that I had to think of my career now. I'd given him a year of the Kershaw Dad-and-Son show.

"Hatch, you still there?"

"Yeah."

"Listen, I don't want to broach it with Rebels management unless we're sure."

I should have been jumping at the opportunity to get away. To reset. But something in me resisted. "Can I think about it?"

"Sure. Just don't think too long."

We hung up with plans to check in after a day or so. I had made career decisions before based on my gut. I wasn't sure how well it served me.

Look at the events of today.

"Hi."

Summer stood at the entrance to the living room, swimming in a pair of my sweatpants, rolled up at the ankles, and a faded University of Michigan tee. That was my alma mater. I'd given her my clothes because I felt odd about borrowing stuff belonging to my family.

Her hair was wet and sleek down her back. She must have found a hairbrush in the bathroom. All her make-up was gone, and before me stood Summer, stripped to basics.

The basics were beautiful.

"Hey," I said, after five awkward seconds of gawping at her. I hadn't reckoned on the impact of seeing her wearing my stuff, how it created this weird tug in my chest—and other areas.

She stepped in further. "Thanks for the clothes."

"Sorry there's no underwear. Well, there is, but I didn't think you'd want to wear my boxers or anything belonging to my great-gran."

Her mouth twitched. "This is fine."

Which meant that maybe she had no underwear on? Definitely braless, I'd made sure of that.

"You hungry?"

"Not really."

She hadn't eaten all day and now it was close to four in the afternoon. "I'm going to make a sandwich."

She followed me into the kitchen. "You had food here already?"

"I put in an order to the local grocer yesterday."

Her eyes widened. Such a lovely shade, that violet-blue with flecks of gold. "You were already planning to come here?"

"I usually spend time here every summer." I gathered

sandwich supplies and started putting one together: Muenster cheese, turkey, lettuce, tomato, mayo. I held up the mustard and gestured in offering. When she didn't respond, I reasoned, "You already gave your crackers away to the ducks."

"Okay. No mustard."

I topped the sandwich with a thick slice of country wheat and placed it before her.

"Water okay?"

At her nod, I filled a glass from the Brita filter. Then I set about making my own sandwich. "Don't wait for me."

She waited anyway. Hell, she wouldn't last long in the Kershaw house where no one waited for anyone. I needed her to eat—it felt important that she get some sustenance—so I finished up quickly and took a seat at the kitchen table.

I picked up my sandwich. She picked up hers and took a bite, chewed, moaned, swallowed, then took a sip from her own glass. I was fascinated by the bulge of her slender throat.

"God, I've missed cheese."

"Cheese?"

"Yeah, I've been dieting, so I cut out dairy. Which kills me because cheese is my favorite thing in the world."

I too loved cheese, but I didn't have a raging hard-on for it. "What's your favorite?"

"Triple crème brie."

"This is a cheddar house. Though we have a soft spot for Pinconning, because, Michigan."

"Might have to do a cheese-off." She smiled and there it was again, that weird lurch in my chest.

I focused on my sandwich because the last thing I needed was to have that sunshine smile affecting me.

"Why did you help me?"

"Because you asked."

"I expected you'd let me hide out at your condo in the city. But this ..." She looked around. "This is better."

"Sometimes you need distance to acquire perspective." How wise I sounded. I'd tried for distance for years, for all the good it had done me.

"But I can't stay here forever, can I?"

"Maybe you should sleep on it."

"I've been sleeping on it for five years."

My gaze snapped to hers. What did that mean?

"Or maybe I should say, sleepwalking. Through my life." She shook her head, like she was arguing with herself. "I can't believe I let it go this far."

As the altar? A streak of anger bolted through me. All these people hurt, and she had made me an accomplice. This woman was something else.

I needed to get out from under the spell she had over me.

"Think I'll take a shower myself." I was still wearing my tuxedo pants and shirt. The tie and jacket had been dispensed with a while ago, but I needed to change and restore some sense of normality.

Or as much as I could with Summer here.

She watched me stand and put my plate in the dishwasher. Those violet eyes assessed me.

"You're mad at me." Not a question.

"Why would I be mad at you?"

"Because I've placed you in this awkward position. With a teammate. With your team. Maybe even with your family because you brought me here."

"I'm not mad. I don't feel anything about this situation."

Her lips curved slightly. "Oh, you're mad alright. Absolutely pissed at yourself for stepping in and at me for forcing your hand."

"You were kind of sad and lost there, so how am I gonna resist that?"

"Just doing your good deed for the day."

"Uh huh."

"Even if it makes you look bad to others."

What was this? "I don't care how I look to others."

"Doubt that. We all care. What I can't understand is why you did it."

"Like I said—"

"Right, you couldn't resist my sad and pathetic presentation, and you're a sucker for a damsel in distress."

I didn't respond. Just looked at her as she shot sparks through her eyes. Why she was angry at me for doing her this favor I had no idea.

But part of me liked it. Because seeing this side of her meant I might have misunderstood her before.

There might be a whole other Summer I could learn.

Instead of a fire blanket, I opted to throw paraffin on the flames. "You suddenly don't seem all that grateful."

"Oh, I am. I'm also confused. Because why would you do this when you so obviously hate my guts?"

CHAPTER SEVEN

Summer

THERE, *I'd said it.* Hatch Kershaw had never liked me, so his assistance today was incredibly confusing. I needed to know what was happening inside that broody head of his.

"Now wherever did you get that idea?"

Not denying it, then. "Oh, every single time we meet. If you're not glaring me into the ground, looking down your nose at me, or sneering in my general direction, you're usually ignoring me even when I speak to you. It's incredibly rude."

"Believe me, I have never ignored you."

"Yes, you have. Back in February, you came in for a meeting with Ryder and while you were waiting, you put in your earbuds. After I spoke to you directly."

He shrugged. "So I didn't hear you."

"Anytime we're in the Empty Net, you look at some point over my shoulder."

"There's always a prettier girl."

"And if I ask you a question, you act like I smell bad."

"I'm allergic to your perfume."

This. Liar. I had experienced enough gaslighting from my fiancé, I wasn't going to put up with it here.

"I might be a lot of things, Hatch, but I'm not stupid. Evidently, I offended you at some point in the past."

He crossed his arms over his chest, displaying rolled up sleeves and incredible forearms. All the players had amazing physiques, big shoulders and thick thighs. Hatch had always struck me as so imposing, even more so than Dash.

"You're mistaken, Summer. I really don't have any opinion of you."

I pointed. "Impossible. At this point in our relationship—"

"We don't *have* a relationship."

"Everyone who spends time in the same circles has a relationship. Hell, I have one with your dad and I barely know him. But he's a player on my fiancé's team"—*still my fiancé, I reasoned, if only for the purposes of this example—* "and on the team I help support"—*still my job, though I was no longer employed by the Rebels.* "We have a professional relationship. You and I don't even have that because you decided at some point that you would prefer to be rude or to ignore me. I'm even friends with your sister, but for some reason I really piss you off. I'd like to apologize for whatever it is I did."

"You didn't do anything. Some people just don't ... gel. That's all there is to it. No need to read anything else into it." Apparently, he wasn't falling for my strategy to induce him to come clean. He pushed off from the counter, with all that easy grace that made him a star athlete. "I'm going to take a shower in the pool house."

"You guys have a pool?"

He smirked. "Yeah, we have a pool. Good night."

He walked out to the patio while I did my best to ignore how good he looked leaving. Better to assure myself that his leaving was good *for* me.

Maybe he was telling the truth. I'd met people and quickly deduced they weren't on my wavelength or that they rubbed me the wrong way, but I liked to make an effort with all the players on the team. These were the assets for the organization where I worked—past tense—and my job ran more smoothly if everyone got along.

But Hatch had obviously decided I wasn't worth his time. I initially put it down to the fact I worked in administration, was merely one of the little people even though I was engaged to a fellow player. Likely he thought I was a social climber, shooting way above my station. Hatch Kershaw was hockey royalty, the son of a legend, part of a family that ate, slept, and breathed hockey 24-7. I was clearly below his interest, so he was doing me a great kindness in coming to my rescue.

I would do him a similar one by leaving him the hell alone.

I TOOK A NAP.

Well, I dried my hair first with a hairdryer I found in Hatch's great-grandmother's bathroom, then I slipped under the covers. It was too hot, so I removed the sweatpants, kept the University of Michigan T-shirt on—Hatch's alma mater, if I recalled correctly—and closed my eyes. I hadn't slept well over the last week, the last month, to be honest, and I expected it would be tough to fall now given the chatty hamsters riding wheels in my head. But I soon slipped away. When I awoke, the darkened room told me considerable time had passed. The sun set around 9 p.m. this time of year in the Midwest, so I reckoned I'd slept for at least five hours.

After switching on a nightstand light, I looked around. I hadn't paid too much attention before and now I expected an old lady room, but this wasn't frilly or filled with weird figurines or whatever women of a certain age liked. The walls had interesting art—prints of Rothko, Lichtenstein, and Basquiat—ones I recognized from the online lectures I'd taken during my "Crash Course in Culture," one of the early lessons for Project Summer.

The room also had a dressmaker's mannequin in the corner, draped in flowing scarves and a *Grease* Pink Ladies-style jacket, worn by members of Aurora's fan group for her grandson, Theo's Tarts. (They used to dance in the seats at the home games, before she retired after a hip replacement.) Two dressers were covered with framed photos of her family and its multiple generations. What must it be like to be so proud of your family you wanted to record it over and over like that? I couldn't imagine it.

I'd spent the last ten years unable to imagine it.

My stomach rumbled. I'd already eaten today but I was hungry again. If the wedding had gone ahead, we would have been long past the dinner by now. Most likely, this would have been the time to do the rounds and visit with the guests, most of whom I didn't know. Mrs. Carter had taken care of the guest list—it was the one area I'd been happy to let her control, not realizing that giving her that inch would result in her taking a mile.

"What about your family, Summer? Surely there are some long-lost relatives in the woodwork who would like to join a beautiful society wedding?"

Even Dash, for whom his mother was usually beyond reproach, had frowned at that dig. "She already told you they died when she was little."

Mrs. Carter shrugged. "I just thought there might be a responsible uncle or cousin at the ready. Who's going to give you away?"

"I'll give myself away."

She hadn't liked that, but I did. I'd been alone since the age of sixteen. I was completely responsible for making it this far, so why shouldn't I walk myself down that aisle?

I could finally say goodbye to Shelby Mae.

I would know so few people at the wedding except for the friends I'd made since I started working at the Rebels. First, Rosie, then Adeline, Hatch's sister. Both were daughters of Rebels players and a few years younger than me. I knew Rosie better but had gotten better acquainted with Adeline over the last few months.

Yet they didn't know me at all. Because I was a liar. Or more accurately, an expert in omission. Every now and then, my accent would slip, and one of them—usually Adeline—would give me a look. But I would recover quickly, utter something cheerful or inane, and get us back on track. No one would, or could, know I was Shelby Mae Landry, backwoods Mississippi girl, made over to Summer from the Bay Area, the girl most likely to succeed at anything she chose.

I pulled on the sweats, visited the bathroom, and ran a brush through my hair. The dark circles under my eyes were less bruised. New color pinked my cheeks.

Back in the bedroom, I picked up my phone and switched it on.

I had multiple messages. Dash. Mrs. Carter. Rosie. Adeline. Even one from Ryder Calloway, the Rebels GM and my former boss. I listened to that one first.

"Hi, Summer, I'm probably the last person you need to hear from today, but I just wanted to check in and see how you were doing. No need to call back. Just know that we're all thinking of you."

I swiped at a tear, marveling at how he could be so kind. I'd jilted one of his players, yet here he was reaching out when he could have just ignored me.

Anyone might wonder why I'd decided to hear Ryder out before tackling Dash. Well, I was starting to realize that I had a major problem, beyond the immediate one of Dash and everyone he knew hating my guts.

I needed money. A job. *My* job. So I had given notice a month ago and had even helped train my replacement, but perhaps there was a chance the Rebels would employ me again?

Sure, Summer, you sweet dummy. They'll be just dyin' to get you back on the payroll after you made one of their players look like a loser.

Shelby Mae, you are supposed to be dead to me!

Cue backwoods cackle.

That ornery bitch was right, though. Ryder might call me out of a fatherly concern for my well-being, but he sure as hell would not be offering me a job now. One other person might be in my corner, though. Scott Kincaid, the assistant head of scouting, had been mentoring me over the last year. One evening in the owners' box, I'd made a comment about the NCAA Frozen Four to Scott, and we'd had a great chat about hockey prospects. When I told him I made slide decks for Ryder and even sometimes added my own commentary, he asked if I was willing to do some research for him.

So began my first meaningful professional relationship. I didn't have the cajónes to ask Ryder for true mentorship—and what would I say? *Oh, Mr. Calloway, any pointers for the woman who makes your coffee and picks up your dry cleaning?* (Dash's digs had taken residence in my head.) But Scott was willing to sit with me at lunchtime in the staff break room and answer my questions about the hockey business and scouting. And when Dash was on the road, I spent my evenings trawling college websites and creating reports, desperate to prove there was more to me than a powerful man's personal assistant.

Then Dash found out. One night, I'd fallen asleep on the sofa with my laptop open, only waking when Dash shook my shoulder at five in the morning.

"Waiting up for me, honey?"

We didn't live together then. We'd dated for close to four years, had even broken up several times, when I suspected Dash had not been faithful to me on away trips. He never admitted anything but inevitably he would draw me back in. It was hard to work for an organization and ignore one of the assets. So, we would start dating again because I was lonely and thought he was charming, if a little immature. Definitely not husband material. But he had a key to my apartment and usually slipped into my bed after an away trip, freshly showered with no trace of another woman.

That morning, he had sat beside me on the sofa as I shook myself awake.

"What's this about?" He pointed at the laptop screen

with its rows of data in spreadsheets. "You ranking other guys?"

"Just a little work for Ryder," I fudged. "Scouting prospects."

"Babe, you shouldn't be doing this off the clock. He's taking advantage."

"I don't mind. I like learning about how the business works. I don't want to be his assistant forever."

"No one says you have to do that. You've got so much more going for you, Summer."

At the time, I'd interpreted it as encouragement, the water my arid heart needed. I floated on a cloud of happiness, confident I could do anything. That I was more. Six weeks later, Dash proposed in the Empty Net in front of the entire team and its fans, and against my better judgment, I accepted, mostly so as not to embarrass him.

Later, he put any doubts I raised at ease, and I let myself be persuaded that we would be a super couple of hockey. The star on the ice, the brains behind the scenes. Our story was still taking shape, the outlines fuzzy. But if I continued to work with Scott, learned the ins and outs of the franchise business, I would get what I wanted. All the way from Thunder Creek, Shelby Mae Landry would have completely reinvented herself.

Instead I had let Dash steal my shine. Turned out that when he said I had much more going for me, he meant my ascension to the role of Mrs. Dash Carter.

Now, I looked at the message thread from him. I went back to the beginning, or rather the beginning of the end, starting with my text to him.

Please forgive me. I can't do this.

Then the texts started flowing.

> Summer, where are you?
>
> We can talk about this. Just come back.
>
> Why aren't you answering?
>
> Did my mother say something?
>
> Summer, this is childish.
>
> Fine, be like that.

Texts seemed inadequate at this point, yet I wasn't ready to talk to him.

Summer, you sure are a coward. So much for reinventin' yourself.

I had no response for that one. As usual, Shelby Mae was right.

CHAPTER EIGHT

Hatch

THE KERSHAW KINDER chat group was away to the races, led by my younger brother Conor.

CONOR

Can't believe we missed more Rebels drama! First Nyquist's baby mama drop off at the Net. Now Carter gets jilted.

LANDON

We did see Dad punch Nyquist at a game though.

CONOR

Yeah, classic.

Anyone here? H? Addy? We need details from the insiders. Mom and Dad are useless.

ADDY

Yes, I'm here. And no, I have zero information for you.

LANDON

Find that hard to believe. You were on site when she skipped out, right?

ADDY

I was outside talking to Lars.

CONOR

Jesus. Way to drop the ball, sis.

ADDY

Rosie said Summer went into the bathroom and never came out.

LANDON

Like the Twilight Zone. Or Hotel California.

ADDY

I'm sure she had her reasons.

CONOR

You mean you haven't spoken to her? What about Carter? How's he taking it?

LANDON

Sounds like you really care, bro. Such heartfelt concern.

CONOR

So Carter's a fuckwit but even I wouldn't wish that on anyone. Not sure what Summer's game is but he can't be happy about it.

LANDON

This would be a great time for Dino Boy to weigh in. Hatchling? Oh, brother where art thou? Got anything to add to bring the level of this discourse down even further?

No, I did not. Usually, I would be all over this chat because I enjoyed a good gossip as much as the next person. The twins, Conor and Landon, were home for the summer, living at the family home on Chicago's North Shore, after graduating from the University of Michigan a month ago. Conor was due to start at training camp in the fall for the Detroit Motors. Landon didn't play hockey; he was an app developer and was currently working on securing funding for a dating app he'd created in college.

We were all close, a product of the tight-knit family environment my parents and great-grandmother, Aurora, had crafted with care and love. There was nothing I wouldn't do for them, no secret I wouldn't share.

Except when it came to Summer.

How could I tell them she was hiding out here in the family's vacation home when I barely understood it myself? All I had to do was take her to my place in the city, let her compose herself, then send her on her way. Adeline could have helped. Rosie, too. Instead of approaching it logically, I'd brought her here.

Because you can't help yourself. This woman has had her barbs in you from the beginning.

I needed to say something on this damn chat.

ME

Once I realized the wedding was off, I left for sunnier climes.

CONOR

How's the Tuck?

LANDON

No one calls it that, dude.

CONOR

Dad does, and he's the OG Tuckman!

ME

> The Tuck is fine. They opened a new restaurant on the pier. Nice looking grill place from the pics.

ADDY

Did the hydrangea hold up over the winter?

ME

No idea.

ADDY

Send me pics of the garden! Tomorrow when the sun is out.

CONOR

Gardening, Adeline? Where are your priorities? I can't believe you haven't heard from Summer. Or that you won't tell us what happened. Don't make me get it out of Rosie.

ADDY

Good luck with that. The day I see you guys sharing anything is the day Hatch can actually recognize a hydrangea bush.

That made me smile. Rosie and I were good friends, Conor and Ro, not so much.

ADDY

As far as I know, Summer's already been in touch with Dash. It's between them.

I didn't know that. Of course, she had to talk to him at some point, but something in me balked at the idea. Would she go back to him? Would he try to fix things with her? After all, "Carter's Cool Crew" implied the groom thought Summer's sprint was merely a hitch.

While the Kershaw Kinder chat bubbled away without

me, my phone buzzed with a call from Rosie. She'd already left a couple of messages, so I answered.

"Yep."

"Don't 'yep' me, Hatch Wayne Butler Kershaw. What the hell is going on?"

She couldn't possibly know, unless Summer had said something.

"You're going to have to be more specific, Ro."

"You were in the wedding party, but you didn't even stick around for the fireworks."

"Carter and I aren't buddies. You know his mom only wanted me in there because she thinks some of Dad's glory will rub off on her." Which made little sense when the Carters were billionaires with their own glory cloud. "He's got people closer to him to help him through this."

"Well, I'd love to know what's going through their heads here. Dash told NoBo that Summer was okay. But she's not answering my texts or calls, so I'm not sure I take her ex-fiancé's word for it. What if he ... did her in?"

My friend, the drama queen. "He did not do her in. At least not personally. He'd outsource it."

"Not funny. I just wish she'd call."

Guilt at being in the know and unable to put Rosie at ease pinged me. But it wasn't my place. Neither did I want anyone to know I was involved.

Because that's what I was: *involved*.

"How long are you staying in Saugatuck?"

"A week, maybe two. I said I'd come back to help with the Rebels Youth Hockey Camp when the U-14 session starts up. For now, I just plan to chill."

"Any word on your dad's plans for next year?"

"You mean, since you asked me yesterday?"

She clicked her tongue. "I think you should talk to him. Tell him you're looking to play for another team."

Rosie and Special Agent Lauren were the only people I'd confided in about my desire to move.

"He would be so disappointed, and I don't want him to make a career decision based on whether I'm here or not. Me telling him I'm looking to leave would hurt him. And that's the last thing I want to do."

If my father knew about my special guest, he wouldn't be too pleased either. I was the golden child, and I didn't usually make mistakes.

Maybe Summer wasn't the only one who had gone a little mad back at that church.

CHAPTER NINE

THE HOUSE WAS DARK, so I switched on lights as I headed downstairs and wandered around. No sign of Hatch.

A chill coursed through me. I'd wanted to be alone, but I had hoped he wouldn't abandon me on my first night in a strange house. I stood in the kitchen, looking out into the backyard. I couldn't see a pool, so not sure what that was about. But there were tiki torch lights and the silhouette of someone in a chair.

I considered leaving him alone, but I craved human contact, even if it was sub-standard. Feeling a touch chilly, I picked up Hatch's tuxedo jacket from where he'd draped it over a chair and shrugged it on.

Sniffing the lapel, I inhaled the citrus-cedar scent. It smelled incredible.

Aftershave? Or something more? Most tuxedos were

rentals or were worn once then cleaned. This shouldn't smell of anything but dry-cleaning chemicals, yet I detected it, a masculine scent different from Dash's. More potent.

I stepped outside onto the patio. Hatch looked up from one of the wicker armchairs.

"Sleep okay?"

"Surprisingly, yes."

"I'm guessing you haven't had much lately."

Maybe I'd said, or perhaps he assumed because that was the lot of a bride in the weeks before her big day.

"Okay if I sit?"

"Sure."

I took a seat on the sofa across from him. "I borrowed your jacket. I hope you don't mind."

"Not at all." He placed his phone down on the table in front of him. He'd changed into board shorts and a Rebels T-shirt. The light of one of the tiki torches illuminated one side of his face while the other remained in shadow. I couldn't help seeing that as a metaphor for his personality, or at least the sides he presented to me.

"Did you need something to eat?"

I couldn't put him to any more trouble, though I was quite hungry. "I'm fine. I just wanted to check out the pool."

"I might have lied there."

"It looks like a nice garden, though."

"Yeah, Aurora used to take care of it before she moved to Chicago to live with us. Now we have someone come in and landscape."

"What's that place back there?"

"That's the pool house, so called because there's no actual pool. Inside joke."

I tried to smile but it got stuck. I could feel myself shutting down. While I had no doubt leaving Dash was the right move, why had I waited until the last minute? I could have pulled this stunt at any time but today, five minutes before I was supposed to hit the aisle?

Suddenly, Hatch was sitting beside me. A large, capable hand covered my small one, fisted in my lap.

"W-what?"

"You're shaking."

I snatched a breath, but my lungs wouldn't fill. I tried again. Shook my head. A warm weight touched my back. Hatch's other hand rubbed in a tight circle, and that sure, gentle touch brought me back. I inhaled, and finally something went in.

"I screwed up so bad." My accent came out there. *Sooo ba-yad.* I didn't care.

"Better to find out now, right?"

"I had five years to find out. But apparently, I prefer buzzer-beater decisions that destroy lives. I even gave up my job."

"You said that before." He was close to me, his thigh pressed against mine, like it didn't matter at all.

Except it did. Because Hatch Kershaw was gorgeous.

I had always thought so. Dark angel gorgeous. But I'd never moved beyond an objective assessment of his attractiveness because of his attitude toward me. I found it difficult to completely appreciate outer beauty when the inner self so obviously hated my guts.

"I quit a month ago. Well, I gave my notice and stayed on to train someone else. Lainey. She has my job now."

"And you want it back?" He sounded a touch incredulous, with good reason. I couldn't return, not after what I'd done.

"I liked working there. I liked learning about the business, supporting behind the scenes. I thought—" I broke off, aware of how absurd I sounded.

"You thought what?"

"It's stupid."

"Tell me."

"That I could learn the hockey trade. Be a scout or an analyst." I had even agreed to continue research for Scott after I left. If I kept my hand in, I might eventually convince Dash that I could contribute in more ways than just hockey wife and mother.

"Addy loves the stats stuff, too."

"Yeah, we've talked about it sometimes. But I didn't push for what I wanted."

"I'm sure you can find another job."

His hands were still touching me. He seemed to realize that and removed them, sending a chill through me.

"Is there a train back to Chicago?"

"You want to leave?" The words came out gruff.

"I can't stay here, Hatch. Time to face the music."

He leaned back and brought his ankle up to cross his leg. I was momentarily fascinated by the shape of his calf, the dark hair that looked eminently touchable. I had no idea calves could be sexy.

"Maybe take a couple of days."

"The longer I leave it, the worse it'll get. All my stuff is at Dash's place. I'll need to move out and start over." No job. No fiancé. Virtually no savings. I'd spent so much of it in the last year trying to keep up with the Carters. I had insisted on contributing to the wedding even though the cost of it would barely make a dent in their fortune. I'd paid for the rehearsal dinner and the floral arrangements, only to find my choices had all been superseded by Dash's mother and sister.

Roses? Oh, no one does roses at weddings.

I had thought roses romantic, but romance wasn't important to a wedding, evidently. Roses were out of style. Romance, too.

But I'd stood my ground for my bouquet. Pale pink roses, that was what I wanted. Then I'd left it behind at the church, along with this life I'd blown up.

Hatch considered me, wearing that familiar expression I knew. Disapproval. When he was looking at me at all. Sometimes I would glance his way in the Empty Net or at a team gathering and our gazes would clash. He would look away, as if disgusted.

Now I wasn't so sure.

He wasn't looking away now. The tiki torch light mimicked the flutter of a flame. It caught his cheekbones, shaded them like a sculptor revealing beauty in the stone.

"Why are you looking at me like that?"

"Like what?"

"Like you can't figure me out."

Was that why I held some weird fascination for him? Did he wonder how someone like me could have carved a niche into this life where she so obviously didn't belong?

"I don't get why you stayed with Carter for so long. Why you waited to do this. It wasn't like a whirlwind romance where he swept you off your feet and before you know it, 'Here comes the bride.' You had ages to figure this out."

The criticism abraded, but I could take it. I had Shelby Mae as my constant companion, my own best critic, so Hatch Kershaw was following a well-trodden path.

"I was a frog in slowly-heating water. I didn't realize how complacent I had become, how accepting I was of that brand of toxicity until it was too late."

"Anyone could see what a jerk he was to you. Addy and Rosie talked about it."

"Not to me." But then we weren't as close as I wanted to believe. I kept a certain distance from the girls, worried they might want to know more about me. About my past. Trying to fit in required the walls stay at a certain height. "Excuse me for not having it all figured out. Must be nice to be so sure of yourself. Your life mapped out, your path so clear."

"That's what you think? I have it all figured out?"

"Don't you? Son of a legend, destined to follow in his skate glide, part of the great Kershaw legacy. I was there when the front office brought you on—you'd swear royalty had descended."

"Doesn't mean my life is mapped out. We just lost the Cup. And I played like a donkey."

So he hadn't played his best. But this was a team sport. Victory didn't rest on the shoulders of one man.

"You're what? Twenty-five years old? You have another ten, fifteen, maybe twenty years with those Kershaw genes. You have everything in front of you, this amazing family who adores you, the world of hockey at your skates. You've never screwed up and if you did, you'd have your family and friends ready to catch you."

I was twenty six and had nothing. I came from dirt, and I was back in the mud yet again.

He didn't apologize, which was fine. He felt the way he did, and I was the bitch who bailed on his teammate.

"I'm going to go eat some cheese now."

Defiantly, I returned to the kitchen to make myself another sandwich. When I looked out to the patio again, Hatch was gone.

JUST BEFORE 6 A.M., the next morning, I snuck out of the house like a thief.

I was getting used to this. Not that I had to climb through a window this time, but my cat burglar reflexes were on point.

I couldn't impose any longer. I had raided Aurora's closet and found a pair of coral capris that fit me with the addition of a leopard-skin belt to hold them up. I also "borrowed" a pair of Gola pink tennis shoes—very Aurora—and a cardigan to cover up the Michigan tee. I couldn't leave the wedding dress or underwear behind, so I stuffed it all into a Jansport backpack I found in the closet. After washing the borrowed clothes, I would return them to Aurora once I was back in Chicago, or to Hatch if he wanted to keep my visit a secret.

The pool house, where my ogre rescuer slept, was quiet. I slipped out the front door to a waiting Uber and was at the Amtrak station in Holland, Michigan, seventeen minutes later in time for the 6:49 train.

A sign at the station read: *Train delayed. The 6:49 train to Chicago will now depart at 7:10.* Okay. I could do that. I tried to buy a ticket with my Wallet app on my phone, but it wouldn't work, so I had to dip into my cash reserves. Thirty-seven dollars gone, sixty-three left.

I went through all my texts and listened to the messages. Dash had left voice mails after the texts, each more irate than the other.

"Summer, let's talk" became "Summer, you can't do this to me!" in seven tries.

I called him back. He didn't answer, but as I was leaving a voice mail, his return call came through. I inhaled and answered.

"Hi."

He didn't say anything, just let the silence hang.

Finally, he spoke. "Are you out of your fucking mind?"

I laughed nervously. "Probably."

"Probably? That has to be one of the more stupid moves you've ever made, Summer."

I could feel my body flushing with embarrassment. He was right, but did he have to make me feel so small?

"Maybe. But I can't say I regret it. And I think you're going to realize soon it was for the best. I wouldn't have made you a good wife."

"Not really for you to decide, though, is it? I think I'd know what a good wife looks like."

The logic of that escaped me, but I let it slide. "I'm sorry I didn't talk to you face to face."

"Worried I'd change your mind for you?"

"Yes, actually. You're very persuasive." He had spent the last year convincing me that we were good together.

He snorted. "And you don't know what you want, Summer. You never have. I had to tell you what to eat, what to wear, how to behave. My mom said you must have only ever eaten at fucking Olive Garden or shopped at The Gap. We could have taught you so much, how to be someone important. I can't believe I wasted so much of my time on you."

I couldn't believe it either. He was being a dick, but he had a right to be.

"So where did you go? No one knew where you skipped out to, not even Adeline or Rosie."

I squirmed on the train platform's plastic seat. "Out of town. It seemed to be for the best."

"On that we can agree. I'm heading to St. Bart's today, *on my honeymoon*."

"You'll have your family. That'll be good for you."

He made a scoffing noise, but it wasn't loud enough to mask something else. A woman's voice in the background. "Baby, it's *soooo* early! Come back to bed."

I shouldn't have been surprised, but *wow*.

"That was fast."

"You're going to criticize *my* choices on our wedding day, Summer?"

"No. I can't do that." I tried for a calming breath. "I'm on my way back to the city. I can come by when you've left for St. Bart's."

"For what?"

"To pick up my stuff."

"No chance. Security has strict instructions not to let you in. I'll be back in two weeks, at which point I'll let you know when I'm ready to speak to you or allow you to come by. Until then, think about every stupid fucking decision you've ever made."

He clicked off.

I stared at the phone, not quite believing what just happened. Another woman in our bed. Locked out of our apartment. My credit cards, keys, laptop were all back there. My gaze fell on an ATM in the train station waiting room, one of those no-brand ones that charged a shit-ton in fees. I had never been so grateful that I'd resisted joining my finances with Dash. He had told me *what's mine is yours, babe*, but deep down, I knew that was a fallacy. I might need to run.

I'd done it before.

On shaky legs, I approached the machine, inserted my card, and selected the option for a one hundred dollar withdrawal. A message flashed on the screen in a weird dingbats-like script. I waited, but nothing happened. I pressed every button available. Nada.

The damn machine had eaten my card!

Was it possible that—? No. Dash's family was incredibly wealthy, but not even they had the power to control an ATM in a tiny town, miles from Chicago. I hoped.

Shaking, I opened up the bank app on my phone. My login worked—thank God! My balance was lower than I would have liked, but at least it was mine. I had access to money, but I would need a replacement card.

I mentally scrolled through my options. Unfortunately, all of them were Rebels-related. For the last five years, my world had revolved around Dash and the team. Rosie and Adeline might help, but how could I face them after what I had done? I needed to get to the condo, work my magic on Victor, our doorman, and pick up the essentials.

"Where the hell do you think you're going?"

I looked up and met the startling green, you-are-so-fucked gaze of Hatch Kershaw.

CHAPTER TEN

Hatch

SHE HAD SNUCK AWAY before the sun came up. Getting to be a habit with this girl.

I knew the train left a few minutes before seven, and that it was often late. I arrived at the top of the hour to find Summer in the waiting room, looking at her ticket.

She peered up, baffled. "Why are you here?"

"You left." *Without saying goodbye.* Not that she owed me that, not after how I'd behaved last night. "I could have given you a ride."

I took a seat beside her, one of those plastic deals that dug into my hockey butt. Now that I was here, I wasn't sure what my play was. Wish her well? Persuade her to stay? Something else?

"Are those Aurora's clothes?"

With a nod, she pulled down on the brim of a Detroit Motors ball cap, one of the Rebels' biggest rivals in the league. "I was going to wash and return them when I get to Chicago."

"Were you planning to see Carter?"

"I just spoke to him. He's heading to St. Bart's with family, so I think he's in good hands."

She sounded a touch bitter. Annoyed, perhaps, that he wasn't begging her to return?

"How did that go?"

"It was a tense conversation. He's obviously hurt about what I did. I'll give him a day or two to settle before I try again."

Silence fell, neither of us in the mood to fill it, though it wasn't awkward. I came from a talkative family, and we were all chatty, except for Adeline who was the quiet one. I liked not having to compete for air. The station was empty except for an old guy with a walrus mustache on a bench a few feet away. He squinted at us, then went back to his newspaper.

A slow rumble started up, the noise of the incoming train. Summer looked at her ticket, then out at the track.

"I should go." She stood and stepped away, and my feet followed, drawn to her like a bee to nectar. I had to right this ship, eliminate my feelings from the matter. She needed someone in her corner, so the first step toward that was to offer assistance.

"Summer, stay." And because that sounded weird, I added, "Take some time for yourself. When's the last time you did that?"

She blinked in surprise, either at my apparent care for her well-being or the acknowledgment she might not have engaged in much self-care lately.

"I can't impose any longer." But she sounded less sure than before.

"It's not an imposition. You're a guest of the Kershaws." Putting it that way made it seem less personal. Just one of my family's many waifs and strays.

The train pulled into the station. It had been a while since I took it, but my recollection was that it would wait for two or three minutes. She turned to me, eyes wide and shiny, filled with emotion I didn't know what to do with.

"Last night, I was too harsh," I said. "It's none of my business. You and Carter."

"You feel loyalty to him. I understand. And I hate that I've put you in this position."

"I knew what I was doing."

Our gazes locked, some new knowledge passing between us. Eventually you had to admit that circumstances weren't the boss of you and that you had a certain level of control over your actions.

I didn't have to drive her out of that church parking lot.

I didn't have to squire her all the way to Saugatuck.

And I certainly didn't have to drive to the station to beg her to stay.

But I did. Time to own it.

"I don't have any money. The ATM just ate my card." She gestured at a machine in the waiting room.

"Not your week, is it?"

That made her laugh. I joined in, and for a moment, we were on the same page. Walrus Stache got on the train, and it slowly pulled out of the station.

"Looks like I'm staying. I'm really grateful, Hatch."

I released a held breath, my relief both palpable and annoying.

"How about we get some coffee?"

WE STOPPED AT NOVEL GROUNDS, a coffee shop just off Water Street, the main drag in Saugatuck.

"Well, if it isn't Hatch Kershaw!"

I smiled at Gemma, the owner. "Hey, Gem, how's business?"

"Not bad. Had a good Fourth and now we're in full swing." It was early enough in the day to be a little quieter, for which I was grateful. "How's your dad? And the rest of the family? Are they coming out soon?"

"Next month, maybe? Mom's finishing up some work and Dad's getting the back deck ready at the place in Riverbrook."

"And has he decided what he's gonna do?"

"He's still mulling it over." I didn't really want to get into the weeds of my dad's storied career. "So, I'd love an Americano and ..." I turned to Summer, who had pulled the bill of the Motors cap down further.

"Hot tea?" she mumbled as if unsure this coffee shop in the sticks would have such a thing.

"We can do that," Gemma said. "English Breakfast, Earl Grey, or Jasmine?"

"Oh, English Breakfast, please. With milk on the side." She sounded so pleased, like this one little thing could improve her day a hundredfold.

Like a heathen, she tried to offer cash, but I insisted on paying. She didn't order a pastry, so I got two bagels—growing boy and all that—and cream cheese.

Gem winked. "Sit down. I'll bring it over tout de suite."

We took a seat in the back, and Summer threw a furtive glance over her shoulder.

"Do you think she knows who I am?"

"Maybe. People are pretty in tune with the team because of my family's connection to this town. At the same time, you don't really look like any of your pictures online."

"I don't?"

"The disguise is working."

She tugged again at the cap brim. "I grabbed this in the dark. Didn't really think it through."

"That hat belongs to the enemy."

"Uh, it was in your great-grandmother's closet."

I nodded. "She's from here so she has allegiance to the local team. Plus, Conor's starting there in the fall, which will likely muddle our loyalties further. You're probably okay."

"Except for the fact I'm wearing Motors merch." She did a fake spit take that made me chuckle. "So you *can* laugh."

"Of course I can. Until now, you've never said anything to amuse me."

"Hmm. So we've seen each other off and on for five years—"

"Not that long."

She pointed, rather dramatically, I thought. "Yes, it is! We met at a Rebels holiday party almost five years ago. You've barely spoken to me since."

Five years. I knew it but I didn't want to acknowledge it, or acknowledge that she had never been far from my thoughts all this time.

"I hardly saw you over the years. Only when I started with the Rebels last season did we start running into each other regularly."

"And you either ignored me or looked at me like I was something on the bottom of your skate."

"Like ice, you mean?" This was my cue to explain myself, but I'd rather undergo Lasik surgery with a rusty skate blade than do that. Thankfully, Gem appeared with the toasted bagels and beverages.

"Here you go." She hovered, ready to settle in for a chat. "So, you look familiar, honey. Have you been in here before?"

Keeping her head down, Summer dunked her tea bag. "No, first time. Just got one of those faces."

The last thing I needed was this juicy piece of gossip escaping into the wild. Before I could jump in, Gemma had her hand out.

"I'm Gemma."

Summer shook it. "Shelby Mae. Pleased to meet you."

Shelby Mae? Gemma was squinting at Summer, so I needed to put a stop to the interrogation.

"How's Baz?" Asking after her son seemed a good strategy to deflect.

"Still working down at the harbor. I expect you'll be taking the boat out soon. You should call him to pull her out of storage."

"I might just do that. Is he still with Marla?"

"Nah, she's runnin' around with some motorcycle freak from Douglas. Baz was crushed, I can tell ya." We chitchatted for another minute or so, only stopping when more customers came in. "Okay, back to work. You say hi to your pop for me. Tell him we all support his decision but that we'd prefer if he kept playing forever!"

I gave a dutiful chuckle. "Sure will."

Once she was out of earshot, I caught Summer's eye. She looked amused.

"What's so funny?"

"People are kind of obsessed with your dad around here."

"He's a native son. Well, he wasn't born in the town, but

he spent his formative years here. The townsfolk are proud of the connection."

"How does it feel?"

I sipped my coffee. "How does what feel?"

"To have such a legend for a dad?"

"He's a lot to live up to, a larger-than-life character. People look at us and think I should act like him as well as play like him, but we're different people."

Did I sound defensive there? I couldn't help it, I supposed.

Summer sipped her tea. "I never thought you were like him."

Silently, I smeared cream cheese on my cinnamon raisin bagel and pushed the blueberry one toward her.

"He's the cap," she went on. "The lovable team leader. *The* Theo Kershaw. And you're your own person."

"So, you've noticed."

She waved the cream-cheese covered knife. "Meaning I can understand why it might bother you. I think I said something once to you about you being his clone and you did *not* like it."

The night she accepted Carter's marriage proposal, just over a year ago. I'd left that bar in a foul mood and my summer had only gone downhill from there.

"I might have been a bit touchy about it."

She looked sympathetic. "Well, I think anyone who's met you will realize you're not a mini version of Theo Kershaw. So you've got the gorgeous green eyes and the killer cheekbones and that hair I'm sure women love raking their fingers through. Physically similar, otherwise not a chance."

She slathered cream cheese onto half the blueberry bagel. More than fifty percent, which meant she would have less for the second half. I wasn't sure why that bothered me.

"You think my eyes are gorgeous and my cheekbones are killer?"

"Don't forget the running of fingers through your hair."

"You said raking."

She held the bagel to her lips. "I did, but it sounds weird. Like you're taking a gardening implement to your head. You know in Portuguese they call it 'cafune' when someone else does it to your hair or you do it to a lover's."

She took a bite and chewed.

Something weird was happening here. It was like we'd leapfrogged the getting-to-know-you and landed in the middle of some kind of 'ship. Relationship. Situationship. Friendship.

Attractionship.

Knowing that Summer thought my eyes were gorgeous and the rest made me uneasy. I might not be Carter's biggest fan but there had to be some adherence to the bro code.

She swallowed her bagel bite, took a sip of coffee, and stared at me.

"Have I made it weird?"

"No. Okay, yes. We're not … friends."

"And this feels too friendly?"

I pushed the remainder of my cream cheese toward her. Given her usage so far, she might need it.

"A bit."

She held up her hands. "Got it. Let's keep it strictly … well, how would you define this?"

"Helping out a … work colleague."

That pleased her, which strangely pleased me. Fuck, I was losing the plot.

"A work colleague. I can get down with that. So, I have a hugely important question to ask you." She cleared her throat. "Any chance we can hold some work meetings ... on this boat of yours?"

I couldn't help my laugh. "If I can get it out of storage soon, we can go out tomorrow if you like."

"Really?"

The way her face lit up sent my pulse into outer space. She leaned in like she wanted to hug or kiss me, and my cock stirred, anticipating either, yet knowing neither was good for my mental health.

At the last second, she sat back and said, "Thanks, Dino Boy."

I groaned. "Why'd ya go and ruin it?"

She chuckled. "Did your dad really conceive you while wearing T-rex-themed underwear?"

Unfortunately the public was far too knowledgeable about my parents' sex lives. I had my dad to thank for that.

"Hard to conceive while *wearing* the underwear."

"I dunno. I'm guessing some guys are spurty enough to break through the cotton barrier."

I shook my head in disbelief. "Spurty enough? You're assigning *way* more power to any guy's sperm than it deserves. And I really don't want to think about my dad's swimmers."

"Even when it resulted in the miracle that is you?"

That drew another laugh, deep from my belly, and loud enough to attract Gemma's attention.

"Especially that."

CHAPTER ELEVEN

Hatch

NOT LONG AFTER we got home, I had a call from my dad, he of the barrier-busting swimmers.

"Hey, Hatchling, how's it going?"

"Fine, fine."

"So, we're not going to talk about what happened at the church yesterday?"

I inhaled. "Bit of a shit show."

"Didn't see you after. Or before."

"Wanted to get on the road to Saugatuck before I got sucked into the drama. How's everyone?"

My dad talked about the latest thing that my four-and-a-half-year-old sister Tilly was obsessed with (fig jam) and the latest thing that my twenty-one year old brother Conor was obsessed with (trying to nail a puck in the tree hole of the big oak in the backyard).

"I stopped by Novel Grounds for coffee this morning.

Gem was asking about your retirement, then Baz at the yacht club had plenty to say."

He sighed. I felt for him, having to deal with all this speculation about his career. Working with him, side by side, over the last year had been both amazing and intimidating. This was *the* Theo Kershaw we were talking about, a legend in the game. I hated thinking that it would be better for me if he retired, that I could finally get out from under his shadow.

"Have you given any more thought to that?"

"I think of practically nothing else. I'm guessing you're sick of hearing about it."

"Nah."

My dad chuckled. "It's good for you to get away from all the drama, family, hockey, and otherwise. So what's the latest on Carter and Summer?"

"You're worse than the twins. Is this why you're calling? Looking for gossip?"

"Of course it is! Your mother's been at me to get the scoop, not to mention Aurora. I know you're not that close to Carter, but I figured you'd know something. I always liked Summer, too."

"Based on what? You barely know her."

"Wouldn't say that. As a Rebels-*cough*-legend-*cough*, I spent a fair bit of time in the front office in my role as honorary GM, coach, and team psychologist. I had plenty of chats with Summer and she always struck me as a total sweetheart. Guess we never know what's going on beneath the surface."

The truth of that struck me hard. I'd made up my mind about Summer quickly, and now I had no clue what her game was. Just because she had ditched Carter didn't mean she was suddenly a good person, though. She was hiding something. I just didn't know what.

"Carter said she changed her mind. Well, I didn't talk to him directly, but the guys texted to say he seems to think it's just a glitch in the matrix. That they'll sort it out eventually."

Though judging from Summer's reaction to talking to him this morning, Dash was playing a different game with her.

My father hummed. "That's a big hurdle to climb. But hey, maybe this means you can finally take your shot."

"Uh, meaning?"

"I was always surprised you didn't make a play for her. I remember when she came on the scene, the first time you met her at the Rebels holiday party a few years back."

Unfortunately, my dad had the recall of an elephant. I braced myself for a blow-by-blow account of this fateful meeting, but first I argued my case.

"Dash brought her as his date and they've been together ever since."

"Not all the time. Believe me, I've listened to his whining every time they split up and happened to bear witness to all the times he found some bunny to help him get over her. Then a month later, they were back on the hamster wheel of love. Not exactly inspiring."

It was not, but some couples thrived on the drama. "And what makes you think I wanted to take a shot?"

"Because you were smitten that first time you saw her."

I scoffed. "No, I wasn't."

"Oh, Hatchling, I remember it well. You were struck dumb. But I get how you wouldn't want to make a move on another guy's girl."

Ladies and gentlemen, my dad, the shit stirrer.

"I can barely recall meeting her."

Neither did you rescue her from the church, squirrel her away in your family's vacation home, or convince her to stay as long as she needs, either.

"Guess I got it wrong. That was the night I learned your mom was pregnant with Tilly, so maybe I already had empathetic pregnancy brain."

If he had any idea of the bride's current whereabouts, I'd never hear the end of it. The call left me uneasy, closing in on bad-tempered.

Summer wasn't helping.

Having refused my offer of a ride back into town for an "essentials run" with her non-existent ATM card and minimal cash, she was now assessing the roadworthiness of Adeline's bike, an ancient red Schwinn she found in the shed.

"It's going to crap out on you before you're halfway down the drive."

Hopping on it, she cycled twenty feet toward the gate then back again. She had changed into a pair of what I assumed were Aurora's shorts, and even though my great-grandmother was petite, Summer was even more slight. The shorts rode up, revealing smooth, gilded skin.

"It's totally fine."

"I can get you there in eight minutes."

"And this will be amazing exercise. I can't have you driving me everywhere. People will talk."

She was right, of course. Gemma from the coffee shop was probably telling Cassandra at the bakery who would no doubt share with Sam at the library. As far as I was concerned, she could stay as long as she liked, but we needed to be discreet.

I kicked the front tire of the Schwinn. "How'd you come up with Shelby Mae?"

She stilled, then did a slo-mo check of the brakes. "What do you mean?"

"In the coffee shop when Gem asked your name, you came out with it whip-fast."

Another squeeze of the brakes, then a glance behind to see them in action. "I just tried to imagine what kind of name would piss off Dash's mother—I mean, even more than Summer, which she thought was trashy—and it came to me in a blinding flash of inspiration! If I'm gonna go trailer, may as well double down."

I detected a twang there. It wasn't the first time I'd heard it.

"Where are you from, originally?"

"The Bay Area. Small town no one's heard of about thirty miles from San Francisco."

She might give off California summer vibes, but she had never struck me as a West Coast girl.

Before I could comment, she clambered off the bike, lay it against the wall, and picked up a backpack that looked familiar. It had the red-headed Disney princess on it, the one who could shoot arrows.

"That looks like Tilly's."

"I figured as much. I hope she won't mind. I'm going to head into town to pick up some toiletries and ... duh, duh, duh ... underwear."

"Why the big announcement?"

"Because I mentioned needing some spares earlier in the car and it seemed to bother you."

She had. It did. "Your underwear seemed to bother me?"

She nodded enthusiastically. "Yeah. You gripped the

steering wheel really, really tight. Because ... duh, duh, duh ... underwear!"

Maybe I had. Or maybe everything Summer did had me holding on, bracing myself for the next dip of the roller-coaster.

"Did Carter know how weird you are?"

"If he had, I probably wouldn't be in this mess. Okay, wish me luck!"

SHE HAD YET to come home.

It was close to four o'clock and there was no sign of her. I should have taken her number, but I hadn't, and now I was worried because she was riding that pile of rust and had probably fallen into a fucking ditch.

I got in my car and started driving. No sign of her on the road into town or near the harbor. My relief at finding her walking the bike along Water Street pissed me off so much that I was already rolling my window down as I pulled up alongside her.

"Where the *hell* have you been?" Dad energy to the max.

Those violet eyes went wide at my reaction. "Didn't know I needed to check in."

"What happened?"

"Flat tire." She wiped her brow and pushed a strand of hair behind her ears. "I didn't have your number. It's only a thirty-minute walk."

More like forty. "Guess we didn't think that one through." I got out, grabbed the bike from her, and put it in the trunk. The action provided a much needed moment to cool down. "How did it go?"

She patted her backpack. "I got a few things, tampons and the like." If she was expecting me to be embarrassed by the mention of menstrual products, she'd be a long time waiting. I had dealt with enough estrogen in my life to be able to handle that.

To prove how evolved I was, I asked, "Pick up any underwear?"

"No. The boutique places in town are too expensive. I didn't go into any of them, but I can tell."

"So you don't have any clean undies?"

"Don't you worry, Dino Boy. I can wash out my single pair every night before I go to bed."

Which meant she would be sleeping naked.

I really needed to stop thinking of Summer naked.

"Let's take a look."

"At my single pair of underwear?"

"At Saugatuck's clothing emporiums." If necessary, I'd drive her into the next biggest town, Holland, but I'd rather check out the local options first.

She got in the car, grumbling, "what a waste of time and money" and "I believe it's empor*ia*."

I fought to ignore how my great-gran's shorts rode up her thighs and how her smooth, golden limbs had me itching to touch. Two minutes later, we pulled up outside one of the Main Street boutiques.

"How about some retail therapy and then something to eat?" This was already going against my resolution to be discreet, but she had the Motors cap, and I was confident we could fool the lot of them.

She brightened. "I can buy you dinner. To thank you!"

"With what? I thought you were broke."

"Maybe we can find a hot dog stand?"

Even in Saugatuck, they cost a fortune. "Keep it for your underwear. Come on, let's go."

Once out of the car, she squinted at the window of Tanya's Treasures. "I think this boutique might not be for me."

"You said you needed underwear."

"I do, but I don't want to blow my limited funds on one pair of knickers. Where's the nearest Walmart?"

"Grand Rapids. If you start cycling now you could be there in, oh, four hours. Once you get your tire fixed." I touched her back and gave her a gentle shove toward the store. "Let's take a look and if it's no good, we'll come up with another plan."

"I wasn't expecting you to take such an interest, Dino Boy."

"Just being a good host. Would you prefer I wait in the car like your driver?"

She made a low growl in her throat. "Always the drama with you."

"Says the woman who climbed out a bathroom window on her wedding day."

She pushed open the store's door and the bell above gave a little tinkle to announce our arrival. I wasn't a fan of these kinds of boutiques. They were usually too small to keep a low profile and held little interest to me as a consumer. But Summer was clearly in need, and I didn't like the idea of her running around with no underwear on.

Or I liked the idea a little too much.

Someone called out from the back. "Be right there!"

"Take your time," Summer replied, then in a whisper to me, "Ninety-five dollars for a T-shirt? I don't think so."

That did sound pricey, but if it was a choice between a Walmart five-pack and an overpriced scrap of lace, I knew where my preference would lie. With the unerring male knack for being magnetically drawn to the lingerie section, I walked to a corner in the back. Frilly panties and bras were laid out like a tempting buffet. I picked up one of the bras and tried to imagine Summer in it—it wasn't hard.

But something else was.

"Did you find anything?" Summer came up behind me and raised an eyebrow. "Oh, these are pretty. Do they have your size?"

"A little small for me," I said as I stretched the waistband of a silky white pair of panties.

Summer checked the price tag. "Nope."

"I can buy you a pair, poor little almost-rich girl." I picked up the skimpiest ones, which retailed at thirty-nine dollars. So something like five bucks per square inch. "If I'm paying, this is my choice."

"You are not paying for my panties!" She grabbed them, but I held on tight, determined to win no matter the cost. Just the sight of her with her cheeks flushed and her eyes as bright as blue suns was worth forty bucks for sure.

A movement sounded behind us, then came a voice I never expected to hear.

"Hi, Hatch. It's good to see you."

CHAPTER TWELVE

Summer

HATCH AND I TURNED, both of us still holding the panties like some weird twist on *The Lady and the Tramp*. Think knickers instead of spaghetti.

A woman stood before us in a lovely halter-top and a pencil skirt that emphasized curves I hadn't possessed since before I became engaged a year ago. Dark-haired, blue-eyed, and storybook pretty, she projected Hampton Beach vibes to the max. But she also seemed a touch ... thirsty.

Like she wanted to drink a tall glass of Hatch.

"Ava? You work here?" His voice sounded rusty.

"I own this place. I opened it a couple of months ago." She smiled. A touch forced, for sure. "I heard you were back in town."

He frowned. "I thought you were in New York with your fiancé."

"Oh, I was. He's still there. I came down to get the shop

up and running. I'm training a manager." Her gaze dipped to the panties we were both still mauling, then back up at me. "Hi, I'm Ava. Ava Grayson."

She seemed older than Hatch, maybe closer to thirty-five.

"I'm Shelby Mae." I hated having to use that name. It felt like a betrayal of how far I'd come, but I had no choice. I had to protect Hatch, who was helping me out in keeping my secret identity.

"Shelby Mae? Can't say I've heard a name like that around here."

There was that smirk, an expression I remembered well. I'd seen it a million times every time someone heard my name for the first time.

Feeling a little bitchy at her superior attitude, I asked, "So were you Hatch's babysitter?"

Her brow wrinkled. "No! I'm an old friend of the family."

Old is right. Though that was uncharitable. The greedy way she was looking at Hatch had my claws out.

She shifted her attention to Hatch, who looked uncomfortable. Was that because of me or her? "Is the family coming down?"

"In a couple of weeks."

"And you and ..." She gestured toward me and left the query hanging.

"Shelby Mae's a friend of Adeline's. She's here to get some work done."

Either no one in Saugatuck followed the Rebel WAGs unless they were intimately connected to a Kershaw, or my disguise of undereye circles, waif-chic, and a Motors cap was working like gangbusters.

"What kind of work?"

"I write romance novels. Under a pseudonym, of course. Very erotic." I thumbed over my shoulder. "Just doing a little research. There's always a scene where the hero buys the heroine fancy underwear and 'instructs' her to give him a naughty show in the dressing room." At Ava's horrified expression, I went on. "Oh, I'm not that method! I just wanted to get a feel for it before I sit down and write. This place is so cute, by the way! I love that ruffle-collared blouse at the front."

I took a few steps forward, banking on Ava's business sense taking precedence over her cougar one. My hunch was rewarded when she followed me to the front of the shop. I held the top over my body and faced a mirror. I was a mess, but this blouse was fire.

"That would be so pretty on you. The cornsilk blue flowers would pick up the blue of your eyes. Such an unusual shade."

"Summer night storms my momma used to say." That hussy Shelby Mae had to have her way sometimes. And as she was on a roll ... I lowered my voice to a whisper. "Do you think Hatch would like it? On me?"

Ava looked at my reflection. "I think any man would."

I gave an aw-shucks shrug. "But he's the only one who matters right now." I turned and handed the hanger off to her. "I'll need to think about it. Hey, Hatch, let's go to dinner. I like the look of that Italian place on the waterfront."

"Sure, just want to pay for this first." He held up the underwear, the fiend.

"Oh, there's no need." It was forty bucks!

"I think there is. Gotta give you inspiration for the book."

I narrowed my eyes at him, wondering what his game

was. I'd pulled Ava away from his orbit because he didn't seem to enjoy being in her presence. Had I got it wrong? Was he trying to make her jealous?

A minute later, we were outside, walking toward his car. He opened the passenger door for me before I even realized what he was doing. Dash never did that. Once, he wouldn't even let me get into his car because he worried my rain-drenched clothes would damage the buttery leather interior.

"Why were you pretending we were a couple?" he asked as soon as he got in behind the wheel.

So he *had* heard me talking to Ava. "Because she wants you and I didn't think the feeling was mutual. I was trying to help you out."

"Maybe you *should* write a romance novel." He pulled out of the parking space.

"So what's the deal with you two?"

"Let's eat, Shelby Mae."

BY THE TIME we got to Bellagio's on the Water, my spirits had picked up because (a) new underwear and (b) I could now use my limited funds for a cocktail.

Our server practically had an orgasm on seeing Hatch.

"Hatch Kershaw, it's been what? A year?"

"Just about, Millie. How's Rich? Still working at the scrapyard?"

"Oh, yeah. He's always finding the best stuff. You wouldn't believe what people throw away. Who's your guest?"

"This is a friend of my sister's."

"Shelby Mae," I offered with my best Mississippi twang. "Charmed."

"Awesome." She turned back to Hatch. "What are your dad's plans for next year?"

"Like he'd tell me," Hatch joked, but I could hear a thread of strained patience in there.

"I'm sure you'd love him to stick around," Millie said. "He's such an inspiration."

Once she was out of earshot, he said, "That Shelby Mae thing is getting a lot of mileage."

"No one would think that gold-diggin' Shelby Mae had just given up her big payday. The disguise is doing its job."

"You can probably take off the Motors hat, you traitor."

When Millie returned, I ordered a lemon drop martini while Hatch ordered a beer. I put my ball cap down on the seat beside me and looked out over the Kalamazoo River. The sun was low in the sky and the shimmer it cast over the water instilled in me a sense of calm I hadn't felt for ages.

When I turned back, Hatch was staring at me.

"What? Should I put the hat back on?"

"You're unrecognizable." He seemed to shake himself out of some trance and returned to the menu. "What are you going to have? Steak looks good."

It better had at a whopping forty-two dollars. Last week, I wouldn't have blinked an eye at these prices.

"Caesar salad for me."

"You ordered a fifteen-dollar cocktail and now, the cheapest item on the menu." Said like I'd drowned a bag of kittens in the river out front.

"I had a snack earlier. Sub sandwich."

"Liar. The lobster roll here is excellent. Drawn butter, touch of paprika, perfectly toasted bun."

My mouth watered, my drooling obvious.

Millie returned with our drinks. "You ready to order?"

Hatch spoke first. "We'll each have a lobster roll, Millie. And a side of the Mac 'n' Cheese to share. Thanks."

"No problem, Hatch." She smiled at him, barely looked at me, and took both our menus.

"Very high-handed, ordering for me."

"Sorry, does it remind you of your former fiancé?"

"He wouldn't dare." When we went out to dinner, Dash reserved his lord-and-master shtick for the staff. It was nice to dine with a man who didn't feel threatened by the people who made and delivered his food.

Hatch raised his beer bottle. "To one day at a time."

I blinked, surprised at his words. That was another of my mantras—or at least since yesterday. Things were looking up. I had exercised, been gifted a pair of forty-dollar panties, and most importantly, had a cocktail in my hand. (I had also lost my ATM card, hurt my fiancé dreadfully, and could feel my myriad mistakes closing in on me like a dark winter's night.)

I clinked his bottle with my glass and took a sip. "Oh, that's nice."

"It's the little things."

"It sure is." I gazed out the window again because lately, Hatch had a habit of staring at me. It was strange—he never used to look at me at all. Often it felt like he was looking straight through me.

But since yesterday at the church, I occasionally found him studying me so intensely it set my body aflame. It was as if he had decided to give himself permission to do so.

Which meant that all these years I'd crossed his path, he had been working overtime not to look at me properly.

I turned back from the window. Still looking.

"What's wrong? Bad case of hat head?"

He grunted.

Okay, be like that. I decided to steer the conversation to more productive avenues. "Tell me about Ava."

"Not much to say."

I scoffed. "You two obviously have history. What's the deal? Romance gone bad? You get into it with this fiancé of hers?"

"I haven't seen her since last summer. And the engagement is relatively new."

But he knew about it. He had expected her to be out of town, and he clearly wasn't enjoying this complication.

"She hurt you."

"Just a summer fling."

Oh, it was more. I just couldn't get a read on what exactly had happened. Cheated? Swindled? Insulted his ancestors? Somehow this woman had done him wrong.

"She's older than you. By a lot." Hatch was twenty-five, a year younger than me.

He eyed me critically.

"Just saying."

"She's thirty-two."

I shrugged. "Looks older. And now she's engaged to someone else. And you wish she wasn't."

He looked at me sharply. "You have no idea what you're talking about."

Millie appeared with our lobster rolls, putting the Ava conversation at an end.

"CAN we go for a walk along the harbor?"

We had just left Bellagio's. I tried to pay, at least for my cocktail, but Hatch had already handled it on the return from the bathroom. I promised to get him back the next time, to which he offered his typical grunted response.

I wasn't ready to go back to the house yet. I liked the town, which was still lively with tourists taking a stroll either before or after dinner. Hatch touched my back, a light brush against my spine to guide me in the right direction. Every hormone in my body spiked.

Something was buzzing between us, an electricity that felt dangerous.

Desperate to not think about where danger like that might lead, I searched for something to say. "So, this isn't one of the Great Lakes?"

"No, it's a tiny one, Kalamazoo Lake. The river connects it to Lake Michigan."

"And you guys really own a boat?"

He slid a look. "Are you interested in me for my boat, Shelby Mae?"

"You bet I am, Boat Boy! Are you serious about taking me out?"

"Any time."

I didn't have a swimsuit, but I could probably scrounge up shorts and a tee from Aurora's closet.

"So what's so special about Saugatuck? I get that it's scenic and all, but it's got a different vibe to other small towns."

"It's a former artists' colony. Back in the 1910s, artists would come here and paint as part of the Ox-Bow school. They set up artists' and writers' residencies, and now it's what the town's known for."

"And for producing the legendary Theo Kershaw."

"That, too."

He spent a few minutes talking about summers in Saugatuck, which made it sound idyllic and a million miles from the summers of my childhood. We had circled the harbor and were back at the Bellagio, heading to the car when a familiar figure emerged from the restaurant, carrying a takeout bag.

The Panty-Purveying Cougar herself.

She was coming our way but hadn't spotted us yet. I wasn't sure what possessed me, but I hadn't liked that melancholy in Hatch's expression when he talked about her earlier. Something had happened between them, and whatever it was, it left him sad and her wanting more.

Hatch went to open the passenger door for me again, ever the gentleman.

So I decided to do a most unladylike thing and take advantage.

Placing both hands on his chest, I pushed up on my tiptoes and pressed my lips to his. I wasn't expecting him to respond. In fact, I didn't need him to respond. I just wanted Ava to know she couldn't have him. She blew her shot with whatever she'd done and now, as far as she was concerned, this man was mine.

His lips were warm, his body hard and unyielding. I had kept my eyes open because this was a fake kiss, a gesture to prove something.

It was also a mistake.

Because Hatch's eyes smoked over with, first, surprise, then a recognition that something significant was happening here. And it wasn't silly Summer's attempts to pay it forward.

No, this was another of Shelby Mae's poor decisions.

He didn't ask what I was doing. He just went with it, like the great adapter he was. I had pulled back, assuming that was enough to get the point across. But it wasn't enough for Hatch. His hands slipped around my back. One fixed above my butt, the other dipped—and dipped—to below it. As in cupping one butt cheek.

I gasped, and he dove right into a kiss so startling I had no choice but to part my lips and take him in. He devoured me, thoroughly, letting me know who was in charge. A couple of seconds later he slowed to sips and soft licks.

But now *that* wasn't enough for me. I angled my mouth for more and moved my hands up around his neck, seeking purchase. His hand tightened around my butt cheek and squeezed, then levered me up so I was inches off the ground.

I found myself spinning, spinning, and landing in the passenger seat of the SUV. Instinctively my legs parted and wrapped around his waist. The kiss continued, then abruptly stopped.

He blinked, retreated, stared, then touched his mouth. His expression was just this side of astonishment.

"Plenty of material for your book, Shelby Mae," Ava called out.

Hatch turned to Ava, who stood there with her takeout bag and a smarmy grin.

"Ava," he said quietly.

"Have a good night, you two." She made it sound indulgent, like she was blessing us. I didn't care. I saw how annoyed she was, and that was all that mattered.

Or, at least, I thought it was before Hatch upped the ante on that kiss. At which point I had tried to pretzel myself around his body.

You naughty girl, Shelby Mae.

I gave an embarrassed chuckle. "Mission accomplished."

He whipped back to me. "What?"

"I saw her coming out of the restaurant, so I improvised." *And so did you. Did you ever.*

"That was for Ava's benefit?"

"Of course it was. I'm not in the habit of accosting men I hardly know in the street." Only I didn't think he knew Ava was there. In fact, I was certain he didn't. Which meant the moment overcame him—and then it grabbed me by the lady balls as well.

His expression turned stormy. "Get in the car."

"Are you annoyed?" I knew he was, but I wanted him to admit it. He was such a hard ass when it came to fessing up. He couldn't even come clean about why he hated me.

"Me? Nah. I'm just peachy."

"You don't sound it."

"You want to walk home or are you getting in the damn car?"

CHAPTER THIRTEEN

Dash Crying in his Mojito in St. Bart's

Chicago Rebels forward Dash Carter is currently licking his wounds at his family's vacation home in St. Bart's. Sources tell us that what was supposed to be the happy couple's honeymoon and a chance for Summer to become better acquainted with the Carter family, is now a somber affair. A close family member revealed that even after several years, Dash's fiancée was "somewhat of a mystery," and there were concerns that she might not fit the Carter culture. It looks like those concerns were well-founded! The "enigma of Summer" deepens as no one has reported seeing her since her pre-wedding bolt to freedom. Even the bridesmaids are keeping their lips zipped.
-@HotGoss

Hatch

. . .

THANKFULLY I WAS SLEEPING in the pool house. Distance was about the only thing preventing me from strangling my guest.

So, she thought she was helping me out. She'd witnessed the vibe between me and Ava, figured Ava might want to pick up where we left off, and saw an opportunity to give me an assist.

Only I didn't know. And because I didn't know, I thought Summer was kissing me for real, which made me so damn happy in that moment. To hell with Carter and the bro code and every reason kissing this woman was a bad idea. I had Summer in my arms, and all was suddenly right with my world.

Until it wasn't.

Until I realized I was another one of her dupes.

The last thing I needed was to be letting a grifter like Summer Landry under my skin or into my bed.

Don't think about bed. Or Summer in a bed. Or the things you want to do to Summer in a bed.

At just after seven in the morning, I had returned from a run that did little to excise this woman from my brain. I could see her in the yard through the window in the pool house. She wore a bikini, or the top part of one with shorts, and had Adeline's bike turned upside down while she examined the tire. A toolbox lay open at her feet, with various implements strewn about.

She didn't look like she knew what she was doing. And all that bending over ...

Her head shot up, our gazes clashed, and I almost ducked. In my own house!

She waved.

I refused to return it.

Realizing how ridiculous this was, I headed outside, along the path to the patio, and stood before her, hands on hips.

"You're doing it wrong."

"I am?"

"It doesn't matter if you fix the tire puncture. You need to see if the inner tube has a hole in it."

She pushed a finger through the slash in the tire. "I can't feel anything else in here."

"Of course you can't. And you need to remove the wheel. Otherwise, it's just guesswork."

Her gaze coasted over me in my sweat-dampened T-shirt and my board shorts. I thought I saw appreciation there, but she was quick to look away. She lifted her hand to her brow and swiped, leaving a black smudge that I wanted to ... *nope, don't want to do anything.*

She pulled on the axle. "Should it just release here?"

"You can open and hold that lever and I'll unscrew the nut from the other side."

"Or you can just tell me how to do it."

"It's easier with two people." It made no difference, but I couldn't leave her now that I'd started even if the mansplaining made me sound like a dick. In a couple of minutes, we had the tire off.

"Now, we need to deflate it." I pressed down on the center of the valve, and we heard a low hissing sound. I worked the tire bead loose to pull it away from the wheel and free the inner tube.

All this took a few minutes, and I was fully conscious of Summer standing there in her tiny, red bikini top and a pair of khaki shorts that must have been Aurora's. But that bikini did not belong to my great-grandmother.

"Where did you find that swimsuit?" I knew it was a bikini but even saying it felt too intimate.

"I'm guessin' it's Adeline's."

I remembered now. "She wore that when she was ten." The tiny triangles barely covered Summer's tits, but because she was thin—too thin—it did just enough and left the rest to my overwrought imagination.

"I hope she won't mind."

"She won't." *But I do. I mind a lot.* "Could you get a basin of water? There should be a small tub under the sink in the kitchen."

"On it!"

Off she went, and thankfully the shorts were loose on her, so I didn't have to deal with that complication. There was the butterfly tattoo on her shoulder, though, like I needed any more reason to be attracted to her. Not that tattoos were instant turn-ons. Rosie had a whole sleeve of tattoos and while I'd had a crush on her when we were kids, it had never gone beyond that. On Summer, even a cliché of a tat was getting me all worked up.

Or maybe I was just remembering the feel of her in my arms last night and the taste of her mouth. That kiss had kept me awake most of the night, and when I finally succumbed, my dreams were sweaty and sexy and filled with Summer.

I took a closer look at the tire damage. It was a clean cut, not ragged at all, which meant Summer cycled over something sharp, like a piece of glass in the road. I examined the tube and found no damage. We might not need that water after all, but I didn't regret sending Summer away for a few minutes so I could gather my wits and adjust my cock. She came out of the house with the basin sloshing water over the sides, and by the time she reached me, her bikini top was soaked.

Nipples. Beautiful, suckable candy peaks I couldn't even see. My imagination handily filled the gaps. Now I had the combination fantasy of Summer's wet bikini and those pretty, pink nipples running a horny riot in my head.

"Just put it down," I barked.

"Okay." She sounded so fucking cheerful. Was this how she acted around Carter when he was in a bad mood? All conciliatory and soothing, the good little woman?

I went through the motions of putting the tube under the water, searching for punctures. As far as I could tell, it was just the main hole near where the tire was damaged.

"Want to talk about it?" she asked.

"It was just a kiss."

"I meant Ava."

I blew out a calming breath that had no impact on my mood whatsoever.

"Nothing to talk about."

"You sure? I get the impression she followed us last night. Stalker vibes."

I squinted, then stood so I could tower over her and tell her what was what.

"Ava's not stalking anyone." So she had been fairly aggressive in pursuing me last summer, but she understood the score now.

"She knew we were going to that restaurant, and then, hey, that's where she got her take-out from. Are you still annoyed about the kiss?"

"I don't care about the kiss. I'd just appreciate a heads-up next time you're planning to dive into one of your many roles."

She opened her mouth, but I was already gone, heading

to the shed to look for a bike repair kit. She had started this business with the tire, but she didn't even have the correct supplies? Annoyed at her effect on me, I rummaged around in the shed until I found what I was looking for. When I turned back, Summer was standing at the entrance. The morning light limned her figure, giving her a haloed silhouette. She might be thin, but she had shapely hips, and lovely legs, and I was sick of the sight of her.

"One of my many roles?"

"Forget it." I moved forward but she blocked the exit.

"No, tell me. What roles have I been playing?"

I shrugged, though my shoulders were so stiff the movement made me wince.

"Tell me."

"Summer, the adoring fiancée. Summer, the perfect assistant to the GM. Summer, the good friend. Summer, the gold digger. Summer, the nervous skeleton bride. And now we've got a whole other part of your repertoire as you move into summer stock. We've got Shelby Mae, the erotic novelist. And is it Summer or Shelby Mae who thinks it's a whole lotta fun to lead a guy on with the best kiss of his life, the same guy whose teammate she just jilted? I guess you contain multitudes."

She stared at me, dumbfounded. I only wish I'd lost my own ability to speak about twenty seconds ago. Had I really just told her that was the best kiss of my life?

"I-I'm sorry. I was only trying to help."

"Well, don't. I've got a bike tire to fix."

After a moment, she stepped aside and I walked by her, ignoring the wide-eyed shock on her face. We certainly had enough of that to go around.

CHAPTER FOURTEEN

Summer

THE BEST KISS *of his life.*

Sure, it had been good. Okay, amazing. But the best? Hatch must have kissed plenty of girls—Ava came to mind, unfortunately—but I couldn't possibly have been at the top of his scale, could I?

It might have been a top-shelf kiss, but Hatch Kershaw was not happy about it. He thought I was pretending—and I was. At first. It started that way and developed into something else and now I was left wondering how to get me more of that amazing mouth.

Which was all wrong, of course. I had just crashed and burned my previous relationship, and now I was thinking about another man less than forty-eight hours later. Hatch was right: I did contain multitudes!

The part of me who was not a trophy wife wannabe or a

bride on the lam needed to think about the future. This morning, I had texted Dash.

> Could we talk?

It hadn't been delivered. I appeared to have been blocked. I understood, but I had hoped he might have calmed down and would want to listen to what I had to say. Of course, he had every right to excise me for his mental health.

Still, I needed to talk to someone, and Hatch was clearly too angry to be a good sounding board. Both Adeline and Rosie had left messages. I suspected Adeline would be more sympathetic while Rosie would be all "fuck that guy" without even caring that I was at fault.

I texted them both on our group thread, Chirpy Chicks.

> Is anyone up for a chat with the most hated person in the Midwest?

ROSIE

> If you're talking about Conor, then it's a pass from me. If you mean you, then of course!

Rosie had the weirdest hate-on for Conor Kershaw.

ADDY

> Summer, we've been so worried about you.
> Can you do a video call?

ME

> Could we just do voice? Not looking my best.

Adeline did not need to see me in her childhood bikini. Good luck explaining *that*. Three minutes and one dropped call later, I was in an audio group hug with the only friends I had right now.

Self-pity much, loser?

Shut it, Shelby Mae.

Adeline went first. "First off, are you okay? Tell us you're safe."

"I'm safe. Honestly. I just had to get away."

Rosie chuckled. "There's getting away and there's *getting* away. That was absolutely wild!"

"I know. I'm so sorry for putting you guys in that position. How awful was it?"

"Well ..." Adeline stretched out the word. "I asked Lars to tell Dash. He was there when Ro came to say you'd left, and he *is* a teammate. But Dash had already received your text by then."

Another person I had to apologize to. "Tell Lars I'm sorry. Tell everyone I'm sorry."

"Listen, you can be sorry for the timing," Rosie said, "but if you weren't feeling it, then it was better you make the break. Any regrets?"

"Only that I hurt Dash. I tried talking to him but he's not ready."

"He probably needs some time," Adeline said.

"He's with his family in St. Bart's, so I'm sure he's surrounded by people who care about him."

"Never mind Carter," Rosie said. "What's going on with you? Where are you?"

"I went out of town for a while. Just to clear my head."

"Okay," Adeline said, likely picking up on my reticence. "I hope you're getting some sun and being kind to yourself. Is there anything we can do?"

These girls were too good to me. I did not deserve them.

"No, nothing. I'm going to call Ryder now and see about getting my job back."

"But they already have a new person in the role." I couldn't blame Rosie for sounding skeptical. "I met her the other day. She's kind of scary."

A bit of a dragon lady, Lainey was perfectly capable of handling Ryder. "Maybe not the same job, but something else in the org." An internship was my goal, though I could see that now being an issue.

"They might be able to help out," Adeline said softly.

"But will they want to?" Rosie finished. "Dash works there, too, and to be honest, they're probably going to take the side of the asset worth millions over the woman who left him at the altar."

"You're right, I know. I just don't want to feel so ... worthless."

"You are *not* worthless." Adeline sounded positively fierce. "Call Ryder. You never know, he might be able to help."

Rosie hummed, which meant she was unconvinced but was biting her tongue not to say anything. "Do you need us to come see you? If you don't want to be in Chicago, we can come to wherever you are."

I would have loved to see them, but I had a problem.

Hatch.

I couldn't reveal that he was my reluctant knight-in-hockey-pads. That he had whisked me away to safety and given me a roof over my head.

That I had tried to repay his kindness with a little role-playing and a kiss for the ages.

"It's okay. I think I should be on my own for a while."

We signed off with promises to check in in a couple of

days. I didn't want them worrying about me or asking too many questions.

They were right about one thing: Ryder wouldn't give me my job back. Onto Plan B. Next, I called Scott Kincaid in Rebels Talent Development.

"Hello."

"Hi, Scott, it's Summer."

"Summer! You're the last person I expected to hear from."

"Did you get the report I sent? It should have landed in your mailbox a few days ago." Three days before the wedding, in fact. I'd worked on it, eager to take my mind off my topsy-turvy life. Maybe I should have thought more about my upcoming nuptials instead of NHL prospects.

"Yeah, I got it. Great work as always. I figured you'd be so busy with everything." He paused a moment, then asked, "Are you okay?"

"Yeah, I am. I know it didn't look good, how I handled it. Anyway, I just wanted to reach out to talk about continuing the work we've been doing together."

If I phrased it as a collaboration, maybe he would be more open to the idea.

"You said you wanted to enjoy married life for a while and that's why you quit your job."

I sighed. "It was more that Dash didn't like the idea of me working. He thought it didn't reflect well on him."

"Okay. So what do you want to do now? I don't see you going back to the front office."

"No, that's not likely. But I had hoped I could be considered for the Rebels intern program. I've produced good work for you, and you had said you'd put a good word in with Ryder."

He hummed. "Right. But things are kind of complicated now. We have Carter to think of, and for us to be offering his ex-fiancée a position—"

"Unpaid."

"All the same. It would smack of disloyalty." He took a breath. "But ..."

Hope flared. "But?"

"You've got a great eye for hockey prospects, and your reports are excellent. I think we just need to wait for the dust to settle and see where we stand."

That was probably the best I could hope for. "I appreciate your willingness to be neutral here."

"Don't know about neutral. But I recognize talent when I see it and I'm not talking about Carter."

I smiled. *This.* This was what I was supposed to be doing. Why had I not put my foot down with Dash and told him this was what I wanted?

Because your instincts are terrible, Summer. Otherwise you wouldn't be kissing Hatch Kershaw ...

"So, now that you're not on your honeymoon and you're out of a job, it sounds like you have some time on your hands."

"Do you need some work done?" Maybe Hatch had a computer I could borrow.

"I'll send the specs to your email."

We had always worked using my personal email because Scott worried Ryder would think I was being poached by another department. *Sensitive office politicking.* Once I ended the call, I felt a little bit better.

Then I remembered my run-in with Hatch. Today's run-in, not the kiss from last night. I would not be devoting any more brain space to *that.*

I threw the University of Michigan tee over Adeline's bikini—I suspected Hatch was annoyed with my skin-revealing outfit—and headed outdoors. He was stretched out on a lounger wearing board shorts and nothing else.

My mouth went dry. Then it watered. Then dry again.

Talk about skin revealing. That body was fact and proof of deities who worshipped the male form. All the Kershaws were beautiful, but Hatch was in a class of his own. Scimitar cheekbones, a perfectly chiseled jaw, those jewel-green eyes. Okay, so I was focusing on the face because dwelling on his body might make my hormones bubble to a boiling point.

I chanced a dip south. He had chest hair. I hadn't expected it, and seeing that smattering of hair, the goodie trail, the flatpack abs, had every part of my body doing a celebratory samba.

He pushed his sunglasses onto his head, gave a Class A glower, and barked, "What?"

"Were you able to fix the bike?"

"No. The tube is shredded. I'll have to get a new one in town."

It hadn't looked that bad before, but what did I know. "I'll get an Uber later. Bring it into the bike shop myself."

"Do you need to be in town today? More underwear to buy? Mayhem to cause?"

"No—"

"Then I'll take care of the bike later."

I figured it wasn't a hill worth dying on, not when there were a million other peaks to climb.

"I just talked to Adeline and Rosie."

"Did you tell them where you were?"

I shook my head. "I thought it best to keep that to

myself." I took his silence for agreement. "Could we talk about what happened before?"

He sat up on the lounger and swung his long, strong legs so his feet touched the ground. I took it as an invitation to sit beside him. My thigh brushed his, and the heat of him wafted into my airspace. Damn, call Air Traffic Control at once.

"I should apologize," he started, surprising the hell out of me.

"Oh, no. That's on me. I shouldn't have blindsided you last night. Yet another example of my poor decision making."

"You had good intentions." He raised an eyebrow. "I think."

"I did. But the execution wasn't the best." I took a chance. "Unless it was?"

"Unless it was what?"

In for a penny ... "Unless it *was* the best kiss of your life. Which I find hard to believe because ..." I trailed off. Why did I find it hard to believe?

It was the best kiss of mine.

"Because ..."

Oh, he was going to call my bluff. "I guess I would have thought you'd have had tons of great kisses. Great kissers tend to produce similar results in the kissees."

"The kiss*ees*? We're making up words now?"

"Sure, why not? And don't change the subject."

"Your reasoning is that I couldn't have possibly thought last night's kiss was the best kiss of my life because I'm such a great kisser and I would have already achieved those lofty heights?" When I merely smirked my agreement, he went on. "You don't think a great kisser could always be striving to kiss better, to improve the kiss experience, to aspire to the best kiss ever?"

He sounded so passionate, and I had to admit I *loved* that. Dash was so blasé about everything. Nothing stoked his fire, not even hockey, yet here was a man getting riled about kissing and the desire to always be improving.

In his passion, he had moved a touch closer, his thigh pressed against mine, the heat of his skin searing mine.

I smiled, unable to help myself. For the first time in weeks, maybe months, I felt lighter. "I apologize for casting aspersions on your mission to become the best kisser in all the land."

He grinned back. Oh wow. "As you should."

And there we were, smiling like fools. We'd achieved some semblance of a truce, though we hadn't been enemies before. Well, he hadn't been mine, but I think he thought I was his.

I would question that later.

His grin faded. "What I said, about the roles you play— that was uncalled for."

"You were right. I do play different parts. I always have."

He waited for me to elaborate. It was one of the many things I enjoyed about him. He didn't try to fill silences. He just let me be.

"I've always wanted to fit in, and sometimes that involves being a chameleon. Becoming who people expect in a particular situation. The perfect fiancée, the good employee, the fun friend." The hard worker, the dutiful daughter, the subservient wife. "I might be a lot of those things you said, but I'm not a gold digger. That's the one thing I take issue with. Dash and I were casual for the longest time. When we first started dating, I had to pay for all our dinners and movie tickets because he wanted to make sure I wasn't 'in the relationship for the money.'"

"What a jerk."

Yes and no. "He had a right to be wary, even if the way he expressed it was weird. I don't think it even occurred to me that we would get married. I wanted other things. A career. A life that wasn't dependent on anyone else. But he was persuasive, and I suppose I fell for his charm and maybe I was blinded by his wealth. I never had that, growing up. Suddenly I'm being offered the world on a platter, and it fried my brain a little."

His stare was so intense, yet I couldn't look away. His close regard fueled me.

"But then I started to see that every day we were engaged, every day counting down to the wedding, felt like a death march. Like I was heading for a life that hollowed out every part of me. And it was all my fault. Not Dash's, or not really. I think he started to realize that he'd invested all this time in me—in us—and he didn't want that to go to waste. But I was in so deep that I couldn't see everything that was wrong with us as a couple. Until he told me to give up my job."

"You liked your job," he said quietly.

"I loved it. And I know it doesn't seem that important, helper to the general manager, but I was learning so much. And I wanted to keep learning. Maybe do something bigger instead of signing on for something smaller. I barely resisted, Hatch. Dash told me I didn't need it, and I let that dream go in service to what I thought was another. Being a rich man's wife." I swallowed. I could hardly believe I'd spoken all these words aloud to this man. "Never again. Now I'm going to focus on me. My career, even if I can't get back with the Rebels. Ryder might give me a good reference, or ... something."

So a bit of a damp squib there at the end. *Go, girl* to *oh no, girl.*

"Sounds like this is the role you were born to play."

I searched his face, looking for hints of humor and saw none. He was being his usual, serious self.

"What role is that then?"

"Summer Landry, the girl with the world at her feet."

CHAPTER FIFTEEN

Hatch

SUMMER NEEDED ACCESS TO A COMPUTER, so I made her a guest login, and she sat out on the patio in her bikini and worked away. She had the decency to cover up with a white shirt she found in the laundry room—my shirt —and I had the indecency to think this was hitting another one of my fantasies.

Summer wearing my clothes. My sweats, my tee, my tuxedo jacket, now my shirt.

Teammates first, H. Always.

I needed to get away for a while. "I'm heading into town to get some supplies for the boat."

Her head shot up. "The boat?"

"Thought we might go out this afternoon. If you're still interested."

"I would love that!"

After that chat about kissing, Summer's admission about

the roles she played and why she let her relationship with Dash go so far had been illuminating. Talking about what had happened before, joking around about the kissing, had eased things between us. Something still gnawed at me, though.

It could have been like this all along.

All this time, I'd made it my mission not to like her. Put her into a box, walled her off, because it was easier than thinking about *what if.* I hated seeing her with Carter, and the fact that he had a few years more experience than me on the team and was more often in the roster mix didn't make it easier. The guy had everything I wanted.

Now I was seeing Summer more clearly. Not that it made a blind bit of difference to the situation. Sure, it was better not to be at each other's throats, but that didn't mean we should be at each other's mouths.

Or other body parts.

"Can you get the new tube for the bike while in town?"

"Sure." There was nothing wrong with the tire, but I didn't want her gadding about town where someone could spot her.

"So what are you working on?" I could have looked at the screen, but I didn't want to pry.

"Just returning gifts. Well, creating shipping labels so I can be ready to print them off when I get back."

"No one else can do that for you?"

"It's my responsibility."

Fair enough. I left her to it and drove into town. In the Gourmet Grocer, I picked up a few things for the boat, all the while wondering about Summer and Carter, and how they had got to that point. I had believed her today when she said she wasn't a gold digger, but I had sure thought that before.

My experience was that a lot of women were looking to land a rich pro-athlete, and if a guy disrespects his girl—especially in public—and she's okay with that, then there had to be a reason. My sister thought Summer was trying to reform Carter. That she was too decent to be in it for the money, but I hadn't listened. Unfortunately, I had personal experience that colored my thinking.

And that personal experience was now walking toward me in the Condiments aisle.

I had to admit that Ava looked good. Since her engagement, she'd acquired a cultured air. Her fiancé was an investment banker, as far as I knew, and Ava had landed pretty well for herself. When I hooked up with her last summer, she was more of a townie, a good time girl not interested in anything serious—or so I thought. I was looking for consolation, a salve to my self-inflicted wounds.

"Looks like the Gourmet Grocer is the place to be on a Monday in Saugatuck." She picked up a jar of wasabi and looked at the ingredients. "How are you, Hatch?"

"No complaints."

"Well, you wouldn't have. You and your girlfriend sure know how to put on a show."

I turned to her, looking for some indication of where this conversation might be going. She'd played her hand with me and lost. But she'd obviously played another and gained a fiancé.

"It's early days."

She smiled serenely. "Any chance we could go for coffee?"

"Why?"

She seemed taken aback at my abrupt response. "To clear the air. I feel like things ended ... not so well between us. I'd like a chance to explain."

"Listen, Ava. There's nothing to explain. After it happened and the dust settled, we realized that it wasn't meant to be. You caught me at a strange time in my life."

"Are you saying I took advantage?"

"I'm an adult and I knew what I was doing. What happened is done and I don't want to relitigate it." I picked up a jar of olive tapenade and put it in my basket.

"Okay, I get it. I just wanted to say no hard feelings."

"None, whatsoever."

***

Summer

WHAT I KNEW about boats could barely fit in one of the triangles of my bikini. But I trusted that Hatch knew what he was doing, and that I was in good hands. Over my itsy-bitsy child bikini, I slipped on a purple-and-white checked shirt. A pair of Aurora's capris in lilac and a floppy-brimmed straw hat completed the ensemble.

This was a motorboat, and smaller than I expected. I'd imagined I'd be stretched out on the deck like a model in a Duran Duran video. While there was room to do that, it wasn't quite the luxury yacht experience I was used to with Dash, which sounded awfully snooty. I had never really enjoyed those summer excursions to the Cape with Dash and his family, though. I always felt too much pressure to be on, and Dash didn't like that I wouldn't take more than a few days off from work.

They won't need you in the summer, babe. Hockey season is over.

I'd tried to explain that the front office staff continued to work in the off season and that the business of running the org didn't end in June. But he hadn't understood. He didn't think I needed to worry about "franchise business" in my lowly position.

Frankly, it was a relief to return home from the Cape to Chicago without him. I could wear cozy sweats and hit Lula's, the cat café (Dash wouldn't allow any pets). I even volunteered at the animal shelter run by Ashley, Rebel player Dex O'Malley's wife, though Dash thought I was just trying to suck up to the partner of one of the team's elder statesmen. Everything was transactional with him.

It certainly didn't feel like that with Hatch, who hadn't asked me for a single thing. Instead I was the one making demands: hide me, strip me, feed me, kiss me.

I needed to stop thinking about that last one.

After about ten minutes on the water, we came to the middle of the lake and settled. Captain Hatch put on a life-jacket, tied a rope to a metal bar on the boat, then lowered the anchor carefully. After checking for something—lake sharks, perhaps?—he let the anchor out fully. Stepping back, he removed the lifejacket and his T-shirt with it.

Oh Mama.

He spied me drooling. "What?"

"Impressive. Your anchoring technique, that is."

He smirked. "Thanks. Didn't realize you were such an expert."

"Oh, I've sailed. Boated. Trawled the waves. Dash's family has a yacht."

"Well, this is likely a bit more humble, but at least it doesn't require a crew."

"Self-sufficiency is good."

"I was thinking more of privacy." He took a seat and

popped the lid of a cooler. "La Croix? Or something stronger?"

I peeked inside, noting cans of soda, flavored water, beer, ciders, and wine coolers. Even a bottle of Sauvignon Blanc. "Wouldn't have pegged you for a wine cooler fan."

"I don't see it as a threat to my masculinity. Neither are pink shirts, liking to cook, nor eating a woman out."

Well, then. "I'll start with water." *Or a bucket of ice, if you have it.*

He passed off a lemon water and took one for himself. I sat on the bench a couple of feet away. I drank about a third of the water, then set it to the side.

All while Hatch watched me. It no longer freaked me out, mostly because I liked when he did it. I liked how my skin tingled and my stomach fluttered.

"Could you tell me what happened with Ava?"

"After how I overreacted to that kiss, I suppose I owe you that." He blew out a breath. "I came down here last summer and we hooked up. I'll admit that I wasn't really that into her, but I was at a low point—" He stopped, restarted. "I used her to make myself feel better. She wanted more. Pushed for labels, for something big to happen. Then she told me she might be pregnant."

My mouth fell open. "Was she?"

He shook his head. "No. I'll admit I wasn't careful the first time with her. But later, I was. I should never have continued when I knew nothing would come of it. She finally admitted the pregnancy was more hope than reality. I knew then that I'd let it go too far."

I felt a little bad about my mistaken read of the situation. I might have hurt her feelings last night, but if she tried to trap him with a baby ... Also, Hatch's assumptions about me being a gold digger made more sense now.

"I'm sorry if I made things awkward with her."

"It's okay. Besides, she's engaged."

"Oh, she'd throw over New York Guy in a heartbeat if she thought there was the slightest chance with you!"

He rolled his eyes. "So I guess you did me a favor after all. Made it clear we've all moved on."

I rubbed my hands together. "See? My instincts were completely right! Summer to the rescue."

That made him laugh, and the ease of it gave me a fizz in my veins to rival this bubbled lemon water in my hand. Something he had said struck me, so I circled back to it.

"You were at a low point when you met her."

He appeared to be choosing his words carefully. "Yeah, I had a thing for someone, and it had just become clear that it wasn't going to happen."

"Oh. And Ava was a way for you to forget."

He nodded. "Not fair to her, but sometimes that's what you need. An escape from what's weighing you down."

True. We were all looking for ways to escape our pain. Our pasts. Often they were one and the same.

Look at me: fleeing my problems, the cliché of a runaway bride, fantasizing about the hot hunk who saved the day. As much as I wanted to, I wouldn't use sex to escape, not even with the god posed like a sunbathing lion before me. Neither would I judge anyone who did.

"Sometimes we can think only of the moment. Of getting through it. My momma was a big fan of numbing the pain with anything that made her feel good. Alcohol, drugs, sex. She let every guy run roughshod over her, treat her like dirt, steal every penny and cheat her. She thought those were the prices we pay for the small sliver of pleasure a man could give you."

"Is that what Carter was to you? A way to escape?"

I'd never looked at it that way, but there might be some truth in it.

"I thought this girl who grew up poor with no prospects and no one to encourage her to do better had finally made it to the pinnacle. Hot, rich athlete, who doesn't beat me or treat me terribly, and if I wasn't a hundred percent in love with him ... well, life is a compromise. To be honest, up until he asked me to marry him, I didn't even think we were going in that direction. We didn't live together. We'd broken up several times over stupid things. I was sure he cheated on me, but I could never prove it. And he had to convince me to marry him. I didn't say 'yes' the first time. Or the second. The third time, he asked me in public because he assumed I wouldn't embarrass him in front of his friends. Shows what he knew."

A tear escaped the corner of my eye. There would be no more compromises. No more subjugating my life to a man and *his* career.

Hatch leaned forward. "Hey, it's okay. You don't owe me any explanations."

"No, I-I don't. But saying it aloud helps me get it straight in my head."

He stared at me for a moment. "Your momma, huh?"

I blinked. "What?"

"You said 'your momma' and it's not the first time that Southern twang has crept into your speech. Where are you from, Summer? Really?"

CHAPTER SIXTEEN

Hatch

FOR A MOMENT, I wondered if I'd gone too far.

Summer had been honest about her relationship with Carter. I understood all too well how you could get caught up in circumstances beyond your control. How a rush of feeling, positive or negative, could override your common sense. She had given hints about her childhood—poverty, neglect, hopelessness, all things she had overcome. Meeting someone rich and successful might look like she'd made it out of the trap of her past.

But there was more. With Summer, I was learning there usually was.

"You're not from California, are you?"

For a moment, I thought she'd make a joke and repel my intrusiveness. But instead she gave a small, relenting sigh. "No, I'm not."

"Where did you grow up?"

"Mississippi. A town that's barely a town, more like a dot in the woods. Thunder Creek, it's called. I ran away when I was fifteen. Then again when I was sixteen. That second time, I managed to stay away, and I sort of reinvented myself."

Not what I expected at all. "In what way?"

"With a crash course in Yankee. Figured out how to dress and talk and act like someone who wasn't from the backwoods of nowhere. I toned myself down. Not immediately, of course. Those first couple of years, I lived on the streets in Jacksonville—that was as far as I could get before I ran out of money. I did odd jobs, gardening, dishwashing, all under the table stuff. Once I turned eighteen, I was able to get better jobs with longer hours, and once I had a place to live and some money set aside, I started on the road to me."

A lightbulb went off. "Shelby Mae is your real name."

"My legal name. I wanted to change it, but you've got to do it in the county where the records are and there was no way I was goin' back there."

There was more to that, but I wouldn't push. Yet. Summer—or Shelby Mae—was running away from more than a mismatched fiancé.

"Were you always a hockey fan?"

"That came later. At night I'd work in this sports bar where the owner was obsessed with hockey. No one in that bar wanted to watch it but he insisted, and I became completely invested. Soon I was giving anyone who would listen my opinion on the games, the tactics, the players, the trades. My boss called me 'Shelby Slap Shot.'

"Then his son made a pass at me, and wouldn't take no for an answer, so that was the end of that. I figured I needed to make my way in a bigger sports town anyway. I had this idea I could work concessions at Wrigley Field or sell beers at the Rebels Arena, and that would be a way to connect to that world. Silly dreams, right?"

"We all have to start somewhere." Every word out of her mouth had me on the edge of my seat. I had a million questions, but I figured it was best to let her say her piece in her own time.

"During the day in Jacksonville, I'd hide away in the conference rooms at the public library and listen to tapes to try to fix my accent."

Ack-zennt. I was picking up on it more.

"Just trying to smooth out my vowels, go more neutral. Not because I was ashamed, but I thought it might make me sound more cultured. Make it easier for me to get a job in Chicago. I thought everyone in the Midwest hates all us Southerners, that I'd be labeled a hick before I'd even gotten a greeting off. I'd saved enough to move to Chicago. I worked as a barista for a while, in a cupcake shop, even a stationery store. In every place, I learned something. Fancy coffee, fancy pastries, fancy paper. The people who could afford those things, who came in every day, I'd watch them, how they acted, how they behaved. And I filed it all away as part of Project Summer."

Project Summer. What she must have overcome to get here.

"And how did you get onto the Rebels front office?"

"I started temping with an agency. I had to fake some credentials. My GED, a college diploma. I still had Shelby Mae Landry as my legal name but every new job I'd start, I introduced myself as Summer. That's who I wanted to be, and no one questioned it, because I think we're all reinventing ourselves in every new situation. I listened to how people spoke, mirrored them during conversations, and soon enough I felt like I was fitting in. Then I saw an ad for the

Rebels, a junior administration position for one of the executives in Hockey Operations. I just knew that job was going to be mine!"

Her eyes sparkled, showing me the Summer she had been hiding for as long as I knew her. Or maybe this was the version I'd refused to see because I was too butthurt to pay attention. Something panged in my chest, sorrow for time wasted and opportunities lost.

"When I interviewed, they asked me all the usual questions and one of the execs ended with the classic: 'give me an example of a problem you've overcome and how you handled it.' I made sure to keep it short and impactful, but I also slipped in some hockey knowledge, like how Dex O'Malley's plus-minus was looking particularly stellar this season, and good thing *that's* not a problem we need to overcome."

"Sneaky."

"It was! But I had them grinning away. They were going to remember me when they looked back through the candidates because no one else in an admin position would have sprinkled her answers with hockey stats. I thought it was so clever. And I got the job! Two years later, Ryder's assistant went on maternity leave, then said she wanted to stay home, and I asked if I could move into that position. A lateral move, but I felt that was where the action was."

"By that time, you were dating Carter."

Her blonde brows dipped together. "Yeah, I was. But it was casual. On again, off again. I told Ryder up front in case it was a conflict, and he said he didn't see a problem."

Now conflicts abounded. "Carter said you had no family living."

"That's what I told him." Two spots of color appeared high on her cheekbones. She was embarrassed to have lied, but especially to have lied to the man she had planned to spend her life with. "I know that makes me some sort of snob, but I haven't spoken to my mother or anyone back in Thunder Creek for ten years. I never felt safe there. She—" She broke off, her eyes welled.

"Sunshine, it's okay." I couldn't help myself. I scooped her up into my lap and wrapped her in my arms. She sank into me willingly. "I'm guessing you had a pretty toxic home life." Why else would she be running away at fifteen?

"You could say that."

"No reason why you wouldn't want to separate from all that. Leave it behind."

She rested her head against my forehead, composing herself. "It seems like another lifetime. In a way it was. Shelby Mae, wild-spirited, but caged. Then I come here, reinvent myself and become Summer. Toned down my wild, only to put myself in another kind of cage. Thinking I had made it when I was merely running in place."

"So you reinvent yourself again. Take what you've learned and figure out what comes next."

She peered at me through the veil of her fair lashes. "Not exactly what you expected when you asked me where I came from, was it?"

"No, but nothing about you has been expected. I like that you told me the truth. That you felt comfortable enough for that."

"You make it easy. It's so strange because ... well, you're not going to believe this."

I let my thumb brush the soft skin at her waist. She shivered, but didn't move away.

"Try me."

"Do you remember the first time we met?"

I nodded. Like I could possibly forget that Rebels Christmas party five years ago.

"That was my first date with Dash, and I'd already met your dad and a few of the other Rebels because I'd worked in the front office for a few months. But I'd never met you."

"I was home for the holidays from college. I went to that party because I had a crush on Giselle DuPre."

She laughed. "Harper and Remy's daughter?"

Harper Chase was the Rebels CEO while Remy DuPre was a former star player and now her husband.

"Uh huh. But she had brought a boyfriend, so I got over it really quickly. She was too old for me anyway."

"I figured you were distracted. When we were introduced, you barely said two words to me, but I was a little boy struck when I met you."

I felt like I'd swallowed a puck. "Boy struck?"

"I had a crush on you, Hatch Kershaw! But then the next time we met—I think it was in the Empty Net when the season was over, maybe four months later—I tried talking to you, asking about your new contract with Denver. You shut me down. Cold!"

"No, I didn't." *Yes, I did.* "I just didn't want to be too friendly with you because you were another guy's girl."

"To the point of being rude?" Another laugh, like it was so amusing, while inside I was dying. I had been rude. I had shut her out. I didn't want to get to know her.

Because knowing her, and not being able to have her, would have broken me.

And yet, not knowing her had the same effect. This last year, especially, had been miserable.

"I hope I've made up for it," I said quietly.

"Oh, you have, Dino Boy. You most definitely have."

CHAPTER SEVENTEEN

Summer

WE LAY out on the lounges, absorbing the sun's rays as the boat bobbed lazily in the water. Each conversation made it easier between us. Unburdening will do that.

Hatch had taken what I'd said and been so damn sweet about it. It felt good to talk to someone about my past, even if it was just a fraction of what had happened to me. If I told him everything, he'd probably jump overboard in terror.

As it was, he knew I was a Mississippi girl, a runaway, a fraudster, and a hockey nut. Surely enough for one day.

"Ready for lunch?"

I looked up from the Joanna Lindsay Viking romance I'd found on Aurora's nightstand (with the naughty bits underlined. Go, Aurora!). On the small deck table, Hatch had set down a cheese plate with figs, walnuts, a couple of spreads, and wheat thins. I could have cried.

"Of all the favors you've done for me, Hatch Kershaw, your provision of cheese is the kindest."

"Can't believe you went without for so long." He was busy opening the bottle of Sauv Blanc.

"I had to cut it out to fit in my wedding dress."

"Well, eat up there, Sunshine. You need to start filling out that junior bikini."

My body sizzled at his nickname for me. I stuffed my mouth with a slice of brie and a cracker, and said with my mouth half-full, "God, you're obsessed with my lack of curves."

He merely frowned at that, then poured a glass of wine and passed it over. After we'd taken sips and filled our plates, he took another look at me.

"What I said about you being a skeleton bride, that wasn't very nice."

"No, it wasn't."

His eyes appeared troubled. "I was angry because of the kiss and because you look like you've been dieting. Putting all this effort into this wedding when it seemed to be really weighing on you. Sometimes I'd see you at various gatherings over the last year and you didn't look happy. I wish I'd been a better friend to you."

My heart expanded at his generosity. *A better friend.* I had needed that, but I would never have expected it from this corner.

"Apology accepted."

I was still curious as to why he'd been so cold to me while I was with Dash. Was it really because I was someone else's girlfriend? Since we'd been more open with each other, he had been a completely different person. Friendly, charming, sexy.

Well, he'd always been sexy. I wasn't kidding when I

said I had a crush on him. It hadn't gone very far—the cold shoulder tended to douse the embers of desire—but it had existed, a dangerous tremor under the surface that threatened to erupt each time we met. If he'd given any indication he was interested, I might have parted ways with Dash and shot my shot.

No "might" about it.

Even thinking that raised a million red flags for my relationship with my ex. I would have happily thrown him over if Hatch Kershaw had deigned to smile at me.

"That kiss," I said.

"What about it?" He turned to me, not just his head but his entire body. He wanted to give me his full attention. It had been a long time, and I soaked it up, my shriveled raisin of a heart craving the sunlight of his gaze.

"We joked about it earlier, but it was no joke, really," I said. "It was ... amazing."

"Because we're both such great kissers."

"The chemistry was there," I observed. "*Is* there."

He waited a moment. Inhaled. "But it's complicated."

"It is." This made him uncomfortable, so I backtracked. "You still think I'm too thin?"

"A little," he said candidly. "But you don't look as gaunt as you did when you flattened me outside that church."

"According to you, this skeleton is too light to have done any damage!"

He arched an eyebrow. "I never said that. If anything, your bony knees almost ended my genetic line."

I stood and waved my wine glass at him in mock drunkenness. "You haven't seen what my bony knees can do, Dino Boy."

He stood and gathered me in his arms. His skin was warm from the sun, his body solid from hard work, and let's face it, winning the genetic lottery. This man was perfect in every way.

"Right this minute, I only care what this mouth can do." And then he kissed me, complications be damned. The taste of wine and him brought my nipples to sharp points and dampened my panties.

"Watch you don't get hurt," I murmured into his mouth. "I'll be careful."

I was kidding around, referring to my bag of antlers slenderness, but the way he responded—he actually worried I would hurt him. And not just physically.

I'd already hurt one man. I couldn't do it to another.

Assuming this man cared enough about you to get hurt, Summer.

It could happen, Shelby Mae.

The kiss deepened, and I felt myself sinking to a place from which I might not return. Anxious, I pulled back. "This hasn't suddenly become a good idea, has it?"

He shook his head. "It gets worse with each passing second."

"We should stop."

"Agreed."

We did not stop.

The kiss went on, deep and sinful one moment, soft and playful the next. His cock felt hard against my hip, his palm hot on my lower back. His fingers teased beneath the waistband of the shorts, but never further.

I wanted further.

But I also knew that as soon as we crossed that line, any chance I had of recovering some semblance of my life would disappear. As it was, I would have to leave here soon. It was far too dangerous for all sorts of reasons.

I drew back. His lips were puffy from my kiss, his eyes

glazed, dark, and smoky. No man had ever looked more beautiful in his abandon.

"We can't, Hatch."

"I know, Sunshine." He pressed his forehead to mine. "I know."

CHAPTER EIGHTEEN

Summer

FOR THE NEXT FEW DAYS, we stayed in our respective corners—he in the pool house, me in the main like the lady of the manor. I did research, worked on scouting reports, and kept an eye out for my name on the gossip websites. There were a couple of mentions but nothing particularly scurrilous. A few distant photos taken by the paps of Dash in St. Bart's showed up online, but the family wasn't commenting right now.

In the mornings, before the sun started to beat down, Hatch and I biked on the rural back roads and along the lakefront. In the evenings, he grilled on the patio. My appetite had returned with a vengeance. I ate like a starving woman—steak, shrimp, the best Mediterranean-marinated chicken I'd ever tasted. And cheese. So much cheese.

After dinner we'd sit in the wicker chairs out back and watch the sun set in a watercolor-striped sky. Sometimes we'd dip into TV shows, usually *Taskmaster* and *Downton Abbey*, comfort watches for me. Hatch was new to *Downton* and I enjoyed explaining to him the foibles of the British upper classes at the turn of the last century. (His comment that *Mary was the worst* was spot on. Mary *was* the worst and Edith was done dirty at every turn. Writers, just let her be happy!) My villain origin story was the untimely death of Matthew Crawley, and I loved sharing that with someone.

One night, just over a week from my doomed wedding day, we were relaxing on the patio after scarfing down a particularly excellent charcuterie board. There was a stillness in the air that made me sad, like summer was ending though it had barely started.

I took a breath. "I can't hide out here forever. It's not fair."

"To me?"

"Especially you. I don't want to interfere with the team brotherhood. The longer I stay here the more likely it is that someone will recognize me. Or maybe I'm assigning myself too much importance in the Rebels universe."

He stretched out his long legs, and I averted my greedy gaze. That was another side effect of my recently returned appetite. It came with a ramped-up libido. I wanted to attack Hatch Kershaw like he was a hunk of mature cheddar.

"Definitely. No one would even think for a second that erotic romance novelist Shelby Mae is the former fiancée of Rebels superstar Dash Carter the Third."

"Can you believe there were three people called Dash?"

"It's pretty incredible." His phone rang; he checked and silenced it.

"Who's that?"

"My agent."

"I can step inside if you want to talk to her."

He shook his head. "It can wait. She's shopping me to other teams."

I sat up straight in the chair. "You're leaving the Rebels? But you only just got here."

"I'm *thinking* about leaving. I only agreed to the trade in to play with Dad in his final year."

"It's been great for the team, having you both on it."

He shrugged. "Good optics, I suppose."

"And now he might stay for another year. How do you feel about that?"

"I want him to be happy. But I also want to play without the comparisons."

"You're a right winger, he's a D-man. Not too many comparisons, but I can see why it might be tricky for you. He does suck up a lot of attention."

He laughed. "He does! He always has. I'm not looking to hog that much of the spotlight. Playing under the radar is fine by me. But I played better in Denver."

His team before he came to Chicago. It was true—his stat sheet had slid since his arrival. He hadn't played that well in the Finals either.

"Why do you think that is?"

He considered it for a moment. "I think I've let the media get to me. I go out there, worried I won't play well, that I'll disappoint Dad. Then I *don't* play well, and it becomes some self-fulfilling prophecy, at which point I feel like shit because I'm blaming him, when I'm the problem."

"He did push for you to play on the team in his final year. Maybe that wasn't part of your planned career trajectory, and you felt you'd lost some control over your life."

He looked relieved that I understood. If anyone knew

about the perils of letting someone else take the reins, it was me.

"Have you talked to your dad about this?"

"No. He wouldn't like it. And I hate the idea of blaming him for my bad play. It sounds petty."

I could see how that might not be received well. "I think he'd rather you were honest."

He smiled. "Maybe."

Not for the first time in his presence, a lovely calm settled over me. So strange when before I'd felt nothing but tension whenever I was near him. I looked out over the garden, then snuck a glance back at him, only to find him watching me.

"What?"

He took a deep breath. "I'm just thinking how weird things have turned out. The two of us here, breaking bread, biking the trails, sharing confidences, listening to 'valet' pronounced with a T on some snooty period piece. Basically, getting along like normal people."

"Snap. I was thinking that, too. I guess I'm not sure why it was any other way."

"Does it matter as long as we're friends now?"

"I suppose not." But I still wanted to know what his deal was and why I had offended him so much for so long. I was also torn about the "friends" label, especially when those calves of his made me squirm. Of all things.

"It's such a nice night," he said. "Would you like to go for a drive?"

"I'd love it."

We drove around the lake with the windows down and the wind in our hair. John Cougar Mellencamp's "Jack and Diane" came on the radio, the perfect soundtrack as we traveled the back roads. It was a summer feeling, and reminded me of those days in Mississippi, tooling around in Jez Corden's TransAm. At fourteen, I was too young to be hanging out with boys like Jez, but I was a wild thing who needed freedom to roam. A couple of months later, Momma met Clark, and he saw a chance to make a buck and tame my wildness at the same time.

You ain't gonna be messin' with those trailer trash boys, Shelby Mae. We want you intact for your husband.

I had thought it the biggest joke. Barely fifteen and my marriage arranged by the man who had spent less than six months with my mother. She was too drunk or high to figure out his game. He could have done anything to me, and she wouldn't have noticed. Thankfully he wasn't interested in me that way. Small mercies that my utility was as an asset to be sold.

So I ran away. But Clark found me in Biloxi and brought me back. That was when I realized I needed a plan. A way for him to never find me.

"Oh, that looks pretty." I pointed to an opening off the road.

Hatch stopped and backed up. "That's where the kids park. Overlooks the lake."

"We could just look at the water, couldn't we?" Instead of each other.

"Yep." One syllable, into which he managed to infuse a dumpster truckload of gravel.

A minute later we were parked, facing the lake, the headlights shining on the water. Suddenly the car was the size of a postage stamp, the air leaden like a summer storm was brewing. I got out and stood in front of the hood.

The car door closed behind me. "You want up?"

"Up?" I turned to find him standing close, holding a

light blanket. The headlights provided just enough light to illuminate his thoughtful expression.

"On the hood? If we're gonna park, we need to do it right."

"Oh, okay."

He spread the blanket out. His hands gripped my waist gently, and he took a second to adjust his hold before lifting me with ease and placing me on the hood. For a few moments, he held his hands curled on my waist and stood before me. My thighs itched to part, to bracket his hips, to draw him in like that night we'd kissed outside the restaurant, but he retreated before that impulse could overtake my common sense. He climbed up and sat beside me.

Across the bay, the lights of Saugatuck twinkled. I'd seen signs earlier saying we were officially in Douglas, the next town over.

"Jason's joining the Rebels in the fall," he said. Jason Isner was Theo's half-brother, Hatch's uncle, and a star defenseman for the Boston Cougars.

"I'm so glad that worked out."

He tilted his head. "You knew?"

"I'm the assistant—or I *was* the assistant to the GM. I knew there was talk of bringing him over. We have to be realistic about your dad's longevity. Even if he decides to stay on, we need to build up the defensive bench. Lars isn't getting any younger and MacFarlane is good but not ready to lead. Jason would be a great addition to the D-lines."

He looked surprised. "You *do* know your hockey."

I chuckled. "You don't work in the front office for close to five years without picking up a few things. I've drilled down on the Central Scouting rankings, compiled reports, put together presentations. When Dash was at away games,

I spent most of my time researching the league prospects for the Scouting and Player Development Division."

"Ryder had you doing that?"

"Not Ryder. I brought it up once, but he didn't seem interested. One night at a game, I got talking to Scott Kincaid and I told him a couple of things about one of the rookies, just some strategy analytics. Nothing major." Hatch was staring at me, intense as ever. "I told him that I'd love to be a scout one day. One thing led to another, and I started producing reports for him."

"Is that what you've been working on with my laptop?"

I nodded.

"But you gave up your job."

"I did. I regret that. I regret caving to Dash. But I think I had it in my head that separating myself from this administrative job would allow me to take the scouting option more seriously. That people might take *me* more seriously. I convinced myself that this would be a good step." But then I overheard Dash and his mother talking about getting me knocked up as soon as possible. "And now I've messed it up completely. I made Dash look like a fool and no one's going to take me seriously at all. I'm just the flake who climbed out a bathroom window in her wedding dress. What does she know about NHL prospects or Corsi scores or whether Jason Isner is a good fit for the team? He is, you know! I told Scott all about it when I handed in my report."

I sniffed, which had Hatch looking alarmed.

Woman. Tears. Bad.

"Hey, it's okay."

It really wasn't, though. Love was for suckers. No more. From here on out, I was going for what *I* wanted.

Starting now. Tonight, I wanted to be Shelby Mae again, that girl who scrapped and scraped her way out of the backwoods. I'd leaned too far into Summer, trying to be all things to everyone. Determined to never make waves and accept compromise as the measure of success.

"It's okay," he repeated. He inched closer, and the heat off him burned through me. "You're going to figure it out."

"Right now, I can't see the road ahead." As long as I stayed here in this bubble, I didn't have to look too far. Not with a gorgeous guy like Hatch Kershaw blocking the view. It wasn't his fault. He had been nothing but kindness itself, and here I was taking up so much space.

I raised my gaze to his. "I'm not making things easy for you, am I?"

"You never have," he bit out. And the heated look he gave me? I would say it was hatred but that wasn't right. This was more like ... torment.

"What do you mean by—"

The rest of my query was swallowed by a kiss.

CHAPTER NINETEEN

I HAD ASKED FOR THIS.

So he didn't take much persuading, but then Shelby Mae never had problems attracting boys. Or men. Now Hatch was kissing me like he had no choice. Like I had given him no other option because I was some sort of siren, drawing him to his doom on the rocks.

His mouth moved over mine with assurance, sweet and full of promise, and when his tongue touched mine, the kiss exploded into pure, sexy filth.

I pulled him down into the gutter with me. His weight was perfect, though the hood was hard on my back. I didn't mind. It was summer, and Stevie Wonder's "As" had just come on the radio.

I'll be lovin' you always.

He drew back an inch and looked down at me, his dark head framed by the starry night sky and soft moonlight.

"This is a terrible idea," he murmured. It would be the epitaph on my gravestone.

"I'm sorry." And then I kissed him again because I truly was sorry, but I was mostly angry. With Dash. With myself. With Hatch for being so cold and stand-offish toward me this past year when it could have been *this*. Not that anything would have happened, but he had acted like he hated me all this time and I don't think I realized until now the toll that took on me.

That hasn't changed, dummy. Hate has never stopped a man from wanting in a girl's pants.

Shelby Mae, right again!

So we were both agreed it was terrible, but then the worst ideas tended to feel so good. Maybe it was the taboo, the forbidden, the danger. Or maybe this was simply a reaction to uncommon kindness. The man who had whisked me away to safety, my reluctant rescuer.

So far, it was just a kiss. It could remain there, a bumped line but no further. Unless we pushed the boundaries yet again.

Shelby Mae had *ideas*. She always did.

The minx slid a hand under his T-shirt and splayed it over his abs.

He inhaled on a hiss, expelled on a groan, and the kiss turned feverish, as did his hands. They were suddenly everywhere, like my touching him had given permission to explore in ways he would never have dared. One hand held my head still for the mouth-fucking of a lifetime. The other wandered over my ass, my back, my ass again, then turned braver. He cupped my breast through the thin fabric of the shirt I wore—his shirt—and plumped what little I had in the way of boobage.

Now it was my turn to groan. I would never have

considered my breasts sensitive—Dash hadn't paid much attention to them because they were, in his words, "no bigger than mosquito bites." He had promised to get me a boob job as soon as we were married, not that I'd asked. The idea of owning my tits was hilarious to him.

I had buried that one deep. People mix up love and possession, but they're opposites. My former fiancé thought they were the same.

Hatch lifted his head. "Did I hurt you?"

"No, no, just—sorry you don't have much to work with there."

He remained silent.

"Meaning the itty bitty tittie committee," I explained.

"What the fuck are you talking about?" He sounded annoyed. No surprise there.

"I don't have a lot going on up there so—"

He squeezed my left tit again and I arched off the hood with pleasure.

"Does it feel good?"

"Y-yes."

"You don't sound so sure." This time, he slipped a hand inside the shirt, which had become miraculously unbuttoned, and grazed his knuckles over the slight swell of my breasts, making me shiver.

"You're beautiful."

I took a breath, though it was harder to inhale than usual. Likely because of the man in front of me, looking like I was a golden vision in his dreams.

My lungs filled, my heart rate picked up, my eyes ... watered. What was wrong with me?

His breath was hot on my neck, his hands warm on my waist. I closed my eyes as he moved his mouth softly over my collarbones, brushing them with a feather-light touch. The reverence in it undid me.

I shivered. So did he.

He returned to my neck and moved my hair aside. Neck kisses. I saw this gif once of a guy kissing his lover's neck, which I'd thought the most romantic thing ever, and I played it over and over. Something like a sixties' French movie. This wasn't that.

This was better.

I sighed and our mouths met like it was meant to be. We kissed for a while, exploring each other like we had all the time in the world. Just two kids necking at the lake. But soon, I started to ache. My breasts, my belly, my pussy. The kisses were perfect but not enough, yet Hatch was in no hurry. It was as if he'd found a missing piece from his existence and was determined to make every moment count.

I loved that, but also not. I was starting to feel hot and desperate. I needed to feel his skin against mine, his hardness against my softness. I needed it all.

I pulled at the hem of his shirt—I had to do it a couple of times for him to get the message. He drew back, his eyes wild, his lips puffy from my ravaging. I was topless while he still had his T-shirt on, and that would not do.

I pushed the shirt up and he finally understood.

The headlights of the car gave off enough light for me to see the perfection before me.

"Wow," I whispered. It wasn't the first time I'd seen that killer body, and I didn't think I would ever tire of it.

His mouth kicked up at the corner, then his gaze dipped to my breasts. "Wow, right back."

And you know what? I believed him. This wonderful man thought I was beautiful with my tiny breasts and my skeleton-bride frame. I gripped his arms, barely able to get my hands curled around the biceps, they were so thick.

I ran my palms over his pecs, enjoying the tickle of his chest hair. He felt so solid, so present, and it was all enhanced by how he looked at me. Truly saw inside me.

I shivered again.

"You cold?"

Not physically, but my mind had yearned for a connection this vital. "Warm me up, Hatch."

He covered my body with his, careful not to apply his entire weight. Wrapped up in him, I let myself fall into pleasure. His mouth on mine, my hands on his back, chest to chest with his roughness abrading my nipples. His fingertips found my breast again, but now there was no barrier. He played with the sensitive peaks, using his thumb to tease and stroke.

Merely the appetizer to his tongue.

When his mouth closed over my breast, I almost arched off the hood. I moved my own hand down past the waistband of his shorts and squeezed one hard butt cheek. Moved around so I could undo the top button.

Then the zip—

He left off from suckling my breast with a wet pop and met my gaze. "Nope."

"But I want to."

He smiled. "Not yet, Sunshine."

But apparently those rules didn't apply to him. Three seconds later, *my* zipper was down, and Hatch's fingers were hovering over my panties. The ones he bought for me from his former fling.

As the kids might say, could we *be* any more complicated?

He stroked the lacy edge, then hooked a fingertip beneath the band. "Yes?"

"No," I said grumpily.

"Because?"

"You won't let me touch *you!*"

He smiled. "Is that the only reason?"

"Isn't it enough?"

He lay his palm flat on my stomach. The heat of it seared me, sending shockwaves to my core. I wanted that hand moving down, down, *down*.

He cocked his head. "Have you ever heard of the phrase 'cutting off your nose to spite your face'?"

"Have you heard of 'you scratch my back and I'll scratch yours'?"

He licked my nipple and earned himself a throaty moan. "Or I'll lick yours if you lick mine?"

"Yet you won't even let me touch, never mind lick."

"There's timing to consider here, Summer. If I let you touch me, I'm going to explode before I can get you off. Is that what you want?"

It was what I was used to.

"Or would you like me to stroke your pretty little pussy with these fingers that are dying to get inside you?"

Jesus, that was hot. "Just do it."

"What's that?"

"Finger fuck me, Dino Boy!"

He started laughing and then I started laughing, but not for long. Because he slipped a talented finger inside my panties and delved between my folds.

"Push your shorts down," he ordered.

"You mean, your great-grandmother's shorts?" I didn't know why I was messing with him, but I was enjoying this so much. The teasing made it sexier. Maybe the brain truly *was* the biggest sex organ.

"Shut up and drop 'em."

Giggling, I pushed them down, along with my panties, and let him pull them off. But the giggling died when he pushed my thighs apart and palmed me hard. I was so close that all I could do was squirm as he moved the heel of his hand up and over my clit. Needing leverage, I placed one foot on the hood and opened wide like the absolute hussy I was, giving him as much access as possible.

He continued to stroke, then reapplied his mouth to my nipple, sucking and nipping. His head rose, and he moved closer to take my mouth. Still with the stroking, this time, his fingers inside me, stretching and finding new points of pleasure. His tongue mimicked the rhythm of his fingers, and I dug my own fingers into his arms, holding on as he drove me over the edge.

So good.

I thought that was it. It would have been fine—better than fine—if it was.

But then next I felt him move, slipping off the hood to stand between my legs.

Which he pulled toward him, his hands on my ankles.

Our gazes met, and his was—well, the word "feral" came to mind. He bent his head between my thighs and started to lap at my pussy.

That's—oh my Lord. Soft at first, belying that beastly gaze I thought I saw a moment ago. But soon hunger took over and his hands gripped my ass and lifted them so he could get even closer. His tongue speared inside me, then the flat of it moved over my clit, and again, I broke apart, sobbing with the unbridled pleasure of it.

And he groaned, too, deep and heartfelt, like my taste

was better than anything that had ever passed his lips. A moment later, he was back on the hood and had taken me in his arms, settling me into a post-coital cuddle.

As the haze of the orgasms wore off, I shot up to a sitting position. "What about you?"

He was lying back, his arm behind his head. "Don't worry about me."

I moved to touch him where all the action was. He grasped my wrist.

"I said don't worry."

I blinked, as a chilling realization dawned. "Is this your way of staying loyal to a teammate? If you don't get off, then you can say nothing happened?"

He narrowed his eyes. "I'm fairly certain *something* happened."

"Too right it did! But apparently if I don't touch your dick, you're absolved of all blame here. Only Summer gets an orgasm—"

"Multiple orgasms," he interjected.

"Multiple orgasms! So she's the big old cheater."

I slid off the hood in a move that would have made one of those no-good Duke boys proud. Then I was forced to hunker down to search for my underwear, in a move that wasn't quite as cool. The bikini top had landed a ways away, while the shorts were at the back tire. No sign of the panties, which I didn't care about because they were tainted by the seller.

"What are you talking about?" Hatch slid to a stand and faced me, bare-chested. The top button of his shorts was open in a very fetching manner, revealing a V-cut and a hint of pubic hair that should not have been attractive, but of course was.

"Maybe you get to hold this over me, huh? Punish me

for being so weak?"

I made do with the shirt, which was thankfully long enough to cover my assets.

"You seem to think that me giving you an orgasm—"

"Multiple!"

"Multiple orgasms, is punishing you for being ... what are we arguing about here?"

I stabbed one leg into the shorts, realized it was the wrong leg, and tried again.

"You won't let me give you a hand job. And maybe it's because you feel bad about Dash, so this is your way of dealing with that. If you don't take any pleasure out of it, you don't have to feel you've betrayed him."

He grasped my arms before I had a chance to poke a second leg into his great-grandmother's shorts. Like I said: *complicated*.

"You think I didn't take any pleasure in what we just did?"

"I think I got off and you get to be St. Hatch of the Blue Balls!"

He pulled me close and kissed my forehead. Such a sweet gesture that I almost lost my fury. Almost. I obviously felt guilty at what we'd done, and I was resolved to take it out on him under the guise of any excuse imaginable.

If only I'd enjoyed this level of self-awareness while I was engaged to another man.

"Summer, I would happily let you give me a hand job but there's not much point."

I peered up at him. *Oh!* "Because you ... can't perform?"

He had said if I touched him, he would explode, but that could have been standard sex rhetoric.

"I can perform just fine. In fact, I already did—without your hands-on assistance."

"No!" I clamped a hand to my mouth.

His grin was rueful and this side of cheeky. "Congrats, Sunshine. The taste of you was enough to make this grown man come in his pants."

CHAPTER TWENTY

Hatch

I WAS PRETTY DAMN happy and it wasn't even about the sex.

Okay, the sex was a big part of it. I wanted more sex with Summer because I suspected it was going to be amazing. All of the interactions so far had been: the kiss, the hood, even my early fucking arrival. However, if full-on, fist-the-bedsheets, break-the-bed sex wasn't on the table, I would still have been thrilled.

Because I was connecting with this woman in a way I'd never connected with anybody. Whenever I thought of the reasons why this was a bad idea—*Carter, Carter, and what's that you say? Carter?*—a rain cloud zoomed in and dumped a shit-ton of water on my Summer-filled head. So I raised a metaphorical umbrella, put on a mental windbreaker, and blocked it the fuck out.

Summer had shared with me her fears, her insecurities,

things that made her relationship with Carter clearer. It didn't fix the fact that he was my teammate, but it gave me more clarity about *her*.

That was all I needed.

The drive home was about ten minutes, and we spent it sharing goofy smiles and linking fingers. I was holding hands with Summer Landry and heading home to spend the night with her. Maybe more ...

Let's not get ahead of ourselves.

As soon as we parked in the driveway, we turned and looked at each other. The lightheartedness of before had vanished, leaving gravity in its wake.

I broke the silence. "Would you—"

"Yes."

"How about—"

"Definitely."

We exited and circled the hood—ah, memories—to meet in front of the car. She still wore my shirt, but no bikini so her sweet, suckable nipples poked against the thin fabric. Her shorts, the ones that belonged to my great-grandmother, hung loose on her hips. That should have made it weird, yet I had never wanted anything more.

Instinctively we moved into each other's arms and kissed, the force of our melding like a flash fire throughout my body. After embarrassing myself tonight, I knew I had to pace this better. First, privacy. Second, a bed. Assuming I could make it.

I would make it.

I scooped her up, loving the sexy gasp she expelled, and loving even more the raised eyebrow she gave me as I walked around the side of the cottage, the pool house my goal.

"Show-off," she murmured as she applied gentle kisses

to my cheekbones and nose and eyelids (one at a time, thankfully, so I didn't trip). The house was unlocked, which was probably not the most sensible, but I was sure as hell glad of it now. I would stand for no barriers.

Once inside, I moved toward the bedroom on the first floor. Finally, I lay her down, but I didn't let her go. Parting from her seemed like the worst idea, so I lay over her, cupped her sweet ass and wrapped her leg around my hip.

"How long do you think you'll last this time?"

I shut my eyes. Smiled. Opened them again.

"You're never going to let me forget that, are you?"

"Nope. As a first-time story, it's one for the books." *A first-time story*. As if we were building a history here, with that hood fumble as one of the building blocks. "I might even have to invent a nickname for you," she added.

"No nicknames. I have enough nicknames."

"Right. Dino Boy. Boat Boy." She thought on it, though not for long. "Maybe Minute Man or Hatch the ... Flash! You'll need to show me a hundred more orgasms before you make me forget The Hot Hood Chronicles."

"Think I can manage that. If you let me." I kneeled up and peeled off my T-shirt, forcing the laugh to die on her lips.

"You are something else, Hatch Kershaw." She leaned up on her elbows and shrugged off the shirt. I helped with her shorts, then kicked off my own.

Brushing a hand over my cotton-clad erection, she curled a finger in the waistband and pulled me toward her.

"You don't have to take it slow," she said, clearly pitying me for my earlier performance.

"Don't rush me." I wanted to savor every second. I'd already seen her under the moonlight, and she was just as beautiful gilded in the muted lamplight.

Earlier, she was nervous—about the size of her pretty tits, the feel of her rib cage under my hands, the fact we were crossing lines. Now, she looked up at me, her gaze clear, true, ready.

How had I gotten so lucky?

I ran my palm over her breast, used my thumb to peak a nipple. Coasting my palm down over her stomach, I cupped between her legs. She planted her foot on the bed, opened to give me access, and arched into my touch.

She was already soaked. My fingers picked up the moisture, plucked, swirled, and stroked.

Feeling wasn't enough. I needed to see.

And taste.

I spread her thighs wider, then kissed the soft skin inside her leg. She quivered as I moved closer to the beating heart of her. Touching my lips to her pussy, I tasted her again, the perfect combination of heat and sugar. Instantly hard, I began to doubt my stamina once again. I had already made her come a couple of times, and I was determined to yield more orgasms from her.

I could run hockey stats. Dad's were better, but I didn't need to be thinking of him right now. To be honest, I wanted to stay in the moment with Summer.

She grasped my hair. I peered up.

"Hatch, I'm not going to last."

"Not fun, is it? Though, it's kind of the idea."

"But ..."

I leaned up. "What, Sunshine? Tell me."

"I—I hate to talk about what my sex life was like before, but this is already a million times better."

It would be immature to gloat right now. Later, maybe. "Tell me how you want it. Slow, dirty, fast, raw? I'll give you anything you want."

"I like it ... slow and like you can't get enough of me."

"That won't be a problem. You taste so good, Summer. I could eat you out all day, so how about you let me get down to the business of making you feel sexy and wanted?"

"Yes, please," she whispered.

Two minutes later, she screamed my name and bucked against my mouth. Thank God, because I was about to blow myself.

I checked in as I grabbed a condom from the nightstand. "I'd prefer to be inside you when I come. Is that okay?"

"Well, as I missed the main event before—"

"Dammit!"

She laughed. "Permission for your trigger-happy dick to climb aboard, captain."

I rolled on the condom, and despite my burning need, I still managed not to act like getting to home base was my only concern. Summer liked it slow, so that's what I gave her. One long, consuming stroke into her, then a moment of stillness to take it all in.

I interlocked my fingers with hers and grasped her hand tight at the side of her face. Holding her gaze was a revelation.

She didn't look away.

I couldn't have if I tried.

"You feel amazing," I whispered.

She squeezed. I groaned.

That made her chuckle. And *that* made me pinch her ass.

"Hatch!" With her accent, it sounded like *Haa-itch*.

"That's what you get for your sass, Sunshine."

"I think I can handle any punishment you dish out."

And then I kissed her, loving how connected I felt to

this person I had wanted nothing to do with for so long. Now she was here—and I had no intention of letting her go.

My mission, if I chose to accept it: give this woman the best night of her life.

A slow build, just how she liked it, each thrust deeper than the last, each stroke bringing me closer to release and to something else. Something indefinable.

Something so special I wasn't sure it was real.

CHAPTER TWENTY-ONE

Hatch

I WOKE to the sound of my phone buzzing and the unease of an empty bed. I assumed Summer had gone up to the house to start breakfast, but first I would have to deal with the Kershaw Kinder text thread, already in full flow.

CONOR

I can't believe Jason is moving to the
Rebels before me!

LANDON

You already have a job, dickhead.

CONOR

But they were supposed to hold the
Kershaw legacy slot open for me.

Despite Conor already being contracted to start with the Detroit Motors in the fall, I was willing to bet someone at the Rebels was thinking of a way to get him to

Chicago. Gotta keep the Kershaw money machine pumping.

ADDY

You don't play the same position. They need another D-man, so that's Jason.

CONOR

But they don't even know if Dad's staying on. Unless they do. Has Dad already decided?

ME

Not that I know of. But you could ask. You live in the same house as him.

CONOR

Addy, what does Lars know?

ADDY

Nothing. Dad's still weighing his options. I think it's great Uncle J will be back in Chicago.

CONOR

Fucking Jason. Stealing my job. Probably my women.

LANDON

Whoever Jason's banging is not the same demo as you.

CONOR

Speaking of puck bunnies, any news on the Carter and Summer front? Hot Goss doesn't even know where she is, and those guys always have the inside track. They're offering a "Where's Summer?" reward.

I shot upright. Offering a what?

I checked the *Hot Goss* site and sure enough they were monitoring "sightings of Summer" and offering an unnamed sum for information on her whereabouts. So far she'd been spotted in Miami, Vancouver, Bismarck—I snorted at that one—and in such far-flung places as Ibiza and the south of France. I smiled to myself. No one would even think of looking for her here.

> **ADDY**
>
> She's taking some time for herself, as she should.
>
> **CONOR**
>
> Yeah, but what happened? NoBo said she ran off with a firefighter.
>
> **LANDON**
>
> No, he didn't. He said she would have had to call the fire department because how else did she get out of that bathroom window without help?

Shit. Boden had seen me right under that window before the service was due to begin.

Calm the fuck down. If NoBo suspected anything, he would have reached out.

Unless he told Carter first.

I shook myself awake and pulled on my board shorts. No one knew anything. It was all speculation because everyone loved to gossip, and this was prime tabloid fodder.

> **ME**
>
> Maybe she was a gymnast in a former life. Or she has cat DNA. Or she jumped no fucking problem.
>
> **CONOR**
>
> In Jimmy Choo heels?

I growled. I was going to kill my brother. Still, Summer

would probably get a kick out of it. She had eased up over the last few days, and I was happy to say I might have contributed to that. Thinking of her as she lay on the hood of my car, her beautiful skin gilded by moonlight as I brought her off made me unaccountably happy. And that was before she spent the night in my bed.

There were obstacles. A fuckload of reasons why this couldn't work. But after last night, I was determined to figure them out.

I headed up to the house, feeling like one of those idiots in a cartoon, prancing through the forest while woodland sprites and baby deer frolicked around me. If I strained my ear, I could hear bluebirds chirping and butterfly wings flapping because the world was in Technicolor and life was good.

Summer wasn't in the kitchen. It was spotless so maybe she had headed straight to the shower.

I shot off a text.

> How about breakfast, Sunshine?

I started on the coffee, then looked for the griddle to make French toast. My dad's famous recipe was called for here.

My phone buzzed with a reply.

SUNSHINE

> I'm already on the train back to Chicago.

> Thank you for everything. I'll never forget it.

The runaway bride had struck again.

CHAPTER TWENTY-TWO

OF COURSE I couldn't stay.

I had just exited one relationship and the way I was gravitating toward Hatch, I was about to make a huge mistake and jump into another. With my ex-fiancé's teammate, no less. Simply impossible.

You already destroyed one player, Summer. Why not go for the team?

Shelby Mae might be the sarcastic voice in my head, but I agreed with her on this one. This was absolute madness.

On the train back into the city, I indulged in a memory from this morning: Hatch stretched out on the bed, the cover slipped enough to reveal the curve of his gorgeous glutes. His dark, tousled head lay on the pillow and lovely, sooty eyelashes dipped like a delicate fringe on his cheek-bone. I captured a mental snapshot for the lonely nights ahead, then continued my cowardly slide out the door.

Retaking the reins of my life required that I leave all that behind. My first stop was my apartment building in Riverbrook where I usually received a lovely smile from Victor. But not today. Showing up with a wedding dress stuffed into a backpack was definitely a vibe. I hated treating it with such disdain, but I couldn't leave it behind.

"Hi, Victor. How are you?"

"Good, Miss Landry." I could tell he was thinking that it should have been Mrs. Carter. "Mr. Carter isn't back yet from his"—he cleared his throat—"vacation."

"Oh, that's fine. I just need to pop in for a spell." He winced. "And I'm guessing you have strict orders not to give me access."

"The locks have been changed, and Mr. Carter didn't leave a spare key for you, I'm afraid."

Just as I thought. "The thing is, Victor, I need to get my belongings. Would that be possible?"

"Sure, Miss Landry, I can do that."

Wow, that was a lot easier than I expected. Maybe I still retained some of my Southern charm after all. I followed him to the elevator bank and gave him a genuine smile as we entered the car. But instead of using his master key to access the penthouse floor, he pressed B.

For Basement.

"What's going on?" The elevator landed with a thud instead of the usual smooth arrival that heralded the upper echelons of the building. The doors opened to a dark, dank —okay, it wasn't that bad. It was quite well-lit and smelled merely a little musty.

"Mr. Carter packed up your belongings and put them out for trash pick-up. I managed to save most of it."

He did what? I followed Victor to a corner of the basement near what looked like an incinerator. Beside it, several cardboard boxes were piled high as if ready to be thrown in.

Cautiously, I approached one and unpeeled the flaps. Clothes. Another one contained skincare products and toiletries. It didn't look like everything, but it was hard to know how many boxes comprised a life.

I opened a couple more, frantically searching for—oh, thank God. My laptop was here. I could replace most everything but that would wipe me out.

"You said most of it." I turned to Victor. "Did some of it get thrown out?"

"It was by the dumpster, but I had a feeling you'd come back for it. A couple of boxes were already mashed by the truck by the time I realized."

I threw my arms around him and gave him a hug. "Thank you! I know I'm no longer a tenant, so I appreciate you going out of your way to help me. I'll take it away today."

"Your car's no longer here, Miss Landry."

Not *my* car, of course. A lease that Dash gifted me last Christmas because he was tired of looking at my "clunker," a perfectly respectable ten-year-old Honda Civic. So, no transport.

"Anything else I need to know?"

"Something came for you from the bank, maybe a credit card."

"My ATM card! Do you have it?"

He smiled. "In the back office. I talked to the mail carrier before she delivered to the mailbox. Just in case there was anything for you."

What a life saver.

"Mr. Carter did ask that I call him if you show up. I don't have to."

I kissed him on the cheek. "I don't want you getting into trouble, Victor. Tell him I came by and looked miserable. Would it be okay if I took your number so I can call you about picking up this stuff?"

He smiled, relieved I was being so easygoing about it all. "Of course."

AIMING for discretion in the coffee shop, I pulled my Motors cap down because this was Rebels country and even the baristas knew who I was. When the sales associate asked for my name, I said "Shelby."

She barely looked at me, but she did give my hat significant side-eye.

I took a seat in the back with my eye on the door. Three minutes later, Adeline arrived and beelined right for me. I let her take me in her arms, just like I'd done with her brother several times over the last week. I also thanked my stars that I'd grabbed a change of clothes from one of the boxes. Wearing Adeline's or Aurora's duds would not have been a clever move.

"Are you okay?" Adeline asked. "I've been so worried about you!"

"I'm fine. Trying to stay under the radar."

She nodded. "But you're good?"

"I am. I mean, there's a lot that's not great, but I feel okay."

She held me back. "You look better. Less drawn."

Praise cheese and Hatch-made orgasms. "I've finally allowed myself to eat a full meal."

"Well, hello, stranger." Rosie had snuck up on us and was standing behind Adeline with a cheeky grin.

Adeline nudged her. "She's going incognito."

"In a Motors cap around here? Could work, I suppose."

Adeline rolled her eyes. "I'll get the coffees in. Summer, you're good?"

"I am."

As she walked away, Rosie and I sat. She took both my hands and squeezed. "You look good. Ten days on the lam has put some color back in your cheeks."

Plenty of reasons for that, but I wouldn't be going into details.

It shouldn't have been a big deal. I had been lying—mostly by omission—for years. But this was different. This involved people we knew—Dash, Hatch, the Kershaws.

It might seem strange to have asked Rosie and Adeline to be my bridesmaids when I didn't know them all that well. Since I started dating Dash, he had isolated me so that I didn't have many deep friendships. Coupled with my reluctance to share about my past, this resulted in surface acquaintances that I wasn't sure I could trust. I had followed these girls' world travel adventures online, madly jealous of their free-spiritedness and tight friendship. To have Rosie and Adeline in my corner now was amazing.

"Where were you?" Rosie demanded. "Okay, hold on until Addy comes back and you don't have to repeat yourself."

We chatted a little about Rosie's job in a tattoo parlor and about some of the hot guys who were regulars. Her ink was amazing, and she wore it with such confidence. I'd always admired her punk aesthetic and bad girl vibe. All I had was my tiny butterfly tattoo. Some rebellion.

Adeline returned with coffees and a selection of pastries "for the table."

"For my mouth, more like," Rosie said. "Okay, Summer, go."

"Where do I start?"

"How about the church bathroom window? How did you even jump without breaking your ankle?"

On the train, I'd had time to think about my story, so I tried to keep it as truthful as possible. An Uber instead of a grumpy hockey player. A motel in the sticks instead of a lake house in Michigan. Time alone to reflect on my sins instead of lazy days on the patio, sunny spins around the lake, and orgasms on the hood of a car.

"What about Carter?" Adeline asked. "Have you had a chance to talk to him?"

"Briefly. He's obviously not ready and I want to give him space. He did, however, change the locks, return my car to the dealership, and throw out all my belongings."

Adeline's eyes went wide. "What a dick."

There was also the woman he took to our bed on our wedding day, but I could hardly talk, could I?

"He's angry, and he has a right to be. I handled it poorly and I let my life become enmeshed in his in such a way that untangling comes with consequences. But I still have a separate bank account, so there's that." Not that I had more than a few hundred dollars in it after I set aside money for rent on wherever I would be living. So much for disaster preparedness.

Rosie squeezed my hand again. "What do you need from us?"

Tears sprang into my eyes. "Just being here and listening is amazing."

"Have a pastry." Adeline pushed a cranberry-orange scone my way. "We're also bringing these to the party."

I broke off a corner and popped it in my mouth, loving

the buttery flakiness and sharp pop of fruit. "My next step is finding a place to live. I've already started looking at Craig's List for roommates—"

"Oh, you're staying with us." Rosie shared a quick check-in glance with Adeline, who nodded enthusiastically.

They had moved in together about six months ago. I would have expected Adeline to live with her boyfriend Lars and his little girl Mabel, who she had nannied for last year before they fell hard for each other. But they were taking it slow like the mature, grounded individuals they were. I could learn so much.

"But you guys don't have room for me." *Please say you have room for me.*

"We have an office with a pull-out sofa," Rosie said. "It's very small, but there's a closet in there and we can probably squeeze a dresser in, if you need it. Unless you'd rather room with complete strangers like a weirdo."

"Which we get," Adeline said. "Rosie is kind of a grouch before her morning coffee, so I'd understand your reluctance. Oh my God, are you crying?"

I stroked away the tears. "I was so ashamed of how I behaved. That's why I-I didn't talk to you much. And now you're being so forgiving and wonderful."

Rosie shook my shoulder. "Nothing to forgive! You prioritized your mental health when you could have bowed to peer pressure and gone with the flow. Don't you worry, we have your back."

CHAPTER TWENTY-THREE

Hatch

I WALKED into the kitchen at my parents' house on Chicago's North Shore around lunchtime. My mom was rinsing a plate in the sink while my baby sister Tilly sat at the counter playing with Cheerios.

"Hey!" Mom grinned and reached out to hug me, holding her wet hands aloft. At the last second she streaked my face with them.

"Mom!" I wiped my damp face dry with a dish towel. So annoying.

"Sorry, couldn't help it. I love seeing this beautiful face."

Since moving back to town a year ago, I'd lived in a condo closer to downtown Riverbrook, but this was where I grew up and where I gravitated to in times of stress.

Or when the woman I wanted left me to marinate in misery at the lake.

"Hatch!" Tilly held out her arms, and I did as nonverbally ordered: lifted her up off the stool.

"Tilly-Billy, you are such a big girl! How ya been?"

"Good. I found a snail in the garden."

"Oh yeah? Sounds like the best place for it."

My mom grinned. "She was exploring with Franky earlier."

Francesca St. James was Rosie's stepsister and a world-renowned expert on snails and slugs. Someone had to do it, I supposed.

"You're getting heavy, Til. What have you been eating?"

"Cheerios. And naan. And bag-it." That was *baguette*. My girl was a bread fiend. "But Mommy won't let me eat snails. Franky says they eat them in Fratz."

"Yeah, I heard. Sounds gross." I set her down on the counter stool and took a seat beside her. "Everything okay here?" I asked my mom.

"Not bad. Conor is doing the hockey camp with your dad, Jason, and Gunnar this week."

Every year my dad, former Rebel Gunnar Bond, and my uncle Jason indoctrinated the youth at the Rebels Hockey Camp. It held special meaning for them as it was how my dad and his half-brother Jason became close after Dad connected with my grandpa Nick later in life. This was Conor's first year and my third.

"Yeah, I'm looking forward to it." It would be good to focus my mind on something else.

"And Landon's working on his app thing." Conor's twin Landon was a software whiz, about to launch a dating app that did something no other dating app did ... I had no idea what he was doing to separate it from the pack, but I trusted my brainiac brother would make it work.

"Where's Aurora?"

"Meeting with her Tai Chi girls for lunch. How's the cottage? Did you get some rest?"

"Uh huh. Nice and relaxing."

She tilted her head, raised an eyebrow, and gave me a look that pierced right through my bullshit.

"What?"

"I had a chat with Gemma. From the coffee shop in Saugatuck? She said you came in one morning with a pretty blonde."

I'd forgotten Gemma and my mom were buddy-buddy. "Just someone I chatted with over coffee. No big deal."

"She sent me a photo."

"And?" I brazened it out. I'd have heard about it by now if Summer's presence in Saugatuck was common knowledge.

"She had a ball cap on, so her face was hidden."

"Imagine that. Someone who would prefer privacy in this crazy media-conscious day and age."

My mother grinned. "So you won't be bringing this mystery woman home to meet the family?"

"No, Mom, I will not. Any news on the contract front with Dad?"

Mom looked at me squarely. "What do you think about it?"

"I think that Dad must be so"—I covered Tilly's ears—"fucking tired. You, too, Mom."

She laughed. "A little. But your father keeps me young."

"You said I keep you young, Mommy!" Tilly looked up from her Cheerio art.

"Such a smart girl." To me, she said, "He's loved playing with you on the same team, but sometimes I worry that you get overshadowed in the Theo Kershaw show."

While I agreed with that, I didn't want my family to be

of the same mindset. If they knew I was looking to move to another team, they would be hurt. In truth I wanted to stay in Chicago. I loved being close to my family and all the friends I grew up with. I loved playing for my home town team.

And then there was Summer.

"Plenty of time for me to take a starring role. Though by the time Dad retires, Conor will somehow make it onto the Rebels and steal all my thunder."

"Sounds like your brother." She took a closer look at me. "I know you weren't so keen to join the Rebels at first. You did it because your dad asked."

My phone buzzed with a text from the man himself, saving me from an awkward conversation.

Meet for lunch? Sunny Side Up?

"Looks like I have a lunch date with Dad. You want to come?"

"I'd love to, but I have a client call in half an hour." My mom ran an information consultancy business and worked harder than anyone I knew. "Go and spend some time with your dad. Oh, and bring Landon. He's going to lose his eyesight if he stays in front of that screen any longer."

"Not why he'd go blind, Mom."

"Oh, jerk off jokes. Hilarious. Don't forget who washed your sheets during puberty."

"Jerk off!" Tilly popped a Cheerio in her mouth and gave me the Kershaw grin.

THE SUNNY SIDE Up Diner was busy when Landon and I arrived, but Dad and Conor had already snagged a booth, so we headed over and slid into the red leather banquette. Everyone did the usual fist pumps and then all eyes turned to me.

Usually, I wouldn't care if I was the focus of a Kershaw face-off involving multiple members of the fam, but today I was extra sensitive because of nosy Gemma and my mom's questions about the mystery blonde. My concerns were proved to be founded when my dad kick-started the inter-rogation.

"So who is she, H?"

"Already got the third degree from Mom. I had nothing to tell her."

"You tell your mother anything and she assumes you're getting married."

Married. Just the thought of Summer's lucky escape made me squirm.

"Someone I met and had coffee with, that's all."

Conor eyed me over the menu. "Gemma said you came *in* with her, not that you met her there."

"Could've met her outside," Landon commented a la Sherlock, Cumberbatch style. "Or on any number of dating apps."

"How's that going?"

Landon smirked. "No chance, dude. You will change the subject when we *decide* you change the subject."

I pursued the menu. A stack of pancakes would be nice with a couple of scrambled eggs. "This subject is at an end. I've nothing to say, so you may as well move on. How's camp going?"

My dad held my gaze for a second, then took my cue. "Great. There are several flyers this year. A couple of girls, too." Each year, more girls joined in, which we all loved to see. "With Gunnar going on vacation next week with Sadie and the girls, and Conor so busy sexting—"

"Hey!"

My dad ignored Conor's interjection. "It'll be good to have someone with more maturity there. Also, I have someone else starting, and you can show him the ropes."

Before I could enquire further, Landon cut in.

"There's Addy."

We all turned to the entrance. My sister and Rosie had just come in—and behind them was Summer.

I shouldn't have been surprised. She had said she needed to sort things out with her apartment, with her job, with Carter. But a part of me had thought we wouldn't run into each other so soon. That I could prepare.

I was not prepared.

My sister waved and because we weren't sociopaths and actually liked each other, she headed over with Rosie and Summer in tow. Thankfully there was no room at the inn, and they would have to sit elsewhere.

"Hey, guys! Fancy meeting you here." My dad grinned and elbowed Conor to get out of the way so he could exit the booth.

"Sure, Dad." Addy grinned. "Fancy meeting you at the diner where they've named an omelet after you."

"The Theo is amazing. I recommend it." Dad gave Addy a hug, Rosie a kiss on the cheek, and then stood before Summer.

"How are you doing, Summer?"

She peered up at him, her eyes wide and glossy. "Okay, Mr. Kershaw."

"I've told you, it's Theo. You need a hug?"

Her bottom lip quivered, and she nodded, whereupon

my dad wrapped her up and held her for a few seconds. God, he was such a good guy.

The entire diner had ground to a halt: servers stopped delivering coffee, diners paused with forks half-raised, and all watched as my dad made it clear that Summer was one of us. She might have done one of the team dirty, but she wouldn't be a target, not on Theo Kershaw's watch.

He drew back. "Pretty brave to come back."

Summer exhaled. "I have a life here, too."

"Yes, you do." And then to the rest of the diner, "Carry on, R-drama fans! Nothing to see here."

That yielded a few chuckles, and everyone continued about their business, but with one eye on our corner.

Addy said to Dad, "We're just going to grab a table over there. Talk later?"

"Sure, Twinkle. Have a nice lunch."

I watched them go, silently urging Summer to look my way. There was a flicker of a glance in my direction, and then they were off to a table far enough away that I could pretend she wasn't even here. Rosie caught my eye and raised an eyebrow. I gave her a quick smile.

Dad retook his seat.

Landon adjusted his glasses. "That was a nice thing to do, Dad."

"I've always liked Summer. I know it had to be a tough decision for her. She's going to be under a lot of scrutiny for a while."

Conor picked up his menu again. "Well, it's a good thing she doesn't have anything to do with the hockey camp."

Weird thing to say. "Why's that?"

"Because Carter will be joining us as a mentor next week."

CHAPTER TWENTY-FOUR

I'D ALWAYS THOUGHT of myself as a reasonably good actress. First there was the smoothing of my accent, then culturing myself so I wouldn't sound like an uneducated rube. Learning how the middle classes did things helped me to become a character that was a million miles away from Shelby Mae.

I called on those skills now.

I hadn't expected to see Hatch, and even though he was a fair way off, my Shelby senses had tingled and pointed my nipples right at him. He should have been on the other side of Lake Michigan, enjoying his vacation. Instead, he was here, confusing my hormones when they needed calm and quiet.

We took a seat at a table on the other side of the restaurant, and I accepted the menu handed to me by the server. Suddenly I'd lost my appetite. How could I act normal while he was here? Or while every set of peepers was locked onto me, waiting for ... what exactly? For me to knock back my chair and sprint out of here?

I had history after all.

But I wasn't running. Not anymore. When Mr. Kershaw—Theo—had hugged me, I almost broke down in tears. These people were so kind. Too kind. I didn't deserve such consideration, but the Rebels captain's gesture placed me under his protection. No place felt safer, except perhaps that vacation house in Saugatuck with the man's son.

But then I caught Hatch's eyes, those all-seeing windows, and I realized I wasn't safe at all.

I put in an order for coffee and a bagel and got a disapproving look from Adeline who thought I wasn't eating enough. We had just inhaled a picnic-basket's worth of scones at the coffee shop but apparently I needed to be shoveling the carbs non-stop to get meat on my bones.

"Back in a second."

In the bathroom, I checked my reflection. I looked pale, but the circles under my eyes had faded, and I felt better physically than I had in months. While my life had imploded, I was taking small steps to get it back on track.

I would probably need to increase my stride if I wanted things to happen more quickly. I knew what I needed to do this afternoon, after Lars helped to move my life-in-boxes into Adeline and Rosie's place. I sent a text and left the restroom.

Hatch was waiting against the wall.

Rather than luxuriate in the god before me, I flicked a quick glance down the corridor toward the restaurant. No one was in my sightline, but that didn't mean this was safe. Before I could complain about the audacity, Hatch opened a nearby door and ushered me inside.

He turned on the light. We were in a utility closet.

"What are you doing?" Though it was rather obvious.

"I need to talk to you."

"Anyone could see."

He passed over my objection. "You shouldn't have left like that. I was worried about you."

I swallowed. "I had to go. I couldn't rely on you anymore." I had enough of that with Dash, and though it didn't feel the same, there was the risk I would fall back into those old patterns.

"Sure, but I could have driven you back to the city. It wasn't very efficient. Or good for the environment."

That made me chuckle. "You think we should have been cooped up in a car together for three hours to save the planet?"

He moved in closer. "Carpooling is always the way to go. Like shared showers. And body heat to save on energy costs."

His body heat was certainly not saving any energy costs in this small space. I placed a hand on his chest. Yeah, leeching heat all over the place.

"How many times have we said this is a bad idea?"

"Too many to count." He sounded so resigned, which made me smile. He inclined his head further, and our lips were close enough to …

No more kissing. Or orgasms of the Hatch-made variety.

I pushed him back to give myself room to breathe. "Your dad is awesome."

"True. Though married."

I rolled my eyes. "Your sister, too."

"Spoken for."

"I'm staying with her and Rosie until I can get back on my feet."

He didn't seem surprised. "I'm glad they have your back."

"They've been kind and non-judgmental. Now I need to work on getting my life on track. And this"—I waved between us, my knuckles grazing his chest. His hard, unyielding ... *focus*—"is not helping."

"We can't pretend nothing happened, Sunshine."

"Oh, yes, we can. I would have thought you'd be thrilled for me to be out of your hair. I ruined your vacation."

"Vacations are all about sex, sun, and more sex. You're denying me two out of three."

"Could you be realistic about this? I had to go, to sort through the rubble of the life I just blew up. I couldn't do that in Saugatuck." I tapped his chest lightly. "I'm very grateful, though."

"Not looking for gratitude," he said moodily.

"Well, you have it. I don't know what I would have done without your help. Not just the ride out of Dodge, but everything."

"Don't thank me for the orgasms."

"Okay, I won't."

He was still annoyed, and I was rather miserable about the whole thing myself. "Are you going to stay mad at me forever?"

"Not mad at you."

"Oh, please, Dino Boy! I'm having flashbacks to every run-in over the past year. I *know* when you're mad at me."

He growled.

"So. Mad."

"I just thought we were getting somewhere."

He sounded so woebegone. I felt his—I wouldn't dare

say heartache, but something more like disquiet—in my soul.

"We were. We're friends now, aren't we?"

He blew out a breath. "And if I want more?"

"You don't think the Rebels have had enough teammate drama after your dad and Lars last season?"

"It's not the same. Carter and I aren't close."

"It would still be a shitty thing to do to a teammate. And a shittier thing to do to the man I left at the altar." Plus, I needed to figure out things on my own.

He leaned into me, and just the nearness of him almost undid me.

He cupped my jaw, and I found myself curling into his touch like a fool. It would be so easy to let him hold me, to lose myself in him. But that was my mom. That was me with Dash.

"Tell me you can stop what's happening here, Summer."

I shivered. "I'm not going to deny my attraction to you, Hatch. But if we were to follow through on this, it would look ... incriminating. Like I planned to jilt Dash for you."

"No one would think that."

"I already look like a flake, and with you, I would look like a cheating flake."

He studied me. "Do you feel like this is cheating?"

"No. I feel like it's ..." *More than I could have ever wished for. And definitely more than I deserve.* "Getting out of control. I just exited a long-term relationship and I'm not ready to jump into another one. My life has too many loose threads right now and if I pull on this one, the whole sweater will unravel. Not that you want a relationship—"

"I do."

The shock of it, those two little words—the ones I had

not said to Dash in the church—now repurposed in a different context almost knocked me over.

"But you barely know me. Up until a few days ago, you didn't even like me."

"And today I know you a bit better. And tomorrow I'll know you a little more. And the only way that's going to happen, properly, is if we continue to get to know each other. But I understand that this is a confusing time for you. You need time to think. To figure out your game plan." He took one of my hands and placed it against his chest. His heartbeat thrummed under my fingertips, vital and life-affirming. "Let me tell you mine. You. You're my end game here."

My pulse hammered wildly. I couldn't think straight around this man. It had always been like this. He confused the hell out of me with his coldness one minute, and his intense, scorching heat the next. I was a bird in the vortex, buffeted by the wind, trying like hell to survive.

I resolved to stay firm, though part of me wanted to surrender.

"I need to sort things out."

"Got it." He still held my hand, and the sight of his big one around my smaller one did strange things to me—as if I needed more strangeness! Raising my hand to his lips, he pressed a sweet kiss to my thundering pulse.

Not. Helping.

"I should go." *Before I cave to the shelter of you.*

I wouldn't say "see you later" because the look on his face made it clear.

Later was just a heartbeat away.

CHAPTER TWENTY-FIVE

Summer

RYDER CALLOWAY WAS A VERY handsome man. Close to forty, he was young to be a general manager, but the Chicago Rebels had a history of taking chances on newer talent both on and off the ice. He had been in this role for three years, and the most recent season saw the Rebels get to the Cup finals. He must have been doing something right.

Today, he sat behind a large oak desk, the perfect picture of the franchise executive. I had known him in a professional capacity as his assistant for the last two years, and the day I quit my job was sadder than the day I jilted my fiancé.

At this point, the red flags were practically slapping me in the face.

"I'm glad you're safe, Summer. You had us worried."

"I'm sorry about that. I wasn't exactly thinking straight."

He waved it off. "You don't owe me or anyone here an explanation. So how are you? Really."

"I'm ... figuring stuff out. Dash and I still need to talk properly, but until that happens, I'd like to get my life back on an even keel. Getting a job is number one on the list."

He nodded, tapped the desk. "Well, as you know, we've filled your position."

"Right. I was hoping to be considered for an internship, maybe in scouting. For the last year, I've been creating asset packages and reports of franchise prospects—"

"You have? I know you've done some of the slide decks for the talent meetings, and your work has always been excellent. Which reports are we talking about?"

"This was on my own time. I gave them to Scott Kincaid. Creating a portfolio, if you will."

He frowned. "Why didn't you talk to me about them?"

"I mentioned the idea to you once and you didn't seem all that interested. One day I was talking to Scott, and he said he'd love to see what I had to offer."

He took a moment. "I wish you'd come to me, Summer. I know you said you had, but maybe you caught me on a bad day because I don't recall."

"I didn't want to nag you about it. Scott was kind enough to offer to read them."

He didn't look pleased. I should have run it by him, at the very least clued him in that I was providing this data for Scott. Now it looked like I'd gone behind his back.

"Be that as it may, Summer, I'm not sure we can offer you a position here, internship or otherwise."

My heart sank. "Because of Dash?"

"I know I said I didn't foresee a conflict of interest, but obviously I was wrong there." As if these particular circumstances could have ever been predicted. "It would be one thing if you hadn't quit your job, but you did and employing you again wouldn't be fair to Carter."

I should have known I'd be perceived as the villain here.

"But ..." he continued.

My heart leaped.

"I could enquire at another franchise, assuming you were willing to move to a different city." The implication was that it would be better all-around if I did. Still, this was kind of him. He didn't need to do a thing.

"Thanks, Ryder. I would really appreciate that."

I was used to starting over. If that's what I had to do, then I could do it again.

* * *

Hatch

SO THERE'S this old tune called "Jesse's Girl" about a guy who has it bad for his friend's woman. Carter might not be a friend, but in all other respects, I was living this fucking song.

Since I'd gotten to know Summer better—in all the ways—the next step should have been obvious.

Make her mine.

I wanted nothing more. I wanted to be her knight, to shelter her from the storm, away from the rest of the world. Away from family and friends and the city we both lived in.

Away from Carter.

Only now we were back in the cauldron. I couldn't make a play for Summer because (a) she had told me she wasn't interested and (b) even if she was, Carter would be sore about it. Summer was right. No one would believe it hadn't been planned, that we hadn't been hooking up before the wedding that never was.

But that didn't mean it could never happen. I would merely have to bide my time.

Carter was the last person I wanted to see, but my father had invited him to Rebels Youth Hockey Camp. *This'll be good for him,* Dad had said. *Get his mind off stuff.*

I was of the opinion that staying in St. Bart's and fucking anything that moved would have helped the guy more.

Carter was already sitting in the locker room alone, taping his stick, when I arrived ahead of camp. He looked tanned, rested, and remarkably untroubled.

"Hey, how are things?"

He raised an eyebrow.

"Sorry, dumb question."

He shook his head. "Nah, you're alright. Your dad roped you into this, too?"

I took a seat on the bench beside him and started untying my sneakers. "I've done it for three years now. It's a lot of fun."

"Yeah, and good PR for me, which never hurts. I'm looking forward to whipping the brats into shape."

Jesus, this guy. "The kids are actually great." I moved on. "How was St. Bart's?"

"Amazing. We have a house there, so it's the perfect place to get away from it all. Though there were helicopters trying to get photos. My mom was *not* pleased. She blames Summer."

"And you don't?"

"For helicopter paps? Nah. They've been following me

around for years. I can't buy a condom without someone reporting about it."

I was having a hard time figuring out what Summer ever saw in this guy. Maybe he had presented a different front to her, like a Jekyll and Hyde deal. She saw Dr. Dash and I saw Mr. Carter.

"You heard from Summer?"

"One call with her sobbing about how sorry she was. I told her she would need to wait until I'm ready. Best to let her stew. Figure out how bad things are without me. Then" —he snapped his fingers—"I'll decide if I should bring her back in."

I stared at him, barely able to hide my incredulity. "You mean, you'd get back together with her?"

"Maybe, maybe not. Don't get me wrong, I'm pissed at her. But she's always been indecisive. Took her two tries to get her to say yes." Summer had said three, but I didn't correct him because I wasn't supposed to know that. "And she wanted to keep her job, but I convinced her to cave there, too. Now she's unemployed and homeless. Once she realizes how cold the streets are, she'll come around."

I had come in here, thinking that Carter deserved my sympathy. I was now convinced he deserved jack shit.

There was a reason we weren't that close: he made everything about him. Maybe that was the result of growing up the scion of a billionaire family. Sure, my family was wealthy, but we weren't allowed to coast or rely on that wealth. Hell, Dad made me get a part-time job at Saugatuck Yacht Club every summer from the age of fifteen. Said it would teach me the value of hard work.

Of course, Carter had worked hard to make it in the NHL. No one got to this level without putting in the effort, but he had always been the kind of player who skated by on his natural talent. I was gifted but not as much as some of the other guys. Not as much as my dad, my uncle Jason, or even my brother Conor who was going to outdo us all in the legend stakes. The kid was phenom with a capital P.

No, I worked my ass off every day and made sure no one doubted my worthiness to be on a pro-hockey team. Carter didn't see his hockey career in the same light. This was a side hustle for him rather than the main event—the main event being Dash Carter the Third.

"But why would you want her back after what she did?"

"Not sure I do. And frankly I could get anyone, y'know? But she always played hard to get, even when we were dating. Like she didn't think I was good enough for *her*. Women don't usually put up that kind of resistance with me. It's kind of hot."

The guy was jilted by his bride on his wedding day, and it made him want her ... more? Summer had told me they'd broken up a few times. Maybe this was just part of their drama cycle, taken to the next level.

Too stunned to respond, I pulled off my T-shirt and started dressing for camp. Because this was the equivalent of light practice, I forewent the full padding and kept it to warm-up gear. I was lacing up my skates when Conor walked in.

He approached Carter with his fist already closed, going for the bump. "Carter! I cannot *believe* you are showing your face in this town."

That was my brother, the closest we had to a Theo Kershaw clone. Over the years my dad had become more tactful, (slightly) less embarrassing, and more likely to think before he spoke.

Enter Conor.

The guy had picked up the mantle of my dad's lack of

filter. But because he was such a good-natured bro about it, a shocked Carter just held up his fist and accepted the bump.

"I'm guessing you found some island hottie to cheer you up."

Carter smirked, instantly mollified. "You know it."

"Sounds like Summer landed on her feet, too."

"What? You mean, she's with someone?"

My brother shrugged and ... side-eyed me. *What the—?*

"No idea," he said to Carter. "I meant that she found a place to live. She's staying with Addy and Rosie. Is it true you dumped her stuff on the street? That's cold, man!"

That *was* cold. Also, the first I was hearing about it. My fist clenched at my side.

Carter gave a negligent shrug. "Girl's gotta learn."

Conor caught my eye, winked, and placed his palm over his heart. "Well, miracle of miracles. The Lord saw right to save that sinner's possessions and make it so she could find them again."

Bafflement knitted Carter's brow. "The Lord saw what now?"

"Guess her stuff didn't get thrown out after all. Addy sent Nyquist over to pick it up because he's whipped. Or he's a sucker for a damsel in distress." Conor looked pointedly at me then back to Carter. "Jesus, dude, do you want her walking the streets naked? Huh, maybe ya do."

Carter had no response to that, and now my dad had come in, so the conversation was at an end. As we headed out to the rink to start the camp, I pulled Conor back.

"How come you know so much about this Summer situation?"

"I make it my business to keep up with the R-drama. Knowledge is power, bro."

I delivered my best slant-eyed look of death.

He chuckled. "It was so nice to see Summer at the Sunny Side Up. Glad she's getting back on her feet."

"I suppose."

"And who knew she was a Motors fan? Just like Aurora." Punctuated by the perfect Conor smirk. Off he went, leaving me gaping like a trout.

CHAPTER TWENTY-SIX

Summer

ADELINE WALKED into the kitchen where I was seated at the table on my laptop. I had just finished a report for Scott but given what I'd heard from Ryder about my career prospects, I wasn't sure whether to send it to him.

"How were the little ones?"

Adeline smiled as she placed her guitar case near the door. "So cute. Usually I just sing the classics—'Wheels on the Bus,' 'Baa Baa Black Sheep,' etcetera—but today they were actually calling out requests for original material."

My new roomie had found her calling singing for kids at JiggleJams, a class devoted to crawlers and toddlers at the Chicago School of Folk Music. She had the sweetest voice and the best temperament for working with children.

"So what did you give them?"

"I have one called the Banana Peel Song and another about dragons."

"*Game of Thrones*, PG version."

She laughed. "Exactly. So, how are things?"

"Not bad. Still no response from Dash, though he's back in town according to that finest of tabloid rags, *Hot Goss*."

"Yeah, he's working at the hockey camp with Dad and my brothers."

Dash? Working with Hatch? I had no idea what to make of that, only I was fairly certain I didn't want them in the same locker room together, never mind on the same rink.

Adeline continued. "Conor said Carter wasn't too pleased to hear you managed to recover your belongings. In my little brother's words, it looked like he'd swallowed garbage water."

Of course, he'd rather punish me. I understood it even if I hated it.

Adeline's phone buzzed and she quickly checked it. "Summer, I advise you to never have three obnoxious brothers."

"Oh yeah?" Weirdly, I wanted to hear about Hatch.

You ain't weird. You're just horny.

If I could strangle my alter ego, I would. I silently pondered on how to kill her dead for good.

Another *zzz*, and Adeline scanned her screen again. "The Kershaw Kinder thread has been buzzing since we found out Hatch has a secret woman stashed away in Saugatuck."

My heart jumped into my throat. "He does?"

"Yeah, some nosey Nelly from the town sent a photo of them getting coffee to my mom, and now everyone's trying to squeeze more information out of him."

There was visual evidence? I smothered a nervy chuckle. "Have you seen this photo?"

"Yeah. Some blonde piece, Motors fan. Sounds like he

picked up a townie. Which wouldn't surprise me because he did that last year according to Conor."

That would be Ava.

She handed over her phone and there it was: Hatch and me at the coffee shop. The cap was pulled down low, the bill shading my face. I recognized me but no one else would. I hoped.

"Maybe it's all innocent." *It's not. It is so not.* "After all, it's just coffee."

"Perhaps. But Conor keeps saying she looks familiar."

Conor? I think I'd met him twice in my lifetime. What the hell was this kid doing playing detective?

I handed the phone back, trying to keep my hand from shaking. All the more reason to stay away from Hatch. I was a pariah with half the Rebels org, I certainly didn't want to lose the support of the other half.

"Rosie's already got a date lined up, which is her standard response."

"Her standard response to what?"

She grimaced. "She has a crush on Hatch. Or did. Well, it comes and goes, and I think she's in the 'goes' phase. Which is good, because Hatch has been kind of moody lately."

Rosie liked Hatch? I should have known this but of course, I didn't know either of my bridesmaids that well. Since they returned from their travels, the last year had been all about me and my wedding planning. What a terrible friend I was.

"Does Hatch know Rosie likes him?"

She chuckled darkly. "He's a man, so I'd say he's clueless. There have been many stages in their relationship. She wanted to marry him when she was twelve. I think she kissed him in a closet at a birthday party when they were fifteen, and they both claimed it was 'the worst.' But just before we went traveling, I would catch her staring at him. She's usually coy about it, but I worry about her getting hurt. And I don't want to be caught in the middle."

Neither did I. Thankfully, I was on a no-Hatch diet, and this new information further firmed my resolve.

"So, how did the meeting go with Ryder?"

I filled her in on the current thinking of the Rebels GM.

She looked sympathetic. "Not a complete surprise, then. I'm pretty impressed about these reports you're compiling, but it's not really cool that Scott used your labor like that and didn't give you credit."

"Oh, I don't see it that way. It was good practice and got my foot in the door." Except it didn't really. Scott hadn't returned my calls either.

Adeline didn't push the issue. "I know you might not be feeling it, but have you thought about getting another job while you wait on the dream to happen?"

"I've been checking online sites. What I really need is something I can start quickly."

She clapped her hands. "I was hoping you'd say that! I have an idea."

***

THIRTY MINUTES LATER, I'd had a phone interview with Kennedy Clark-Durand, who was married to former Rebel Reid Durand (one of the hotter, growlier players in his day), and ran a personal concierge business called Can Do. They hired people to walk dogs, do grocery runs, pick up dry cleaning, make restaurant reservations, and more for a coterie of top-notch clients. Many of them were Rebels players who apparently didn't know how to use DoorDash or Open Table.

"Would you have a problem running errands for a Rebels player?" Kennedy had asked.

"None whatsoever unless his name begins with Dash and ends with Carter." Though at this rate, it might be the only way the dick would see me.

Kennedy had chuckled. "The best thing about you, Summer, is that you're unfazed by the Rebels shiny. You wouldn't believe how many bunnies and wannabe star fuckers apply to work with us so they can get close to the players."

"I've seen too many of them naked on locker visits to care about that. Plus, I can safely say I will not be dating any more hockey players."

She cackled. "Famous last words! Okay, I'll email you a list of errands for tomorrow. I just need you to send over a photo of your driver's license and insurance."

"Insurance?"

"Yeah, I need to know you have car insurance."

I didn't even have a car. "Okay, watch this space."

After I hung up, I went into the kitchen. Adeline was on her computer using a music notation app and Rosie was making something that smelled amazing.

"So, I got the job."

Adeline raised her hands and went, "Woot!"

"But I have a problem. I need a car. I could lease one but that might take a while." And money I didn't have.

"How soon do you need it?" Rosie asked.

"Tomorrow? I have to send over car insurance details to Kennedy."

"Borrow mine. I can use my dad's." Rosie pointed to the foyer where the car keys to her Jeep sat in a small bowl on the entrance table. "The insurance card is in the glove compartment—wait, I have a photo of it on my phone."

While she looked for it, I hugged her from behind. "Thank you. I don't know what I'd do without you girls."

"Yay, group hug!" Adeline jumped to her feet and got in on the action.

CHAPTER TWENTY-SEVEN

Summer Returns to Pick Up the Pieces

Fresh back from her "jilt-cation," Summer Landry was spotted with Chicago Rebels player Lars Nyquist outside her former home with Dash Carter, directing the packing of boxes into the flatbed of a pickup. Insider sources tell us that Dash left orders for the boxes to be "disposed of" while he went on his honeymoon-for-one. But someone must have been looking out for the quick-footed bride because they were set aside for safekeeping.

Rumor has it that Summer is staying with Adeline Kershaw, daughter of Rebels captain Theo Kershaw and girlfriend of Lars, as well as Adeline's BFF Rosie Burnett-Moretti. It looks like certain players have picked a side in the latest episode of this R-drama—though Adeline might want to keep an eye on her man now that Summer is back on the market. (She and Lars looked very cozy during the boxes pick-up.)

It'll be interesting to see how the other players respond. Will they come out for Dash, or is Summer working overtime to keep certain players in the "divorce"? Only time—or one hot Chicago summer— will tell!!
-@HotGoss

———

Hatch

LANDON

Just what we need, more Rebels drama.

CONOR

Well, Adeline got her claws into Lars and caused World War 3 all of nine months ago, so we're kind of due.

ADDY

I like how they hinted that Lars is probably going to hook up with Summer because "boxes". LOL.

CONOR

We need to start taking bets on who else Summer will get in the "divorce."

LANDON

She does have the inside track on the players, access to HR records, perfect blackmail material, from her time in the front office. Time to use it.

Speaking of players, H is being pretty quiet.

CONOR

Probably too busy with his coffee shop hottie.

ME

Just waiting for you to get the verbal diarrhea out of your systems. So, what's the plan for Tilly's birthday party?

CONOR

Mom's got it under control. And the adults are talking here … about your coffee-drinkin' cutie.

ADDY

Which you've already mentioned. Two million times.

LANDON

If you have any pertinent information, Con, spill it. Otherwise, quit with the hints.

I THREW the phone down on the sofa. I had yet to talk to Conor properly, and anyway, what would I say? *You think you know what you saw, but you know nothing. And if you do, keep it zipped.*

Just fuel to the fire for my shit-stirring brother. I was amazed that no one else had figured it out.

I sent Summer a text.

Hey, are you okay?

SUNSHINE

Fine. Except for the fact there is a photo of us in the wild from that coffee shop in Saugatuck.

ME

You know about this?

SUNSHINE

Adeline told me. And that it's a hot topic of conversation in your family group chat.

ME

About that. Conor knows it's you.

SUNSHINE

What?!

ME

You wore the hat in the Sunny Side Up and he put two and two together. You need to burn it. For multiple reasons.

No response.

ME

Can you talk? On the phone?

SUNSHINE

I'm kind of busy right now. Maybe later.

Which sounded like code for "never." Fuck.

Halfway through my misery stew, my intercom phone rang. "Your grocery delivery is here, Mr. Kershaw."

"Oh, thanks, Hank. Send it up."

I opened the door and waited for the delivery person to exit the elevator. I was not expecting Summer.

A familiar pattern these days. This girl certainly knew how to surprise me.

Still wearing Aurora's Motors cap, she turned toward me, sighed with her entire body, and moved forward with a couple of shopping bags. I'd ordered a gallon of milk and a ton of fruits and vegetables, so I rushed forward to take them from her.

"Sweet Lord, put your shirt on!"

Not what I usually heard from the mouth of any woman of my acquaintance (except Addy when she was fourteen and I spent the summer of my sixteenth year downing protein shakes, working out, and showing off my newly-muscled body). Now I was sent back in time to my horny teenage years—and in my own home as well.

"Lovely to see you, too. You're working for Kennedy now?"

"Just temporarily." She looked a little tired, and I couldn't blame her. Her life had undergone a lot of upheaval recently.

"We were texting a few minutes ago."

"Yeah, I was parked downstairs, psyching myself up. And then you texted, like it was a sign!" Sign sounded like *sa-hn*. Her attitude made me chuckle. Also, psyching herself up to see me? Was that good or bad?

"It's not funny," she added.

"Kind of is. The universe is throwing us together."

Cue a not pleased Summer. "You've got these?"

"Sure, but could you come in and chat for a second?"

Without waiting for a response, I headed to the kitchen to unpack the groceries. If (a) I remained shirtless and (b) she didn't say "kthanxbye," then we had a chance at a conversation. I looked up over a Whole Food shopping bag to find her hovering on the threshold.

"I'm still on the job. I have to pick up dog food for Noah Boden's Great Dane."

"Snoopy can wait. Just a couple of minutes."

She inhaled, muttered something under her breath, and followed me into my apartment. As I worked, I watched her checking my place out. It was a decent-sized two-bed condo in a nice building but probably had nothing on the luxurious penthouse where she once lived with Carter. She seemed especially interested in the photos of my family on the walls in the entryway.

"Need something to drink?"

Her eyes flashed. "Why? Do you think I'm suddenly parched at the thirst trap you've laid for me?"

"Maybe."

"Oh, please provide me with electrolytes to replenish all the energy I've expended just looking at you, Hatch Kershaw!"

There was the Southern twang again. It came out when she was mad, stressed, or close to orgasm, which I knew because I'd witnessed all three.

I filled a glass from the Brita and handed it to her. Her gaze over my body was appreciative, so yay for shirtless.

"Thanks."

"How are your new digs?"

She brightened. "Great. Your sister and Rosie are so kind. I don't know where I'd be without them." She peered up at me. "Without all the help I've had so far."

I wasn't looking for thanks. I wasn't sure what I was looking for exactly. The word "everything" came to mind.

"Is Conor going to say something?" she asked.

"No. My brother is a lot of things, but he's loyal to the family. He knows that mentioning our connection would cause ructions. He'd prefer to hold it over my head to piss me off."

"Typical brother stuff, then."

"Classic." I smiled, and she smiled back. My heart did a zig-zag around the rink of my chest.

"How's the hockey camp going? I heard Dash is doing it too."

"Yeah, it's good. Could you sit for a second?"

She looked at the sofa like it might swallow her up, then took a seat in one corner, telegraphing a clear signal that I should sit at the opposite end and not try anything. She placed the glass on a coaster on the coffee table.

"Carter seems to think ignoring you will make you sweat. And that somehow, he'll … get you back."

Her eyebrows slammed together. "He said that?"

"More or less. The fact that you ran out on him means you're either playing hard to get, which he likes, or the ultimate game of chicken, which he also likes. But he also wants to make you suffer, which is why he's not answering your calls."

She considered that for a moment. "He must be really hurting."

"Sure, so bad." Women would employ the weirdest mental acrobatics to construe the best in a guy's motives.

She narrowed her eyes. "Some people manifest their hurt by acting out. Dash is used to getting what he wants and when he doesn't, he constructs narratives to cover what he's seeing. Me leaving him doesn't make sense, so he'd rather invent reasons that show him in a better light. I'm indecisive, flighty, unpredictable. Resistant to his charms, but not really. Playing games to get an edge. It's a form of gaslighting, and I won't be falling for it."

Her intuition surprised me. I had thought she'd feel sorry for him, but she moved on from that quickly to a nice deconstruction of Carter's behavior. I had no idea if she was right, but it *sounded* right.

However, her next words sounded the opposite of right. "I need to talk to him."

Everything in me rebelled at this outlandish notion. "Not a good idea."

"He might be a jerk, but I behaved like one, and I have to apologize."

She stood and headed to the door. I chased her down. "Now?"

"Yes—well, after I walk Cody Jacobs' basset hound.

That's also on my list. The sooner I talk to Dash, the sooner we can both move on. If I can convince Ryder that Dash and I are capable of being civil, then I could get my job back. Or an internship."

That made a twisted sort of sense. But I hated—*hated*—the idea of Summer spending any time with Carter. Maybe I should talk to Ryder. Take any leverage away from Carter.

"He wants you back."

She placed a hand on my arm. "Unlikely. But more important, I don't want him. I'm not sure I ever did."

I moved closer, needing to be near her. Craving a moment breathing her air. She was here in my home, a bed, a sofa, a kitchen counter all within range, and I was supposed to let her go to talk to her ex and suffer through his mind games?

She turned the knob on the door and pulled it ajar.

I shut it. "What I said at the diner—"

"In the utility closet?"

"With the paper towels and the toilet paper and the light bulbs as my witness. I meant it. I want to see you. Properly."

"You've seen me properly. On the hood of your car at the lake. Then again in the no-pool pool house. Good Lord, you've seen every inch of me, but Summer is now closed for business." She waved over her body in case I didn't get it, which just made me crave that body more. "I have to piece my life together and starting up something with you cannot be part of it."

She opened the door a few inches and I placed my hand on her hip, pulling her close.

"I thought you were all about honesty these days. Be honest and tell me you're not feeling anything here."

Her hand touched my chest. Burned a hole into my

soul. She peered up at me with glossy eyes, blazing with emotion.

"You're right, I can't tell you that. But it doesn't matter. We can't all be acting on animal instinct and doing whatever the hell we want. I need the space, and I'd appreciate if you gave it to me."

Only a dick would refuse a request like that. Was I a dick? Where Summer was concerned, maybe. But I could also be a dick who respected his woman.

I pulled open the door and saw the flicker of gratitude in her eyes. She was close to giving in, and she needed me to be on board with the assist.

My uncle Jason stood in the corridor. He divided a shrewd look between us. "Am I interrupting?"

Yes, you fucking are.

"I'm just going," Summer said airily.

Jason offered his hand. "Don't think we've met. I'm Jason, Hatch's uncle."

"Oh, I know who you are. I'm Summer and also, a fan. Big fan." She took his hand and shook it. "Welcome to the Rebels!"

"Thanks." He stepped aside to let her pass, then cast a quick glance after her as she briskly walked down the corridor, all sass and cheese-made curves. Annoyed as fuck, I yanked him inside and closed the door.

"Careful, y'asshole!" My grasp had gratifyingly found chest hair.

"How did you get up here? I have a doorman for a reason."

"Hank and I go way back. I used to live in this building, remember?"

He leaned against the door, rubbing a palm over his chest.

"What was the Bride doing here?"

"Delivering my groceries. She's working for Kennedy."

I turned to head back into the kitchen, conscious of Jason's eyes boring into my back. I wished now I'd put on a shirt because my lack of one looked incriminating.

"You gonna tell me what's going on?"

"Nothing to tell."

He snorted. "I've seen the photo."

I stilled with my hand mid-grab of a bunch of carrots. Fuck.

"I didn't recognize her immediately, but the minute I saw her now and the vibe you two were giving off, I knew. Start at the beginning."

Making light of it was my best chance of surviving this convo with my dignity intact.

"Funny story. I was hanging around outside the church before a recent wedding, minding my own business, when the bride dropped out of the sky like the house in *The Wizard of Oz*."

"No shit."

"Yes shit. She was making her escape and used me as a mattress."

"So naturally you took her to Saugatuck."

"She needed a place to collect her thoughts, away from all the drama."

That yielded another snort. "How in all that is fucking fucked did you think *that* was a good idea?"

I shrugged, leaned against the counter, and said with all the stubbornness I felt, "She needed my help."

He looked like he was about to explode. My uncle was a bit of a hothead at the best of times. "Who else knows?"

"Conor guessed from the photo, but I can manage him. And you won't say a word, will you?"

"Sounds like you have it all worked out."

The sarcasm was strong with this one, but I could take it. Jason and I were close. I confided in him more than I did my dad, so I got the impression he was masking with snark his hurt that I hadn't shared this thrilling life update.

"And what happened in Saugatuck?"

I didn't say anything, and he lifted his hands jazz-style.

"Cool, cool. So you don't have a freakin' clue. Any chance she does?"

"About what?" Though I knew. Of course I did.

"That you're head over skates in love with her."

CHAPTER TWENTY-EIGHT

Hatch

MY HEART POUNDED hard against my rib cage.

"I told you once I thought she was pretty."

Jason squinted. "Yeah, but then you said some other stuff. You'd had a few drinks, but you still said it."

"It's in the past. Years ago."

He shook his head, pitying. "Maybe you need a little refresher. How about I tell *you* a story?"

"Always up for a fairytale, Uncle J." I could match his sarcasm, for all the good it would do me.

"Well, this one probably won't have a happy ending. Once upon a time, a doofus college kid clapped eyes on a girl at a Christmas party and fell hopelessly in love."

"Lust is more accurate."

He passed over my clarification. "But she was with someone else. Worse, she was with someone he knew, so he remained a gentleman and never made a move." Jason wagged a finger. "But he did spend the next five years being a total dick to her. Pretending to hate her made it easier, I suppose. Kids and their coping mechanisms."

I examined the label of a granola box. Damn, that was high in sugar. "Kind of extrapolating from minimal facts there."

"Okay, how about these facts? About three years ago, this same kid had a chance to take a job and work with his dear old dad, but he told his agent to resist all efforts to trade him to the Rebels. He didn't think it would be a, quote, good move, unquote."

"I had a change of heart and came on board, didn't I?"

"Only because Theo said it was his last year in the pros, and it would make him so shiny-happy if his eldest jumped in. He doesn't know you turned down the first offer because you couldn't bear to be in the same city as Summer."

"I told you that in confidence."

My uncle's expression turned sympathetic. "I know. And I've never breathed a word. Still won't. But that doesn't mean I'm not going to talk this through with you. Hatch, you made career choices because this woman, who you couldn't have, was living in your hometown. You've spent the last year acting like an asshole to her and now you're harboring her like she's a fugitive?"

"It just ... happened. I was under that window when she climbed out. Do you think I wanted to be the one who rescued her? I didn't even like her. Yeah, I was obsessed with her. But *like*? No. And I wanted to keep it that way because even if she was no longer with Carter, no good could come out of getting to know her better. I couldn't help her one day and look my teammate in the eye the next."

Jason's expression was one hundred percent pity now. I hated it.

"But you did help her. And from the body language I just witnessed, I'm guessing you helped her all the way to a fucking orgasm. I'm even going to hazard another guess and say that the 'not liking' thing is no more. You created a cozy little love nest in the Tuck, and this just got a whole lot more complicated."

How was this possible? Each passing second brought new twists and turns.

Jason's rehashing of events was correct. A few years ago, barely a year into my stint with Denver, I had rejected the push to trade me to the Chicago Rebels because I didn't want to be around her. I didn't want to be around *them*. Watching Carter touch her, kiss her, own her, made me sick with jealousy, so I told my dad I wasn't ready to move. He was disappointed but he didn't push it.

Then I decided to sac up. Knowing it was likely my dad's last year in the pros, I figured that was more important than this ridiculous obsession I had for a woman I had barely spoken to. I could be civil to Carter, indifferent to Summer, and would play my best hockey to honor my dad. I would handle it like a boss.

Then Summer and Carter got engaged.

Right after she said yes, I drove straight to Saugatuck, got drunk off my ass, and fucked a woman without a condom. A woman—Ava—who later told me she was pregnant. That's how stupid love had made me. Jason was right: I had made career decisions based on my pain. Used another woman to numb that hurt, and when she lied about being pregnant, it confirmed everything I thought I knew about Summer. Just another bunny with her eye on a payday.

This last year, I didn't play my best *and* I still had to witness love's young dream in the form of Summer and Carter.

"Yeah, it's complicated, but that doesn't mean Summer wasn't in need. Now she's onto the next stage of her life." And she didn't want my help. She wanted to manage Carter by herself and not reckon with what happened between us.

What *could* happen between us.

Well, I wasn't ready to give up just yet.

Thankfully, Jason moved on—to another third-rail topic. "Speaking of life stages and big decisions, how come just as I move back to Chicago you might be moving out of it?"

"And there I was thinking the agent-client relationship is sacrosanct." Special Agent Lauren had been besties with my uncle since they played youth camp hockey together as kids.

"Nah, that's not where I heard it. Connie seems to think you're looking to trade."

I really needed to have a chat with that kid.

"I didn't have a good year, J. And if Dad's sticking around, I'm not sure the next will be any better."

"Listen, no one knows better than me the pressure of being in the same biz as Theo Kershaw. And I play the same position as him. I'm *never* going to measure up."

Jason and I had never discussed this before. I could feel myself leaning in, desperate for whatever pearls of wisdom he had to dispense.

"Pro sports is as much mental as it is physical," he said. "I know the press has been on your ass with the comparisons to your dad. Believe me, I'm fully prepared to suffer them when I join up, whether my brother is on the roster or not. In fact, I could probably take some of that heat for you if you choose to stick around."

I chuckled. "What, you'd flub a few passes? Make me look like 'the good Kershaw'?"

He grinned. "Family first, Hatchling."

CHAPTER TWENTY-NINE

FIVE DAYS HAD GONE by since the grocery delivery to Hatch, and during that time, I took all the jobs Kennedy offered. None of them led me back to Hatch's door, a sign that I was meant to stay away. It was good to be busy. To feel useful again.

Dog tired after an afternoon walking a chocolate Lab, a Chihuahua, and a Pekinese—which sounded like the start of a joke—I trudged into the apartment and was greeted by a lush wall of sound. Motown, but slower than usual and not so upbeat. In the living room, I found Adeline and Rosie belting out "What Becomes of the Broken Hearted?" and swaying with martini glasses in their hands.

"Summer! Finally!" Rosie rushed over to hug me, her drink sloshing over the glass's rim. "You're missing Martini Monday."

"It's Tuesday."

"Well, I had to work last night so we moved it to tonight, which means Taco Tuesday is now on Wednesday."

"Give her a Scandi Noir," Adeline said. "Oh, and her present!"

This adult beverage was well-known even to me, a martini created by Adeline's great-grandmother in honor of Lars Nyquist's grumpy vibe. With great ceremony, Rosie poured a grapefruit-vodka-vermouth mix into a martini glass, added a twist of lemon peel, and passed it over. I sipped gratefully and took a seat.

"How was work?" Rosie asked.

"Peyton Bell sent me to Nordstrom's to buy him under-wear. I was instructed to get extra-large for his hockey butt."

Adeline made a face. "Was it as weird as it sounds?"

"Actually, not so bad. I thought I'd be embarrassed to be reduced to errand girl for guys on the team after my previous lofty position as WAG, but I don't mind it, really. I love walking the dogs. They're my favorite."

Rosie took a seat beside me and clinked my glass as the Miracles oohed the intro to "The Tracks of my Tears."

"The dogs are awesome. Even more awesome, you got a delivery!"

"I did?"

Adeline put her glass down and picked up a box at the side of the armchair. "Someone sent you a present."

Sure enough, that was my name on the label. The return address was something called Boarderie.

"Open it!" Rosie handed me a steak knife.

A minute later, we were gazing in wonder upon a gorgeously arranged cheese board. A handy legend listed off aged Gouda, Cranberry Wensleydale, a creamy Camembert, Rosemary-pepper crackers, figs, almonds, candied ginger, and more.

"Wow, that looks *soooo* good," Adeline said as she picked up the accompanying card before I could. I knew who had sent it. Please God, let him have had the common sense not to own up to it.

Adeline read off the card, "*Just in queso you need a friend, I'm right here.* No name."

"Cute." Rosie narrowed her eyes at me. "Who sent this?"

"I really can't say." True to the letter, if not the spirit. I hated lying, but there was no way I could fess up.

"Looks like you have a cheesy admirer."

"Someone who really brie-lieves in you," Adeline said with a grin. "*I really can't say.*" She repeated my words, slightly exaggerated. "That accent of yours has always thrown me."

"That's Mississippi."

Rosie's brow lined. "I thought you were from the Bay Area."

"I—well, I might have fudged the truth there. Long story."

Adeline smiled. "Worth telling over cheese? I was going to make pasta but maybe we should have a cheese night. If you don't mind eating it."

"It is very pretty, but yeah, let's smash this thing."

"And then we can settle in for Summer's thrilling backstory and a few episodes of *Downton*," Rosie said. "Got to get caught up ahead of the movie."

I grasped her arm. "You guys are *Downton* fans?"

Adeline's smile was wry. "Of course we are. I'm kind of hoping they find a way to have Bates accused of murder for a third time in this entry. I want to see Anna rushing to the gallows with evidence of his innocence."

Rosie laughed. "And Lady Mary throwing her title

around as she talks down her nose to the prison governor. But to be fair, Bates needs to alibi himself every time he leaves the house!"

I could have cried. How lucky I was to have fallen in with this crew. While Rosie grabbed plates, I headed to my room to change and shoot off a text of gratitude.

ME

Thank you for dinner tonight.

DINO BOY

Glad to feed your cheese habit, Sunshine.

ME

The board is so beautiful. I hate having to ruin it, but cheese.

DINO BOY

That's what it's there for.

How have you been?

ME

Working hard, it's good to be busy.

I didn't mention Carter. He still had my number blocked, and I was tired of talking and thinking about him.

ME

How's hockey camp going?

DINO BOY

Awesome. I love working with the kids. Also, it's been cool to hang with my uncle Jason. We're accountability buddies at the Rebels gym.

And now I had a lovely image of Hatch sweating after a workout, maybe even lifting the hem of his shirt to wipe his forehead and showcasing off those perfect abs ...

I considered asking him out for tea, as a proper thank you for the cheese. It didn't have to lead anywhere.

Sure, Summer. You'll be thanking him on your knees before you can say "Earl Grey, hot."

Adeline called out, "Hey Summer, dinner's up, and Lord Grantham is walking his dog!"

Saved by cheese and the opening credits of *Downton*.

ME

Sorry, got to go. Have a Gouda night!

THE NEXT MORNING, I walked into the kitchen, nursing a Scandi Noir martini headache and a cheese hangover, and found Rosie on her phone. She looked up guiltily, turned the phone over on the counter, and gave me a thin smile.

"Coffee?"

"I'll make tea, thanks. What's wrong?"

Last night we'd binged a few episodes of *Downton Abbey* and I'd told them a little about where I'd been raised. Not quite as much as I shared with Hatch but enough to make me feel closer to them. They had taken it all in stride because they were the best people.

Rosie expelled a weary breath. "I suppose you're going to see it anyway. I'll send you the link."

My phone buzzed and I opened the link she had sent from the *Hot Goss* site. The headline sent my heart plummeting to the floor.

Dash Carter Breaks His Silence: "Summer Checked My Heart."

I CLAMPED my hand to my mouth, then met Rosie's worried gaze. "I'm guessing the title is the nicest part of it?"

She jumped up and pushed me to a chair at the kitchen table. "Have a seat, get it over with, and I'll make you breakfast. Blueberry pancakes."

"You don't have to—"

"This is a blueberry pancake situation!"

She busy bee'd her way about the kitchen while I read the "article." More like a hit job.

Chicago Rebels hockey player and heir to the Dominion Hotel Group, Dash Carter, has finally spoken out about the shocking events surrounding his wedding almost a month ago. In a horrific turn, Dash was abandoned at the altar by his long-time fiancée, Summer Landry.

"If she had come to me and told me how she felt, we could have worked something out," Dash said. "But the way she left? Only someone with a cruel streak a mile wide could think that was a good way to break up with a guy."

Regular readers will recall that Summer exited the church in what some have labeled "a cowardly manner"—she used a bathroom window to make her escape—instead of bravely facing the man she supposedly loved. Over four hundred guests were left speechless when Dash's best man, his cousin, Saxon Carter the Third, made the terrible announcement that the wedding was cancelled due to the absent bride. What happened next reveals Dash's depth of character and resilience.

"I went on my honeymoon alone and did some soul-searching. What was it about me that would have a woman do that? Sure, we had our problems, like any couple. She didn't like that I was on the road so much, even accused me of cheating. Early in our relationship, she slept with someone else, and I forgave her. Because I thought she was worth it. That we were worth it."

"That liar!"

Rosie paused mixing the pancake batter. "The cheating accusation?"

"Completely made up. He cheated on me! Only I could never prove it."

I returned to the phone, my hands shaking.

Many observers have speculated about Summer's motives in taking such drastic action. Dash has his own take on it.

"I know it wasn't about the money because, if she was a gold digger, why not go through with it? And I don't want anyone calling her that. Sure, I gave her some nice gifts. Jewelry, clothes, a car. She definitely did okay out of it. I think she just likes the idea of stringing guys along. It's a power thing."

When asked if he had spoken with his former fiancée

since she left him in front of his friends and family, Dash shook his head.

"I've reached out to her, asking if we can sit down and talk. She's ignored all my calls. I returned to the city to volunteer with the Rebels Youth Hockey Camp, which is dear to my heart, and to see how she is. Summer made sure I was out of town when she came by to pick up her belongings, which I had set aside for her. I guess she prefers to spread rumors that I left them to be trashed. Funny what you find out about people when they're under pressure. She didn't have any family, so I'm not sure she even understands what it's like to connect with people. We wanted to accept her, but she always set herself on some sort of pedestal."

Phew, that's a lot! We asked Dash if he saw any chance of reconciliation?

He likes to think there's always hope. "I'm a big-hearted guy. Always have been. Ask my family, my friends. Ask Summer, if you can get a hold of her. Despite her cruelty, I still think there's something between us. Call me a fool, but then I'm a fool in love."

"He is so full of it!"

I had never once heard Dash talk like this. It sounded like he'd plugged in a *jilted groom, make me look like the victim* prompt into his favorite AI bot and copy/pasted it to this so-called journalist. "He said I won't take his calls. It's the other way around. And he left my belongings for garbage pick-up."

Rosie brought me a cup of English Breakfast tea. "Maybe you should give an interview? Jordan Hunt would love to talk to you." Jordan was a hockey reporter and podcaster.

"Nope. I'm not playing his game."

But neither was I prepared to take it lying down. If he wouldn't take my calls, I would place him in a position where he had to talk to me.

Two hours later, Tara Fitzpatrick, who operated a hair salon in the Rebels practice facility, met me at security to walk me in. I let her give me a trim, a blow out, and a *you-go-girl* pep talk, because damn, I would look good and feel empowered when confronting the ex-fiancé I had terribly wronged.

I was waiting inside the locker room when Hatch came in after the youth hockey camp session. He wore warm-ups and skates with guards and was carrying a stick.

"Summer." His voice sounded warm, deep, empathetic. I hadn't realized how much I missed him.

"I'm here to see Dash."

Disappointment flashed across his features for a second before he schooled them to neutral.

"He's on his way. Still think he's hurting?"

I tried to smile. "He's lashing out, so yes, that is often how hurt people behave. We need to talk. I can't put it off any longer." Not that I had been, but I had to admit a certain relief when a text or call remained unanswered. I could bask in the glow of self-righteousness, but it wasn't moving either of us forward.

Hatch opened his mouth, but whatever he was about to say was drowned by the thunderous entry of more hockey players. First his brother Conor, whose eyes went wide on seeing me. Then Jason, who nodded then sent an inscrutable look Hatch's way. Finally, Dash. No sign of Theo, for which I was grateful.

Dash practically sneered. "How did *you* get in here?"

"I still know people. I hoped we could chat."

Given that he had maintained I was giving him the runaround, he couldn't very well claim he didn't want to talk to me now.

"If you'd talked to me in the first place, maybe we wouldn't be in this mess."

I deserved that, so I took it like a champ, but I could feel the tension emanating from Hatch's direction. I stood and headed to the door, passing by Hatch. I didn't dare look at the man who had rescued me, and who had become so much more than a random knight.

"I'll be in the yoga room whenever you're ready."

Dash turned away, which gave me a chance to catch Hatch's eye. Just a brief glimpse to give me strength before I shut the locker room door.

My former fiancé made me wait twenty minutes. Again, fair. I was sitting on a yoga mat when he came in. He'd obviously taken the time to shower, had even dried and gelled his hair. Fine, we were both going in armed.

"How are you?" I asked.

He lowered himself to the mat beside mine. "Oh, just great, Summer."

Dash's defense mechanisms always leaned heavily on sarcasm, not that I could blame him.

"I know I didn't handle it right. I panicked and saw the window, and before I knew it, I was running."

"Well, how come you decided to run back here? You're just making it worse."

"I have a life here, Dash. And I'm not ready to give all that up." I exhaled. "Surely this town is big enough for both of us."

"Don't think you're getting your job back."

"I wish I hadn't given it up."

He snorted. "Is that what this is about? I was taking *too* good care of you? You could have done some volunteer work like my mom. That's how she spends her time. Or brunching and bitching with her girlfriends. Hell, you would have been pregnant soon."

"I wasn't ready for that. Yet I overheard you talking about it with your mom and arranging for your former nanny to come out of retirement. Don't you think it's weird that you're letting your mother call the shots about our reproductive decisions?"

He rolled his eyes. "So, she's interested. You don't have parents, Summer, so you don't know what it's like when the ones you have actually care about their family and the future of it. I would have thought you'd be pleased to become a part of a family, especially one as important as mine. But you never made an effort with my sister or my mom."

"They thought I was trash. I was never good enough for you."

"Looks like they were right."

He stood and stretched, giving me a glimpse of his abs. It did nothing for me.

This man did nothing for me.

I had handled our wedding day all wrong, but I made the right call in finishing this relationship. Neither did he want me back, and any chatter on that topic was his usual mind games.

I stood and extracted the engagement ring from my

purse, handing it off to him like Charlie surrendering the everlasting gobstopper to Mr. Wonka.

He shoved it in his pocket without looking at it.

"I know it's going to take time to forgive me, Dash. But I'd appreciate it if, in the meantime, you didn't slander me in the press or bad-mouth me to everyone you know. Otherwise, I might have to bite back."

He wagged his finger at me. "You have no power here, Summer. You're just a girl from nowhere, a nobody who's only got connections because of me."

And then he left me to ponder that undeniable truth. Dash might not know a single thing about me, but he'd still managed to hit the nail on the head.

Nowhere Girl. That about summed it up.

CHAPTER THIRTY

Hatch

I SHOULD HAVE PUNCHED Carter in the nose.

I could tell from the smirk on his face when he returned to the locker room that he'd been an absolute asshole to Summer. So maybe she deserved a few harsh words, but to be trashed like she'd been in that article? That was all wrong.

Today was the last day of camp. I'd spent the entire session with the budding hockey champions, staying out of Carter's way because if I got even the slightest whiff of his self-righteous, woe-is-me attitude, I would have checked him through the plexi. Not the best example for the younglings.

Now he was back in the locker room, so damned pleased with himself.

"How did it go?" I asked. *How's Summer?*

"Crushed it."

Conor pulled on his T-shirt. "Made her cry, big man?"

The way he'd said that could be interpreted as standard bro-speak or artful shade. Knowing my brother, it was the latter.

"No. Because I'm a gentleman."

I snorted. Jason flashed his eyes in warning.

Carter narrowed his gaze in my direction. "Something to say, KJ?"

"Nah. You said *all* the words in that gossip rag. Sure showed your ex." I didn't have my brother's sneaky subtlety.

"And you have a problem with this because?"

"No problem. Just the way you talk about her, I don't get why you wanted to marry her. I don't see the connection."

"Connection? Fuck, Kershaw, you reading romance novels now? She was hot and she got hockey."

Conor chuckled darkly. "Hot and hockey, a match made in heaven, C-Dog."

More bafflement on Carter's face. He really couldn't parse my brother's tone.

"I told her that she's done in this town. I know she's crashing at your sister's place, but I can't imagine that'll last long. The Rebels aren't going to rehire her." He picked up his holdall. "Well, Kershaws, it's been a blast. See ya in a few weeks for training camp." With a jaunty salute, he headed out.

"Fucking dick," I muttered.

Conor cocked his head. "H, were you not present when Dad beat the living shit out of Lars during a game last season? Because that's where you and the franchise are headed if Carter gets wind of your shenanigans."

"There are no shenanigans."

My brother side-eyed Jason. "You buying this?"

"Leave him be."

"Ah, so you're part of the trust circle."

"And if he wanted to tell you, he would. Come on, I'll buy you lunch, and we will *not* gossip about your brother. You coming, Hatchling?"

I needed to be alone. "I'm going to shower. Catch you guys later."

Conor was right, though. Like the situation with Lars and my dad last season, this was heading for a showdown. The difference here was that I didn't give a flying fuck about Carter's opinion. I did, however, care about my dad's. He wouldn't like to learn I had messed with a teammate's former fiancée days after she had left him.

I took out my phone and sent her a text.

> If you need to talk, I'm here. No pressure.

I waited a few moments, but no response. Maybe that cold shower would dampen the fury I felt about Carter shit-talking Summer. Grabbing a towel from the cupboard, I stripped and headed into the showers. I was just about to turn on the faucet when I heard a sound from the locker room.

Muttering.

Soft, angry muttering.

I walked out to find Summer with her back to me.

And she had already made her mark.

CHAPTER THIRTY-ONE

Summer

"HEY, BANKSY, WHAT'S UP?"

I dropped the can and whipped around. Hatch stood behind me in nothing but a towel because that was exactly the sort of day I was having.

"What are you doing here?"

He raised an eyebrow. Okay, he had every right to be here. Me? Not so much.

He picked up the spray can from where it had rolled to near his foot. "Just Color Hair Dye," he read off the label, then eyed the jersey hanging above Dash's cubby.

When I came in here, my plan was comprised of a single word: *Destroy.*

I wanted to obliterate something that belonged to Dash. He could afford anything and replace everything, including me. Looking at the vivid pink streaks like Barbie streaks of fury across the front of his sweater, I felt a burgeoning sense of accomplishment. Not in creating something, but in sheer destruction.

After my chat with Dash, I'd sought out Tara, looking for a shoulder to cry on. Unfortunately, she had already left for the day, but her salon inspired me with its gallery of potential mutilation. Touching her scissors was a little like messing with a chef's knives—absolutely verboten—so I focused on the haircare supplies. I found a can of semi-permanent pink hair dye, which I imagined Tara used for fun applications of color for the under twelves and clients who weren't so brave.

Now here I was, a woman scorned, all because Dash wasn't acting suitably damaged by my actions.

"I—I'm sorry."

"Don't be." He handed the can back to me. "Go ahead."

"I've done enough." I didn't want to damage the cubby or surroundings because someone other than Dash would have to fix that. I placed the can down on the bench.

"He was a jerk to you."

"I shouldn't have expected anything else. I'm mostly angry about the lies he's spreading." I swiped at a tear. "Yet, I can't blame him, can I?"

In a flash, I found myself wrapped in strong arms. "Summer, you didn't handle the end of your relationship well. But you're trying to make amends while he's acting like a little bitch."

I chuckled against his chest, which felt so good on my cheek.

He tipped my chin up, and I was suddenly frighteningly aware of how beautiful he was. Not just in looks, but inside, too. He had come to my rescue, sheltered me from the storm, and respected my choices. He'd also made it clear that he wanted me.

I was a data girlie, and that was the data point thrumming through me this minute.

"Don't mind me. I'm feeling sorry for myself."

"That's okay. We all do from time to time."

"Weirdly, the thing that hurt the most wasn't the false accusation of cheating or the hints that I was *definitely* not after his money." I snatched a breath. "It was that dig about not connecting with his family. Like I'm some sort of sociopath who can never belong anywhere."

He growled. "Total and utter bullshit. I've seen you with people, with players in the front office and at the Empty Net. Last Halloween you came to our house party, and the kids adored you and your Taco-Belle Disney princess costume. People feel better when you walk into a room, Summer."

Not everyone. At that party, Hatch had glowered at me any time I caught his eye. The contradictions fascinated me.

He was still talking. "So maybe you've held yourself back a little because of your past, but I know my sister wouldn't have invited you into her home if she didn't think you were worth her time. She's an excellent judge of character. Carter has to buy every connection in his miserable platinum-plated life. You earn it by being you."

His kindness floored me. I wasn't sure I deserved it, but I couldn't deny how special he made me feel.

Unable to help myself, I rubbed a hand along his chest, loving how his breath hitched. *I did that.* I held some sort of power over him, and when you felt as weak as I did, any glimpse of control was heady.

"I'm a little sick of it. The self-pity, the punishing myself."

I hadn't done much of that in Saugatuck. I had let Hatch make me feel good. I wanted to feel that way again.

He merely watched and waited, giving me space to sort out my feelings. But the tension in his body was unmistakable. He was a dangerous predator, coiled, ready to spring, and all I had to do was whisper, "here, kitty kitty."

That *Hot Goss* garbage made me the villain. If I was to do the time, I may as well do the crime.

I reached up and kissed him.

"Oh, fuck," he murmured into my mouth.

I couldn't have envisioned a better reaction.

Until he topped it. He grasped my ass with both hands, scooped me up like I weighed nothing, and pushed me against the nearest cubby.

Dash's.

A small part of me enjoyed that. The majority stakeholder in my brain, on the other hand, preferred to ignore it and let myself be swept away by the moment. By Hatch's hands on me, rough and seeking. By his mouth on mine, devastatingly gentle, then resoundingly passionate. He had said I was his end game, which was absurdly focused and serious. He hardly knew me, yet he wanted me badly.

And I wanted to be wanted like this. I needed it.

But not here against my ex's cubby. Not even I was that messed up.

Oh yes you are.

Go to hell, Shelby Mae!

I pulled away. "Someone might come in," I panted.

As usual, Hatch had the answer. Lifting me up, he brought me through to the showers. More private, and though the water wasn't on, it felt steamier. Sexier. As if it could get any hotter in here.

The next few moments passed in a wild tussle of hands and mouths. My leggings yanked down, a towel ripped away, the bliss of his palm cupping between my legs. Yet again, Hatch was ever generous, giving me what I needed. It was time I returned the favor—and took back some control for myself.

I fell to my knees and tipped my head back to meet his glowing, green-eyed gaze.

His lips parted. Words seemed to fail him. Finally, he managed, "Sunshine, you don't have—"

I didn't let him finish.

At least not yet.

No tentative licks or strokes for me. I took him in my mouth, or as much of him as I could, because not only was Hatch Kershaw gifted on the ice, he was gifted in all areas.

"Oh, Christ!" Followed by a lusty groan that echoed off the tile as I sucked the hard length of him. Grasping his rock-hard butt cheek for leverage, I practically whimpered when the salty sweetness splashed my tongue. I peered up and saw that he had placed one fist against the shower tile. His other hand coasted to the back of my head, and now his fingertips raked my hair—*cafuné*, my favorite Portuguese word!—though his grip was a little harder than that phrasing implied. Less the casual hair rake of a lover and more the sensual grasp of a man needing to fuck his woman's mouth.

His hips rocked, gently at first, like he was trying not to hurt me. But I squeezed his butt, encouraging him to let go. To take what was his. He thrust deeper for a few strokes, but before he could set a rhythm, he pulled me off him and cupped my cheek.

"Look at you," he whispered, his tone one of awe. "Absolutely perfect."

And I felt that with him. With Hatch, I felt like I was a hot mess with potential.

Precome leaked from his slick cock, so I cleaned him up with kitten-like licks, watching as his eyes smoked over.

Before I could restart my very important task, he grasped my arms and pulled me to my feet. Then higher still, as he pinned me to the wall, both hands curving my ass, and pierced me with the cock I'd just sucked. *Oh God.* The feel of him inside me took me out of myself, shot me to a better place.

I didn't last long. Clawing at his back, I bit into his shoulder to muffle my scream of pleasure. He followed me over with a final, powerful stroke that lifted me high against the shower tile and impaled me fast.

I was panting hard, breathing my way back to reality. The one where everyone thought I was an unfeeling, indecisive shitshow. The one where my best ally was the man I once thought hated me.

The one where ... *hell.* "We didn't use protection."

He drew back, his eyebrows in a broody V. Probably wondering how I'd ensorcelled him with my witchy spells.

"That was my fault," he said. "I lost my mind there."

We both had. "I'm on birth control, but you're not my only recent partner." Stating the obvious, but it needed to be said.

"It's been a while for me. The last time I didn't use a condom, I—" He broke off, likely remembering Ava and how she had done him wrong. "I've been tested since, so that side of it is okay. If anything happens, we'll figure it out together."

We'll figure it out together. That assurance fortified me, just as every moment with this man gave me hope that it didn't have to be as it was with Dash. Kind, decent, unbelievably sexy men who didn't view every mistake as a means to exercise leverage over me actually existed.

He had barely softened inside me. After slipping out of

my body, he lowered me gently to the ground and kissed my forehead.

Needless to say, I *loved* when he did that. I felt so cared for.

"Let me clean you up." He threw my clothes outside the shower cubicle and turned the water on. Angling my body so my back was against his chest, he ran lathered hands over every curve, moving his fingers deftly and purposefully. His lips brushed the shell of my ear as he whispered words of loving approval mixed with filthy encouragement.

My sweet girl ... Open up for me ... You feel so fucking good ... Love this pretty pussy ... That's right, baby, I've got you ... Look at those gorgeous tits ... Want to suck them ... Love how you taste ... You need my cock again? ... Fuck yeah, you do ... And it needs you ... So fucking bad ... Come for me, baby ... Yeah, that's it ... Summer ... Summer ... Sum—ah, fuck!

Our moans echoed off the tile as he fucked me again and again, alternately with his magic fingers and rampant cock. Again, no protection. I didn't care because *he* was my protection. Foolish, of course, but I was out of control where Hatch Kershaw was concerned.

After, I pulled up my leggings and handed him his towel because frankly, the man needed to cover up before I dropped to my knees and sucked another orgasm out of him.

The doubts rushed back in. "This isn't really me taking the space I need to get my act together, is it?"

Wrapping the towel around his trim hips, he grinned. "We all find ourselves in different ways. Cheese boards, shower sex, petty vandalism of an ex's workplace."

I covered my burning face with my hands.

Chuckling, he pulled them away and drew me close. "It's okay, baby. You heard some bad news, and you acted out a little. I think you've been putting up with Carter's bad behavior for years and now the freedom has cracked you open. Releasing all that tension is good for you. And I'm *always* happy to help."

"With orgasms," I stated glumly.

"Climbing my way to a hundred."

"While I'm dragging you into my mess."

He dropped a soft kiss on my nose. "No place I'd rather be, Sunshine."

CHAPTER THIRTY-TWO

Summer

I SPENT the rest of the afternoon running errands for Kennedy, that is, doing something that wasn't self-destructive or bad for my mental well-being. I would like to say I hadn't known what I was doing back in that locker room, that I was overcome with emotion and my hormones ruled the day—and while some of that might hold water, the bottom line was that I was not the nicest person. I was using Hatch to make myself feel better, and that wasn't fair to him.

Three dog walks and a grocery delivery later, I headed back to Rosie and Adeline's place. I couldn't call it my home, which made me wonder what the hell I was doing here. Dash was right: the Rebels wouldn't rehire me. Scott Kincaid had emailed to tell me that it was best I no longer do any reports for him—I suspected Ryder told him to stop using my free labor—and now that avenue was closed. I was relying on Ryder to come through with a job at another franchise, which meant if I was serious about working in pro hockey, I would need to leave Chicago. As grateful as I was to the girls for keeping me afloat, I couldn't mooch off them for much longer.

As soon as I opened the door, the smell of cooking made my mouth water and the sound of voices made me anxious. We had company.

A tall, dark-haired guy I didn't recognize exited the bathroom and caught my eye. He had a hot nerd thing going on, though I was probably swayed by the glasses.

"Hello there," he said.

"Hi, I'm Summer." Though I'm sure he knew. Everyone did.

"Ah, the new roommate. Nice to meet you. I'm Sean, Addy's uncle."

Also Hatch's, as well as Jason Isner's brother and Theo's half-brother. The Kershaw family tree was a many-horned beast. He wasn't looking at me oddly, so I wondered if maybe he was the only person on planet Earth who hadn't heard about my dash from Dash.

"Nice to meet you, too. Who else is here?"

"My brother Jason and Lauren—do you know Lauren?"

"I do." Lauren Yates was the sister of Sadie, my wedding dress designer, sister-in-law to Gunnar Bond, an ex-Rebels player, and Hatch's agent. A former professional hockey player in the National Women's League, she had come into the Rebels front office a few times to discuss her clients with Ryder.

Adeline appeared in the corridor to the kitchen. "Hey, roomie! Just in time for dinner."

"Oh, I don't want to intrude."

"Don't be silly. This is for you."

I blinked. "It is?"

"After all that BS in the gossip rags, we figured we'd invite a few people over. Nice, normal, but likely ragingly curious people. So, apologies in advance. Grab yourself a margarita and go mingle until the tacos are up."

Sean smiled. "I can get you a drink. Go on ahead."

I went into the living room, holding my breath. *Don't let him be here. Don't let him be here.*

He was not. My traitorous heart went splat with disappointment.

Lars came forward, hugged me, and growled in a very Lars-way, "Carter's a dick."

I laughed. "Well, that's mighty kind of you to say so." If I'd heard this before I spoke with Dash earlier, I would have made excuses for him. But no more. That didn't make what happened with Hatch in that locker room right, but I needed to move on from the shame.

Lars thumbed over his shoulder. "You know these guys, right?"

"I do." I nodded hello at Jason and Lauren and tried not to imagine what they thought of me. Since leaving my hometown ten years ago, I'd been trying to find a place. Fit in. Yet here I was standing out like a sore thumb.

"Can't believe I considered representing Carter," Lauren said. A tall brunette, she had a bright-eyed, mischievous look that belied a tough-as-nails negotiator. "He told me he would only sign on if I could guarantee him a designer fragrance or a watch deal. Looks like we both dodged a bullet." She punctuated that with a cheeky wink, which made me chuckle.

"Like the guy needs endorsements," Jason said. "He's richer than God."

"It's not just about endorsements," I said. "Goodwill

can be just as important. Dash would have liked to be associated with a brand that made him look better. I suggested he volunteer with some charities, but he said it would be easier to write a check."

"And that's why he's playing the victim in the press," Lauren said. "He knows that people look at him and think, 'rich hockey player who has more money than he could ever spend in a lifetime, I wonder what's wrong with him? Why would any girl not want to be with that?' So he goes on the offensive." Lauren squeezed my arm, though I barely knew her. "Anyone in the business who knows Carter will see right through it. Unfortunately, the readers of those rags are mostly not in the business."

Lars frowned, then looked at me. "But you don't have to care what they think."

Except insofar as it impeded my ability to get a job in the business I loved. I needed to make peace with him so I could tell the Rebels, "nothing to see here!"

Sean came in with two margaritas, one of which he passed to me. "Here you go. So, I just realized that you're Dash Carter's runaway bride. A bona fide celebrity in our midst."

Jason pointed at his brother and smiled. "Dude, you don't even know who Dash Carter is."

"No, but Franky does. She's on her way over."

Jason's easy demeanor changed in an instant. "Just happened to be in the neighborhood, was she?"

"She's doing some research over at the lighthouse, tracking some special breed of snail."

Franky was Rosie's stepsister and a snail specialist, which sounded both creepy and fascinating. I had met her a couple of times at various Rebels gatherings, and I always enjoyed her take on situations. I had no doubt she'd have something to say about mine.

Rosie called out, "Come fix your tacos in the kitchen, people."

As I was closest to the door, I made it to the kitchen first.

Hatch was here.

———

Hatch

I HAD BEEN WARNED by Rosie before Summer arrived.

"You had better be nice to her, Hatch. She's had a bad time of it." She passed me an onion and a knife. Generally a badass, Rosie had always been a wimp when it came to cutting onions.

"Why wouldn't I be nice to her?"

"Oh, I don't know, you tell me." She leveled her dark-eyed gaze at me. "You've always acted weird around her."

"Some people don't mesh. But I can be nice to poor little Summer." I needed to come off as disinterested, mostly for Summer's sake. The last thing she needed was another target on her back.

Rosie tilted her head, assessing me.

"What?"

"You seem different. This last year, you've been so down on yourself, not happy with your play. Now you seem ... lighter."

I attended to my onion chopping. "It was good to get away to Saugatuck."

"Right, the mystery woman. What was that about?"

"I had coffee with someone. Not a big deal."

When I turned her way, I found her looking at me like I was a puzzle. She was the person I could usually trust with my secrets, my fears, my insecurities. But this was the one thing I couldn't share with her. She wouldn't approve, and I didn't want to disappoint her.

Besides, I was soon on the receiving end of Summer's disapproval once she realized I was a dinner guest.

I had agreed to give her space, but neither could I ignore dinner invitations or pretend we didn't now move in the same circles. (To be fair, I knew these people first.) She avoided looking at me, and given the nosiness of my family and friends, I thought it best to do likewise.

The universe heard about that plan and said, "fuck you, guys."

We found ourselves sitting opposite each other at the table, but any awkwardness was lubricated by a pitcher of margaritas. Jason told a couple of funny stories about his hockey teammates on the Boston Cougars while Lauren supplemented his tales with a few of her own, with no names because, "confidentiality." We spent far too much time trying to guess the secret identities, while Addy spent most of *her* time making eyes at Lars, who goggled right back. I was initially down on this relationship given the age gap, the employer/nanny thing, and the fact it had the potential to screw with the team's fortunes, but I could see now how good they were together. I was envious really, because my little sister had her shit sorted out and I did not.

I wanted to be where she was at. I wanted Summer.

This afternoon in the locker room had been so damn sexy, but more than that, I had felt so close to her. Watching her suck me off and fucking her against that shower tile was the definition of hot. But so was listening to her troubles and confiding in her about my career woes back in Saugatuck.

I wanted those conversations as much as I wanted Summer in my bed.

We were debating whether the night warranted another pitcher when Franky arrived. Francesca St. James was in her mid-thirties, so closer to Sean and Jason's ages. I'd always liked her, mostly because she had a direct, no-nonsense way of looking at things. With her dark hair piled into a messy bun, librarian glasses (the bridge wrapped in blue duct tape), and a Lakeshore U sweater over rolled up jeans, she gave off a schoolteacher vibe. Which tracked, because she was a professor of biology at LU.

"Hey, sis!" Rosie jumped up to hug her. "Are you hungry?"

"Starving."

"We were just about to make another pitcher of margaritas," Addy said. "You in?"

"Not for me. I'll just stick with water." She looked around the table. "I thought Sean was here?"

"He's in the kitchen on a work call," I said. Sean was the chief tech officer for a bank in Boston, so very, very important. "How was the slug hunt?"

Her eyes lit up. "Very productive, though in fact, I was looking for snails. Viviparinae Gray to be exact. They're usually found in colder waters of the north but have started to migrate to the lower parts of the Great Lakes and associated waterways."

"Sounds like a wild time," Jason said, with an unexpected touch of snark.

Franky was more friendly with Sean, so I assumed she knew Jason to some extent. Yet I wasn't prepared for her reaction when my uncle spoke to her. Her lip curled in a very distinctive sneer, and she turned away.

Jason shot a quick look of *da fuck* at me. I wanted to laugh because my uncle usually never failed to charm anyone. He was like my dad in that respect—everyone loved him. But not Franky, which amused me greatly.

Rosie set a plate down before her with a glass of water. As Franky picked up the taco, she arced her assessing gaze over the group.

"Have I missed the discussion about Summer's sprint from the church?"

A smiling Summer made a point of not looking at me. "We haven't really discussed it except in surface terms."

"You made the right call. Dash Carter's as spineless as a gastropod." Around her chewing, Franky added, "Slug humor."

Rosie laughed. "Tell us how you really feel."

She sipped from her water glass and took that as a literal invitation to unload. "I once overheard him telling someone at a Rebels fundraiser that he couldn't make a donation because his mother took care of the family's gift-giving."

"Damning stuff," Jason said with an eye roll.

Franky stared at him. "You might think that a meaningless anecdote, but it reflects a negative personality trait that no woman wants in a prospective mate. A man who exhibits that sort of selfishness of spirit is not worth a woman's time. I only wish I'd told you sooner, Summer."

Summer caught my eye—yes!—and rolled in her lips, hiding a smile. "Not sure I would have drawn the same conclusion from that, but there were plenty of other red flags I ignored."

Franky went on. "I imagine he would have provided good genetic material for your children, though. Sometimes that's all you need, especially when we're talking about athletes."

"What does that mean?" Jason asked sharply.

Franky met his gaze over her glasses. They had slipped down her nose while she ate, making her look like a scolding schoolteacher. "Only that athletes aren't the most evolved people on the planet."

Jason looked like he was about to explode. I jumped in to defend my jock brethren.

"Your dad's an athlete, Franky." Not just any athlete. Bren St. James was a legendary center from a Cup-winning Rebels team.

Franky considered that. "My dad excepted. And Uncle Remy, who is probably the most evolved man I've ever met. Uncle Vadim is up there, too, though it took him a while. Russians are tough nuts and Aunt Isobel had to work hard to crack him. The rest of them? Idiots."

"Jesus Christ," Jason muttered.

"I think several of us have a different view of athletes, Franky," Addy said diplomatically.

"Well, you already have proof that Lars can produce a healthy child, so you can check that off the list. And I assume he has other positives that prove he's worth your time. After all, you overcame several obstacles to get your happy-ever-after."

Lars stared at her. I wondered if this was his first direct exposure to the professor.

Rosie looked at her sister indulgently. "All those hurdles definitely make it worth the effort, I'd say."

I considered that. I hoped that one day I would look fondly at the hurdles I overcame to get Summer.

Because I was prepared to knock every single one of them flat to win this woman as my own.

CHAPTER THIRTY-THREE

IN THE KITCHEN, I was contemplating the bombsite Rosie had left in the wake of her meal prep. Don't get me wrong, I loved the results, but I was a big fan of cleaning-as-you-go. This was not it.

Hatch walked in, closing the door behind him. He looked so handsome that I turned away, tired of being blinded by his beauty. I had never thought it would be so hard to sit across from someone. All I wanted was to eat my tacos in peace.

"You okay?"

"Of course I am." My body's reaction to him put me on the defensive, and my next words sounded prim. "Can I help you?"

"Volunteering for clean-up." He gave me a cheeky salute.

"I'll rinse and you load the dishwasher," I commanded.

"Yes, ma'am."

A few moments passed in silence while I sought neutral ground. "Franky's quite the character, isn't she?"

He grinned. "She is. She was a steady fixture in my life when I was a kid because I hung out with Rosie a lot. She used to babysit me and Addy and show us snails in our backyard."

"That's cool." At his casual mention of Rosie, I thought back to their interactions tonight. They had been chatting together in the kitchen during food prep, and their dynamic was easy throughout dinner. No sign of a crush on either side, but was that definitive? I could bring it up with Hatch, but what if Adeline was right and he was truly clueless? I wouldn't want to embarrass Rosie.

All the more reason why I should stay out of his gravity-sucking orbit.

He moved closer. "I'm sorry that people keep bringing up Carter. You probably want to just forget about it."

"It's not so bad. Everyone has an interesting take, most of which paint him in a poor light, which I'm strangely enjoying now that he's shown his true colors. I don't think I understood how much people disliked him, and how isolated my life was as a result." I paused a moment to gather my thoughts. "When I needed bridesmaids, I realized I barely knew anyone, even after four years working for the Rebels. But I'd always liked Rosie, and she was happy to help. Picking at least one person in my wedding party felt like a small thing I could control. I know that sounds pathetic."

"No, not at all. Rosie and Addy are great people to have in your corner. And other people want to be your friend. You're not alone, Summer."

I peered up at him, feeling an earth shock of emotion

with those words. He had a knack for getting to the heart of the matter, and right now I felt vulnerable to anyone who showed me a drop of kindness.

"Thank you."

"For?" He raised a cheeky eyebrow.

"Not for *that*." Would I ever stop thinking of orgasms in his presence? "Okay, yes, for that. But mostly, for being there for me."

He stroked my cheek, and I felt myself melting into him. Again.

"I will always be here for you."

On the door opening, we jerked apart. In walked Franky. She pushed back her glasses, as if needing to get a better look, but made no comment as she opened the fridge and refilled her glass from the Brita filter.

Threading his arms over his chest, Hatch leaned against the counter. "What's going on with you and Jason?"

Franky paused mid-sip, lowered her glass, and instead of answering, cleared her throat noisily.

Hatch cocked his head. "And that means?"

She pushed a strand of hair behind her ear. "I've always subscribed to the viewpoint that if you can't say anything nice, don't say anything at all."

"Have you though?" Because it was clear Franky had no problem voicing her thoughts, warts and all.

She merely smiled, Sphinx-like, and sipped her water. Before Hatch could press the issue, Rosie called out his name, asking him to settle some argument, and he headed out with a secret smile at me.

Franky remained, regarding me with what I could only term as an analytical air. I had to admit being fascinated by this woman and her hot takes on Dash's personality deficits. All night, I'd wanted to ask her a single burning question.

"Why snails?"

No hesitation, she replied with, "They helped me get through my parents' divorce and my father's alcoholism."

"Wow. Not quite what I expected to hear."

She chuckled. "I was a nerdy kid and while everyone else was into butterflies and Barbies, I was fascinated by snails and slugs. I especially liked their little houses. Some therapist would probably say I was looking for a stable home amongst the disintegration of my family life." She smiled at me. "That therapist would be full of shit."

I cackled. We'd met a couple of times at Rebels gatherings, but I'd never had one-on-one time with her. She was quite the tonic.

"So you and Hatch, huh?"

Scratch what I said about enjoying this woman's direct takes.

"We're friend-*uh*-ly."

She hummed. "Rosie used to like him, and possibly still does? Not that it should dictate your behavior, but it might be wise to discuss it with her before you proceed. As a courtesy."

"There's nothing to proceed on. Or with. We're not—there's no future there." I sounded flustered—and guilty. "I'm focusing on my career."

Something like sadness touched her eyes. "That's what I said and look at me now."

Before I could interrogate that cryptic statement, a screech went up from somewhere in the apartment. It was soon followed by thunderous footsteps and the appearance of a wild-eyed Rosie in the kitchen.

"What have I told you about putting snails in the bathtub?"

Franky pushed back her glasses. "Don't?"

"Precisely. There's one on my shower curtain and now I'm going to have to burn it."

"Washing the snail mucin off the curtain with soapy water will remove any harmful parasites," Franky said, a touch cavalierly, I thought.

"Parasites?" Rosie held up a dramatic hand. "Could you deal with your pets?"

"They aren't pets. They're—"

"Franky!"

"Okay, I'll take care of it." Franky inhaled a deep breath and headed toward the door. "Wish me luck."

"With the snails?" I asked, because that sounded a rather fatalistic approach to your life's work.

"Actually, I'm going to ask Sean to be the sperm donor for my child."

I exchanged horrified looks with Rosie, who shut the door to the kitchen and snapped, "Are you kidding?"

"That'd be a strange thing to joke about."

"You're going to ask him? This minute?" Rosie whisper-screeched.

"Yes, this minute. That's why I'm here. Well, I did have research to do in the area, and I love your tacos and *most* of the company, but it coincided with Sean's visit from Boston, and I realized that this would be as good an opportunity as any."

Rosie flicked a glance at me, then at her sister. "I know you and Sean have been friends forever but ... a baby?"

I had an equally important follow-up. "Are you in love with him?"

Her expression indicated that was complete nonsense. "No, I am not. Sean and I are friends, but we are not compatible in a romantic way. I'm not sure I would be compatible with anyone, but I do want to have a child. After much deliberation and analysis of the data, I've concluded that Sean would make the most likely donor."

She took out her phone and opened what looked like a spreadsheet. Excel on a tiny screen was a pain in the ass, but I could tell she had put work into it.

Rosie moved to her other side and said the obvious. "Those are mostly Rebels players."

"All the single ones," Franky clarified. "And a few more men of my acquaintance. Academics and the like."

"But you said athletes aren't the most evolved," I said.

"No, but I don't need that in a donor. That trait can be learned, nurtured. I'm mostly interested in a donor with good genes, no history of disease, and an easygoing temperament. A stud, in the animal sense. Sean meets those requirements."

Okay. "Do you mind me asking why you're doing it this way?"

Rosie cut in. "Summer's right. You're a super interesting woman, smart, capable, and funny as hell. Don't you want to meet someone and raise a baby together?"

She answered with no hesitation. "As clichéd as it sounds, my biological clock is ticking. I'm thirty-eight years old. Even if I met someone today, it would take months, maybe years to develop the relationship to the stage a child was in the picture. Plenty of women manage this alone. I have the resources and the desire. I just need the genetic material."

I took the phone from her and looked the list over. Each candidate had comments beside them, such as "good plus-minus" and "arthritic grandparent."

Hockey *and* health stats as your baby batter criteria?

I noticed Hatch wasn't on there, possibly because he was too close to her family. (She had once been his babysitter, after all.) He was also younger, and this list skewed toward candidates in the thirty-plus range. Jason Isner was on it, but struck through—the only player who was, with the single, damning footnote: "Temperamentally unsuitable."

"Dash is single again. You could put him on here."

"I don't think he would make a good candidate. Likely, his family would require complex paperwork to ensure any child of the union doesn't have a claim on the Carter family fortune. Plus, no offense, Summer, he's a Grade-A jerk."

None taken. It sounded like she had really thought this through.

"Why are you asking Sean tonight?"

"He's going back to Boston tomorrow. I'm prepared to fly out there for insemination visits, but I'd prefer to discuss the details in person."

Rosie grasped her arm. "Insemination visits? Like sex?"

Franky shook her head. "I'll be using what's commonly referred to as the 'turkey baster' method. But I need the donor material to be hot off the presses, so to speak."

"I think you're amazing," I said.

She blinked. "You do? Most people would view it as odd behavior."

"Rather than waiting for something to happen, you're going for it. It's so brave."

Rosie nodded. "It is. I just don't want you to get hurt."

Franky smiled indulgently. "This is purely a business arrangement. No feelings involved whatsoever, except my case of baby fever and the maternal ones I'll have for my progeny." She pocketed her phone. "I'll take care of the snails, then attend to the other."

Rosie gave her a hug. "You can leave the snails until later, if you like."

Once she left, Rosie looked at the door, her gaze thoughtful. "I wish guys could see her the way I do."

"She's lucky to have you for a sister."

"I'm the lucky one. She and Kat—that's my other sister—have always been there for me. Our family is an unusual blend, but I've never been in any doubt that I had these people on my side."

"Seems to be a lot of that with the Rebels. The tight family connections, a network of support you can always rely on. It was one of my favorite things about being part of the org, even though I was witnessing it from the outside. Going to the events, seeing how close you all are, it was lovely."

Rosie's expression radiated sympathy. "And you thought you'd have that with Dash?"

"If Dash was better at making friends, maybe. But he's always seen himself as a cut above everybody because of how he was raised. Not even a team as warm as the Rebels could draw him in."

"Yeah, they're the best. It's like having a million aunts and uncles and cousins—even if you'd rather it was more."

Did she mean Hatch? I was about to ask for clarification when we heard the front door slam shut.

"That doesn't sound good." Rosie opened the kitchen door and stepped into the corridor.

Sean stood there, looking shell-shocked.

"Did you know she was going to do that?" he asked Rosie, with a quick glance at me as if I might have put Franky up to it.

"You better not have been a dick, Sean!"

"I wasn't. At least, I don't think I was. But shit, I can't do that for her. It's too much to ask."

Rosie and I shared a look, a mix of solidarity with

Franky and sympathy for the predicament in which she had put Sean.

"Listen, I've got an early flight to catch," Sean said. "Thanks for dinner, Ro. And if you talk to Franky, could you tell her I'm sorry?"

Rosie grunted, though I wasn't sure if it was agreement or disapproval. We watched him leave, then Rosie turned to me.

"There's always another episode of R-drama waiting around the corner. Still want to be part of the Rebels fam?"

"It's never boring, that's for sure."

Rosie smiled and gave me a hug. "You don't need Dash. You've got us—me, Addy, and the rest of these reprobates. Now you're a member of the crew."

I could feel my eyes welling. "You guys are the best."

Though I wondered how they would feel if they knew I had jumped into Hatch's arms—literally—so soon after jilting my fiancé.

CHAPTER THIRTY-FOUR

AUGUST

Jason Isner has been spotted at Chicago Rebels HQ where insider sources say he is "learning his way around the gym equipment" ahead of training camp, set to begin in just over six weeks. Isner, known in Boston as the Green-Eyed Monster, a nod to his vaunted defense skills, his Kershaw green eyes, and the famous left field wall at Fenway, was brought onto the Rebels roster in a five year, twenty-million-dollar deal, as the franchise looks to strengthen its defensive bench.

When asked if Isner's surprise addition is being rushed so he can play with his brother, Theo Kershaw, for the first time in their professional careers, Rebels PR claimed this was not a factor. We still have no decision on whether the legendary defenseman will remain with the Rebels or if he'll hang up his skates before the season starts. Which leaves us to wonder about Hatch Kershaw's future. As far as we know, he has yet to sign with the Rebels

for the upcoming season. What is the franchise cooking up and what part do the Kershaws have to play in it?
-@RebelsInsider

Hatch

"WHO THE FUCK are these insider sources anyway?"

Jason had been muttering about that *Rebels Insider* piece the entire time we were on the practice ice. He tried to dispossess me of the puck, but I held on gamely and slid it to Conor who slapped it into the open net. Feeling good, I skated over to the bench and grabbed my water bottle.

Conor followed me. "Someone who thinks the gym equipment at Rebels HQ is somehow different from the gym equipment in Boston."

"Well, we can manage more weights on the press than you wimpy Midwesterners. East coast assholery fuels us."

"You grew up in the Midwest." I leaned against the wall and gestured with my water bottle at Jason. "Over ten years in Bean Town and you've become one of *them*."

"It's gonna be strange to be back here, that's for sure. Gotta start thinking like a Chicagoan before the fans start giving me hell."

"That's easy," I said. "Pound Ann Sather cinnamon rolls like they're going out of style."

"Say pop, not soda," Conor offered. "And jabber on about all the different Wackers and how it's 'like a maze down there on Lower!'"

I had a surefire one. "No ketchup on your dogs."

"Truth," Conor said. "And knowing where the lake is at all times is a Chicago superpower."

"Deep dish is for tourists."

This observation from Jason ground the city tips session to a halt.

"Are you fucking kidding me right now?" I yelled. "Pequod's is the best."

Jason made a face. "Like all deep dish, it's overrated."

So that was his hill. Interesting.

Conor pointed at the tunnel. "Get your deep-dish hatin' ass back to Boston, dude!"

We all laughed and said in unison, "And it'll always be the Sears Tower!"

Jason parked his deep-dish hatin' ass on the wall beside the gate. "Hopefully I'll be playing with family because that's one of the reasons I'm doing this."

"Not the twenty million other ones." Conor pulled at his helmet strap.

"Money's not everything, Connie."

"But it sure as fuck helps. Okay, I'll pick up the baton here, Uncle J." Conor eyed me. "Speaking of multi-million-dollar contracts, what's happening with yours, H? Still leaning towards the Sunshine State?"

"Who tells you this stuff?"

"Oh, people *love* to confide in me."

"I don't."

My brother pulled off his lid and dropped it on the bench. "Let me guess. You're thinking of staying in Chicago because a certain coffee-drinkin', Motors-lovin', doggie-walkin' hottie is back on the market."

"Why would I tell you anything when you'll just blab to the rest of the family in Group?"

"I don't blab. I dispense carefully curated breadcrumbs because it's more fun that way."

Jason shook his head. "You're a sneaky little fucker, you know that?"

Conor smirked. "Just like to stay ahead of the goss. And on the topic of steaming hot Double Bergamot Earl Grey, I heard Franky St. James is looking for a sperm donor and the Seanster said nopity-nope."

How did he do it? "Who's your source, asshole?"

"Never you mind. Color inside the lines, please."

Sighing, I turned to Jason. "Did Sean say anything to you about it?"

"Just that he and Franky are friends and it would make things weird."

We all agreed on that score. Yet Franky thought they were close enough to make that request.

"I told her she was out of her mind," Jason added.

I looked at my uncle sharply. "You talked to her about it?"

"I was driving home from dinner at Ro's and Addy's and saw her walking to her car."

"And?"

"And I stopped to ask her what in the hell she was thinking. If she wants a baby so much, surely there are other options. People who would be crazy enough to have a kid with her."

Conor squinted at him. "Isn't that the point? She feels she doesn't have the usual options, so she's resorting to sperm requests from the eligible men of her acquaintance."

Jason snorted. "Eligible? Right. You know she has a list." Before I could ask, he said, "You're not on it, Hatchling. Too young. Neither are you, Connie. Definitely too young."

That was a relief, I supposed. But something about the

way he was acting prompted me to respond with, "Are *you* on it?"

"Apparently, but only as a formality. I don't meet her lofty standards."

Oh, this was only the fucking best. Catching Conor's eye, I could tell he was hearing an angelic chorus of tea-sipping angels.

"You mean your superior athlete genetic material isn't sufficient?"

Jason looked *very* put out. "Some jocks might make the grade. But this one"—he thumbed at himself—"isn't evolved enough. Which is fine because if I had a kid, the entire Rebels roster couldn't keep me away. I'm not like Nick."

That would be Grandpa Nick, Jason's and my dad's father. He had put Dad's mom in the family way as a teen and then left her in the lurch. When Dad tried to contact him after she died, Nick wasn't interested. They eventually made up, but it had rubbed Jason the wrong way to see how his father treated his eldest son.

Conor shook his head. "It's just sperm, man. People need to be less attached to it."

I pointed at him. "And that's the kind of attitude that's going to get you into trouble. You'd better be wrapping it before you're tapping it, Connie."

I'd seen my little brother in action. If there was a league table for scoring tail, he'd be at the top of it. Plus my own recent mishap with Ava had alerted me to the dangers of unprotected sex.

Yet I wasn't nearly so worried about going raw with Summer in the Rebels locker room. Those filthy memories had fueled every jerk off session since. A part of me was almost hoping that something came of it. A baby with

Summer—bonus: one conceived on Rebels territory—didn't scare me in the slightest.

I was so fucked.

"Don't you worry about me," Conor said. "If anyone needs guidance on his sex life, it's you. Is that why you want to trade out? Because you're scared of Carter? Or because Summer turned you down?"

I rolled my eyes. "That woo-woo Jedi mind fuckery isn't gonna work on me. Let's get back to work and see if we can get past the Green-Eyed Monster here."

An hour later, we were back in the locker room when one of the front office assistants, Shona, popped her head around the door.

"Hatch, do you have time to talk to Ryder? He saw you guys on the practice rink and wondered if you could spare a few minutes."

"Sure, I'll be up in ten."

Conor grinned at Shona and made to get up. "Hey, I don't think we've met."

Grasping his arm, I pulled him back to the bench. "Slow your roll, child. Shona, tell Ryder I'll see him soon."

Shona blinked, blushed, and backed out in a Conor-induced daze.

"Do not be messing with the front office, Con. When it all turns to shit, they're the ones who'll suffer, not you."

Conor grabbed a towel and stood, the showers his goal. "Hey, Summer knew what she was doing messing with Carter. But apparently she didn't learn a thing, if she's messing with *you*."

I shook my head as he moved out of earshot. "When did the youth become so wise?"

Jason chuckled. "He comes off as a total bro, but he's the smartest guy in the room. And he does kind of have a point.

I noticed you two were pretty careful around each other at dinner the other night, so I'm guessing that means nothing's happening? Or everything's happening?"

Not so careful I couldn't resist touching her in the kitchen before Franky walked in on us. And before that, "careful" would not be how I described Summer on her knees in the showers behind me.

I blew out a breath, so tired of keeping it in. "I'm fucking crazy about her, J. But she's too close to this Carter situation, to how it's upended her life, to give me—*us*—a chance. I want to help any way I can, but now she wants to focus on her career and on getting a job with a franchise."

I filled him in on Summer's career aspirations before going on.

"There's something between us—I think we could be amazing together—but Carter ruined her trust. And she sees me as one more obstacle, a damn puck chaser whose career will always come first. Getting all tangled up is too risky for her."

Jason looked sympathetic. "She's not wrong, though, is she? As much as we want women who are independent and kick ass, we also want them to drop everything when we call. We are the neediest assholes on the planet."

Wasn't that the truth. But it didn't have to be. I wanted Summer to feel she could have it all, where *all* included me.

"Speaking of being summoned, I'd better head up to see Ryder."

Jason frowned. "Not sure you should be talking to him without Lauren present."

"Not too worried. He probably wants to pump me for info on Dad's plans. This is still Theo Kershaw's house."

RYDER DIDN'T WANT to talk about Dad. I had to admit I was surprised when, after about thirty seconds of small talk, he asked me how I thought last season went.

"For me?"

He nodded. "I want to hear your thoughts."

"I could have played better. I worry that the org put faith in me that I was unable to fulfill. I listened to the press too much, let it get in my head, and frankly, felt the pressure of being on the same team as Dad. I also worry that ... I'm here because of him and not because of me."

Ryder didn't look surprised at my word vomit.

"It's an unusual situation, a father-son duo on the same team, but I'm going to be honest. We don't frame our acquisition strategy around publicity stunts. Of course, the attention has been a bonus for the franchise, but we would never have brought you on if we didn't think you had what it takes to make a real contribution to this team. There's too much money at stake."

He held up a hand before I could respond. "I know we shouldn't be talking about contracts or business without your agent present, but I wanted to get a sense of your mindset as we move into the next season. The contract's on the table but the delay makes me think you're considering other options."

Ryder was no fool.

"You know Lauren has been feeling other teams out?"

"I hear things."

I blew out a breath. "I love Chicago. I love this team. And it kills me to know I've let these outside influences into my head. I don't know what my dad's going to do next year, but if I can't make this team better, then I don't know if I should be here."

Ryder looked pained. "Well, I appreciate your honesty.

We're going to need a decision soon, so maybe talk to Lauren and let us know where you stand."

I nodded. "There is something else I'd like to talk to you about."

"Oh?"

"Summer Landry."

CHAPTER THIRTY-FIVE

Summer

I WAS in Binny's Wine Depot, trying to figure out if a twenty-five-dollar Merlot with a picture of a giraffe on it was fancy enough for Rebels goalie Noah Boden when a familiar voice sounded behind me.

"Hi, Summer!"

I turned to face Elle Kershaw, Hatch and Adeline's mom. I hadn't seen her since … I was going to say the wedding, but I hadn't even seen her then. I was too busy sprinting the other direction. Now it was doubly hard to speak to her without my face turning beet red.

"Hi, Mrs. Kershaw. How are you?"

"I'm fine, sweetie. What about you?"

I must have looked especially pathetic—calling me *sweetie* did it—because next thing I knew I was in her arms. These Kershaws really knew how to hold a girl.

"The stuff in that article," I said, "most of it was untrue."

"I know. Dash Carter is a pinhead and a very, very insecure man."

That was about the long and short of it.

She set me back. "Addy tells me you're working for Kennedy's company. It's good to be busy."

"It is. The perfect way to figure out next steps."

"Well, as long as you don't fall in love with the wrong person while you're doing it!" She chuckled but then turned serious on spotting my deer-in-the-headlights expression. "Sorry, just a silly joke. My daughter was 'figuring out next steps' and then came Lars and Mabel."

"You don't like Lars?" She couldn't possibly have anything against Mabel.

"Lars is wonderful. But there was a time when I worried that he wasn't the best choice for my daughter." She shook her head. "Don't mind me. Sometimes I speak without thinking, which used to be my husband's special talent. The longer you live with someone the more you pick up their bad habits."

"You guys seem so well-suited. Relationship goals, according to Addy. No Tilly today?"

"Oh God, no, I can't bring her into a wine shop. The last time I did that, I was on the hook for a hundred and fifty dollars' worth of Dom Perignon—she loved the shape of the bottle and that was that." She looked at the bottle I had in my hands. "How's that? Any good?"

"I don't know much about wine. I'm buying this for Noah—I think he's got a hot date tonight. My instructions were to 'get something fancy.'"

"Oh, I don't know much either. But this nice young man might be able to help." Elle grasped the arm of a sales associate, and within five minutes, we both had choices made.

"I tend to only buy something I know will wash down the cheese," Elle said as we walked to the checkout.

I laughed. "You Kershaws love your cheese. I had to fight Addy for the Camembert last week."

"If I've done anything right in raising my kids, it's making sure they have a healthy appreciation for cheese."

We paid for our purchases and walked out together.

Elle placed a hand on my arm. "Addy said she asked you to dinner but that you didn't want to intrude. You wouldn't be. There'd be no one commenting on your personal life, except maybe Conor. And possibly Aurora. Tilly would, too, if she had any clue what was happening. But the other half of the family would be very discreet."

I laughed at her defense of her lovely family. "I don't want to change the vibe."

"Oh, please change the vibe. Say you'll come tonight, Summer. We'd love to have you." Her eyes practically beseeched me. "Or maybe you're worried about Hatch?"

My heart stopped. "Hatch?"

"Addy said something—never mind."

"No, what did she say?" Panic raced through me faster than a Formula 1 driver.

"She mentioned that you and he don't get along? Listen, I don't want to pry, but if he's been a jerk to you for some reason, please let me know. I still hold some sway over my eldest's behavior."

Addy had said something to me last Halloween about Hatch, wondering what I'd done to offend him. At the time, I was clueless. Now he claimed it was his way of ensuring he didn't look overly interested in a teammate's partner. I didn't buy it, but if he wanted to keep it to himself, I wouldn't push.

"Oh, it's fine. You know some people don't gel, and I can handle Dash's teammates." It sounded like I was coming to dinner.

Once in the car, I debated whether I should give Hatch a heads-up. I wanted him to be chill, so I could be chill.

ME

Hi! I ran into your mom and she invited me to dinner at your parents' place. I assume you'll be there.

DINO BOY

Well, I will be now.

Damn.

One wine delivery and a shower later, I headed over to the Kershaws' house, a lovely ranch style home close to the lake on Chicago's North Shore. I'd been here a couple of times before for cookouts with Dash, but he always wanted to leave early because the Kershaws were "too much." I'd never thought so, but now I realized he was jealous of how easy and natural they were with each other.

I pulled up and was exiting Rosie's car at the same time as the arrival of Lars, Addy, and Mabel. I had run a couple of errands for Lars over the last week, so I'd had a little snuggle time with his toddler daughter. Addy was holding hands with the little sweetheart, who looked positively darling in a candy-striped pink dress.

"Hi, Mabel!"

"No!"

"Still with the nos, huh?" She was going through a phase of saying "no" to everything. "So tell me, should I have stayed and married Dash?"

"No!"

Addy laughed. "Mabel knows what's what. Are you here for dinner?"

"I hope that's okay. I ran into your mom at the liquor store, and she was most persuasive."

"Of course! Glad she has the magic touch." She turned to Lars. "Could you take her? I wanted a quick word with Summer before we go in."

Lars scooped his daughter up. "Come on, Button. Let's get you inside."

Addy watched them go, then faced me. "So I'm moving in with Lars and Mabel."

"Oh, that's great news."

"It is. But also maybe great news for you, too? If you'd like to graduate to a bigger bedroom, it's yours."

I had been trying to contribute with groceries and cooking meals, but now that my income was more stable, this would be better. Assuming I was staying in Chicago.

"I would love that. If Rosie's up for it."

"Are you kidding? It was her idea. Plus this way, I have a space to retreat to when I need my best girls." She gave me a quick hug. "Okay, apologies for my family in advance. Especially Conor."

Conor was the least of my worries. Heading inside, I steeled myself for a night of ignoring his eldest brother. Hopefully there would be plenty of Kershaws to give me cover, the first of whom ambushed me the moment I stepped over the threshold.

"Summer!" I knew Hatch's great-grandmother Aurora reasonably well, given that she often visited the front offices —the office of CEO, Harper Chase-DuPre, in particular—to chat about what they were doing "to protect her grandson." Apparently, she'd been calling or stopping in for years to ensure Theo was being cared for by the management. Both hilarious and adorable.

"Hi, Mrs. K."

"I've told you, it's Aurora. So I've been working on a new martini recipe. Try this."

Good grief, I was barely in the door! I took a sip. "Let me see. Vodka, limoncello, and ... blackcurrant?"

"Excellent palate! That one's for you. I'm going to call it Rebel Bride, in your honor. A nice combination of sweet and tart."

"Not Runaway Bride?"

"Oh no! 'Rebel' is much more appropriate. It takes a lot of guts to go against the flow of the river instead of letting it carry you downstream."

Tears made my throat tight. Baby Mabel looking as cute as a button, a dedicated cocktail, and this family "Kershawing to the max"? I wasn't sure I would make it.

With my martini and a bottle of red, I headed into the kitchen, arriving just in time to find Theo with his hand inside his wife's blouse. On spotting me, they pulled apart. Slowly. How lovely to still have the hots for each other after five kids and twenty-five years of marriage.

"Sorry, I just wanted to drop this off." I put the wine bottle on the counter beside a very attractive cheese board. A hunk of goat cheese vied for my attention with a harder cheese that was likely a mature cheddar, though the one with walnuts and cranberries also had my mouth watering.

Admit it. You're a whore for cheese, Summer.

Agreed, Shelby Mae. Agreed.

Elle giggled while Theo pulled me into a hug.

"Summer, I missed you at Rebels HQ the other day. Heard you had a chat with Carter, which is more than he deserves after that tabloid slander. So. You gearing up to sue?"

I couldn't tell if he was serious. He had a twinkle in his eye, similar to Hatch when he teased me. "I'll probably take the high road."

"Likely the wiser move." He added a wink. "But just so you know, we're on your side. This is a Summer family."

Another deep voice cut in. "Dad, don't burn your bridges just yet. You might still have to work with Carter next year."

I didn't know Conor well, but I did know one thing: he had the skinny on Hatch and me. He grabbed a dried apricot off the cheese board.

"Unless this is your way of telling us you're finally going to retire and start gardening. Hey, Summer."

"Hi, there."

"Don't rush my decision, Connie." Theo gestured at the cheese board. "Here, make yourself useful and take this out to the living room."

"Oh, wait," Elle said. "We have that Brie, the triple cream one." She pulled it from the fridge and unwrapped it, then sliced off a healthy triangle.

Theo eyed me. "You a fan of cheese, Summer?"

"I'm immediately suspicious of anyone who is not. That Brie's my favorite."

"Hatch loves it, too. He brought it over."

Conor picked up the board. "Imagine that? Of all the cheese boards in all the world ..." With a puckish glance at me, he walked out.

Was I being wooed ... with cheese? I tried to think of a time when Dash had ever learned a thing about me, something I liked or wanted to do. He wouldn't watch *Downton Abbey* or take me shopping for underwear or bike riding around a lake. He wouldn't cook me a meal, and we always ate out or ordered in. To quote him, it was like asking Crosby to teach hockey to toddlers—a complete waste of his resources.

He could buy me anything, but it came with strings and could never compensate for a man who listened.

Theo opened a drawer and removed a pile of red cloth napkins. "Summer, do you mind bringing these out to the dinner table? Just through there."

"Sure. Will lay napkins for food."

I walked in to find Hatch setting the table. He looked up and smiled, and damn, my heart told me what my mind had been trying to deny for weeks.

I had fallen for this guy.

You are one fine dummy, Summer.

Don't I know it, Shelby Mae.

No one was supposed to fall for the rebound. That was why it was called the rebound. It brought you back to life but wasn't supposed to be serious.

"Hi, there, Sunshine."

Flustered, I ignored his soft tone. "Your dad asked me to put these out."

I could have panicked and thrown each napkin haphazardly on a plate, but instead I called on my past server skills and tri-folded the shit out of them. In setting one at each place, I used the mindless task to free up space in my brain for my current predicament and look for ways to neg the conclusion.

I was in a vulnerable place right now, susceptible to a warm smile, killer arms, and a beautifully shaped cock. Starting a new relationship was not on my agenda.

I wanted a relationship with myself first.

But you never liked easy, did you?

Bitch, please.

Shelby Mae had been quiet for a while, but now she was back, exactly when I didn't need her. At the head of the table, I had caught up with Hatch, who watched my final napkin origami effort.

"I think you've done this before."

"Fern's Diner in Biloxi."

"Before or after the hockey fan bar in Jacksonville?"

I loved and hated that he remembered. This man knew me better than anyone, maybe better than myself. It wasn't as comforting as it sounded.

I wanted to be the one who figured out Summer Landry.

"Before. Though we didn't have cloth napkins. I liked folding the paper ones into interesting shapes during the downtime."

"Frustrated artist?"

"Frustrated something." I met his gaze, and there I was, flirting with him again. Time to set some ground rules. "Don't look at me during dinner."

He raised an eyebrow. "At all?"

"If you do, I won't be able to …"

"What, Summer? What won't you be able to do?"

Help myself.

Thankfully I didn't have to answer because Adeline walked in and narrowed her eyes at the two of us standing far too close together.

"H, you had better be nice to our guest."

He clutched his chest. "When am I ever not nice?"

"Just ignore him, Summer."

I moved away in the direction of the living room, determined to shore up my defenses with cheese before dinner.

"I plan to."

CHAPTER THIRTY-SIX

DINNER WAS LOVELY, but really, it was the Kershaws who made it perfect. They were warm and generous, bawdy and rambunctious, exactly how I imagined they would be in each other's company. The contrast to Dash's family was stark, and I hated that my mind went there. After all, I wasn't looking for a relationship with Hatch. His family was not part of some package deal.

But Adeline was my friend, so I contented myself with the knowledge that I was here because of my connection to her.

Most people seemed to have their preferred spots at the table, so I was seated by default opposite Hatch—of course. He made a point of narrowing his eyes to indicate his faux dislike of me, which meant I was already doing what I did not want to do: smile.

Despite Mrs. Kershaw's warnings about her family's

more indiscreet members, no one brought up Dash or the wedding. The conversational focus was on Theo's contract extension, Jason's move to the Rebels, and how the team was in a rebuilding phase.

"Yeah, time for the oldsters to retire," Conor said.

Theo sent him a look. "Who you calling 'old'?"

"I was talking about Lars. You're immortal, Dad."

Lars shook his head. "This kid."

"This kid made the Frozen Four final his sophomore year!"

"What happened the last two years then?" Landon asked his brother.

"We were robbed."

"You kind of were," I said. "They should have put you in more, Conor, especially this last year. Your stats were stellar."

Conor's frown turned upside down. "Knew I liked you."

"But they tend to look for 'solid' instead of 'flashy' at that stage, so I reckon they weren't willing to take the chance."

The table broke out in laughter. Theo pointed at his son. "She's got your number, Connie!"

Conor was still smiling at me. "And you were doing so well. How come you know so much about college hockey?"

"Summer compiled a lot of reports when she worked for the org," Addy said. "She probably knows more about the draft prospects than anyone here."

"Don't know about that," I muttered.

"You do!" Addy gave me a fierce look. Since she'd found love with Lars and embraced her talents as a children's entertainer, she was a champion for other people's strengths. "Didn't you say Lauren asked you for some of your research?"

Hatch's agent had heard from Addy about my side hustle and reached out to me after Rosie's dinner party to ask if I'd mind sending my scouting reports over. Working at The Mallinson Group, one of the top sports management firms in the country, I would have thought she had a team of people to do that, but she said she was curious about how my research aligned with her own.

"Lauren's super sharp," Hatch said.

"Yeah, she is." Theo looked at his son. "Poached you from my agent, didn't she?"

"That was my choice, Dad."

I got the impression this issue had been raised before, and that there was some residual tension surrounding it. The awkward moment was smoothed over by Conor.

"But back to me. The Rebels need a bit of flash. They won't be getting that with Uncle J."

"It'll be good to have some mid-career players in there, for sure," I offered, moving the conversation away from Hatch and Lauren. "That's what a team needs during a rebuild. Stability to ease the transition. Jason's a proven quantity."

"Besides, it's a bit early to be putting you in, bro." Landon pointed a breadstick at Conor. "They probably want to see how much you eff up your first year with the Motors."

"More likely they felt there was a Kershaw cap," Aurora said. "We can only have three of you boys on the roster at any one time."

That produced plenty of laughs.

Conor finished chewing his pasta. "Well, if Hatch gets his wish, I can take his spot."

"Gets his wish?" Theo looked at Hatch, then back at Conor. "Meaning?"

Hatch shot a sharp look at his brother, who mouthed, "Sorry, bro."

"Nothing. Just spit balling." Hatch shrugged. "You never know what's going to happen."

"You looking to move?"

All eyes focused on Hatch. "I like to keep my options open."

"Maybe less of the business talk at the table," Elle said.

I caught Hatch's eye and asked him silently if he was okay. I had hoped he would have talked to his father already about feeling overshadowed on the team and how the comparisons weighed on him. He returned a glance of gratitude, and yet again, something passed between us. Another thread, strengthening our bond.

After dinner, I offered to do dishes, but Elle had put the twins on clean-up duty. Relaxing in the living room, Aurora and I had a nice chat about poison ivy (both the plant life and the Batman villain character), strange KitKat flavors, and which of the US presidents could "get it." She hadn't disagreed when I said Franklin Pearce gave off romantic poet vibes, though she was pretty thirsty for Teddy Roosevelt because a bullet had lodged in his chest during an assassination attempt and *he continued a campaign speech*. We agreed that having a chest so muscled it repelled bullets was indeed the definition of hot.

Addy played a new song she had written about pasta and the different shapes, which Tilly adored, and because Mabel adored Tilly, she spent her time giggling and flirting. I had a soft spot for both little girls, but Mabel was my first love. She climbed into my lap while Addy sang, her chubby fist clumping my hair.

"Mabel, let Summer be," Lars said.

"No!"

I laughed. "She's fine where she is."

Lars smiled indulgently then returned his focus to his girlfriend, all the love he had for her shining in his eyes. Over the years I had watched various Rebels couples together, a touch envious of their vibes. Ones I never felt with Dash. I had assumed that we were just one of those couples who made sense on paper, so what could possibly be wrong?

Only everything.

As much as I tried not to look at Hatch, I couldn't help myself. Tilly was kneeling beside him on the sofa, putting Hello Kitty clips in his hair, which he bore stoically. But after a while, he pulled her close to bring the Ticklemonster.

"Tilly-Billy, what's so funny?"

Tilly screamed, and just the sight of Hatch in his pretty hair clips, being so at ease with his family, filled me with peace and joy. I wanted to feel this happy all the time.

Elle picked up the cheese board from the coffee table. "I'll return this to the fridge."

A chorus of nos went up, and Mabel joined in because it was her favorite word. "That's right, Mabel," I whispered into her fine red-gold curls. "Remember no is a complete sentence." If only I'd learned that sooner, I wouldn't be in this mess with Dash.

Elle stood with arms akimbo. "But you all just had dinner. And you still want cheese?"

Leaning forward, Hatch sliced off some cheddar and Brie and added a couple of crackers. "Mom, we came into this world eating cheese. We will leave it the same way." He set the small plate on the coffee table in front of me, before making up another. It was done so smoothly that I was sure no one had noticed. It would be weird if I didn't say "thanks," though. Weirder if I just accepted it as completely expected behavior from the guy who supposedly despised me.

"Thanks. How did you know?"

He looked up and blinked, realizing what he'd done.

"Just being a good host." Then he turned back to make up mini-cheese plates for Addy and his great-grandmother, which reminded me of the *Friends* episode where Chandler mistakenly kissed Monica, then had to kiss Phoebe and Rachel to cover.

"Wow, it's like we're in Europe," Aurora said after a sip of her wine. "Cheese after dinner."

"Nothing but class here," Addy said.

When I caught her glance, she had a curious expression on her face. Hatch's cheese-serving gaffe had not gone unnoticed.

IT DIDN'T TAKE LONG. I exited the upstairs bathroom to find Addy waiting outside.

"What's going on with you and my brother?"

"Conor's a little young for me and Landon is batting for the other team."

"He's bi, actually, but you know who I mean. He attended to your cheese needs!"

It was one thing not to share, quite another to outright lie.

"We've become ... friends."

She opened her mouth. "Friends? He's making you cheese plates. In front of people!"

"So damning."

She pointed a finger. "Oh my God! He sent you that cheese board. But—how?"

"Could we go somewhere private?"

She grasped my hand and took me behind a door. From the looks of the posters, this was her childhood bedroom. Having slept in my mom's bed as a kid, and then on the sofa when company called, I was always fascinated by the bedrooms of my peers. Before I could examine it properly or explain how Hatch knew about my cheese addiction, Addy spoke.

"You're the woman in the photo." She covered her mouth and shook her head while her eyes danced and her brain joined the dots. "That was weeks ago. Right after ... *did Hatch help you escape?*"

"I swear it wasn't planned. He happened to be there when I climbed out the window. I would say he caught me, but in truth I flattened him like a World Wrestling Federation champion."

I had left her speechless, so I filled the stunned silence.

"He knew I needed to get out of town. To reset. He was already heading for Saugatuck, and he took me there. I stayed for about ten days."

"And you guys ..." She waved.

"Ate a lot of cheese?"

She grasped my arms. "Get out! But he doesn't like you. Unless that's always been some weird pigtail-pulling in the playground deal and he *does* like you."

"No, that's not it." *Was it?* "He was there for me when I needed him, but right now I can't get involved with him. It's far too complicated. And I've done the date-an-athlete thing. Would not recommend."

Addy got a crimp between her eyebrows. "Treating

them like some monolith sounds like Franky talking. Hatch is not the same as Dash."

I knew that. But he had similar career goals—go where he was needed and play where he was wanted. I could see myself getting shafted again because my boyfriend's job was more important than mine.

You don't even have a job, Summer.

Agh, Shelby Mae. I thought you were asleep in your coffin!

"Adeline!" Lars called up the stairs. "You ready?"

Mabel could be heard yelling "no!" at a high pitch. Addy opened her mouth, but Lars called out again.

"Listen, I need to go and I'm staying over with Lars," she said. "But maybe we could meet for lunch and talk more tomorrow?"

I nodded because frankly I was ready to share. I needed to. "Definitely. But please don't tell anyone. It's not a good look for me—falling for the teammate of the fiancé I jilted."

Her eyes went wide. "Falling?"

Oh Summer, you've gone and done it now.

"Just a figure of speech. You should go before Lars blows a blood vessel."

CHAPTER THIRTY-SEVEN

Hatch

ADDY AND LARS had just left with Mabel, Aurora had returned to the coach house, Conor was sweet-talking some girl on his phone, and Landon had returned to his "underground lair," as Dad called it.

I was waiting at the bottom of the stairs when Summer descended on a gossamer cloud. Christ, I had it bad.

"Nice do." She reached up and slid from my hair one of Tilly's clips.

"She's in a hair stylist phase this week."

"She's adorable. You all are."

"Can I give you a ride?"

"My car's outside—well, Rosie's is. But I had a couple of drinks so I'm going to Uber it and pick my car up tomorrow."

"No need for that. Let me."

She tilted her head. "And then what happens?"

"Well, I have this thousand-piece puzzle I just started. Come in and help with that." I waggled my eyebrows, which made her laugh.

She gently brushed my chest with her fingertips. "I think you should stay and talk to your dad."

"I'd rather not."

"Oh, I know that feeling. But it still needs to happen, so why not tell him what's on your mind?"

"Because it would hurt him. Also, there's a good chance it won't happen. I might have delayed it too long." Lauren said Tampa was getting antsy about my wavering. And after my chat with Ryder earlier, I felt a little more hopeful about my place on the team.

"Do you still want to leave Chicago?"

"I thought I did. But then you happened."

She frowned. Had I misread this? I wanted to stay in Chicago for my family and for the woman before me. I would do whatever it took to make it happen.

"You can't make this call based on me. I've told you that I don't want a relationship—"

"And you certainly don't want one with your ex's teammate. But this is where we are."

"Dash does complicate things, but that's not it, or only it. I want to focus on my career, my future, myself. I won't follow you, Hatch. And I don't expect you to make a career decision based on where I am."

Like I already had?

Her phone buzzed. "That's my Uber." She reached up and kissed the corner of my mouth. "Go talk to your dad. Everything else can wait."

I HEADED INTO THE KITCHEN. Dad was tidying up while Mom sat at the island, sipping the last of the wine.

"Tilly already in bed?"

"Yeah, I just put her down." My mom gave me a significant look, stood, and kissed my cheek. "I'm going to head up and do a little work on my laptop."

"Thanks for dinner, Mom."

"You're welcome. It was nice for Summer, I think."

"I suppose it was."

She grinned at me. Damn, did everyone know?

As soon as she left, I leaned against the counter. "Need help, Dad?"

"Just with what's goin' on in that head of yours."

Okay. Straight to it. "I've loved working with you, playing with you, fighting with you, but I haven't enjoyed the comparisons so much. I'm not as thick-skinned as you. And I'm not sure I've played as well on this team as I did in Denver. Look at how I messed up that goal in the last game."

"So you made a mistake. We all do that. Are you really blaming the pressure of being on the same roster as your dad?"

I shrugged. "I don't know. There's pressure. There's always pressure. And I was happy to come on board because this was going to be a big year for you. I wanted to win with you. For you. When we didn't, I worried I'd let you down."

My father came forward and placed a hand on my shoulder. "You could never let me down. So your year wasn't as good as you would have liked. Every player has good years and bad, and the press can be pricks at the best of times. But I wonder if there's more to it."

"Like what?"

"If maybe your mind has been elsewhere. Caught up in the fact you wanted a girl you couldn't have. Believe me, I know what it's like when your personal life interferes with your game."

I met his gaze and decided to choose honesty. "That's why I didn't sign with the Rebels three years ago when I first had a chance. I didn't want to see her. To see them."

He gave a quick nod as if this wasn't news to him. How could I have thought my father was clueless? The man knew everything.

"Then you signed when I told you it might be my last year. You put your pain aside for me because you're a good son. And this past year, you've had to watch Carter and your girl getting ready to spend their lives together. That had to be rough and can't have been good for your game."

"I've wanted to punch him every time I see his stupid fucking face." Some people can channel anger, jealousy, and negative emotions into their game. Apparently, I wasn't one of them. "And then ... she didn't marry him, Dad."

Raising an eyebrow, he leaned back and folded his arms. His expression said, "finally!"

I sighed. "Does everyone know?"

"Conor's not the most discreet. All those hints, and he thinks we're dummies. What happened?"

I filled him in on the details of Summer in Saugatuck, except for the sexier ones, which my father no doubt surmised anyway.

"I didn't expect it to happen. It was like ... suddenly I could have everything I wanted if only all these other hurdles haven't appeared to block me. She's not marrying Carter, but he's still my teammate." Which admittedly wasn't that big of a problem—for me. For Summer, though ... "All these feelings I've repressed for so long can now be expressed except they can't. Not really. She might not want me the way I want her. She might not even stay in Chicago, but I'm working on that."

"Sounds like you might be sticking around after all."

I gave a low chuckle. "Maybe."

"So you were thinking about trading out because you can't share the spotlight with your old man, but now you might suffer in my shadow because this girl you're crazy about is free."

"That about sums it up."

"Tell me this: if I retired, would this even be a question?"

I considered that. "I love Chicago, I love being close to family, it's my hometown team, and it's a dream to play for them. Follow in the steps of legends." But then there was Summer. Maybe she was right. I shouldn't make decisions based on where she would be. She wouldn't give me the same courtesy—and after what had happened with Carter, how she had subjugated her needs to his, who could blame her?

"Well, you'll be happy to hear that I *am* retiring."

I stared. "Dad, please don't do it for me. I can get over myself and figure this out."

He grinned. "I've been leaning this way all summer. I have a couple of ideas about what comes next, but I won't be playing for the Rebels this fall."

I thought I'd be pleased, finally free of the shackles of being the other Kershaw on the Chicago Rebels, but all I felt was sadness. The end of an era.

"But Hatchling, there will still be pressure. This is the team I played most of my career with, and I cast a long fucking shadow. They won't forget about me so easily."

That made me grin. "We get it. Chicago loves you."

"They do. And they're going to love you, if you let them. The thing about pressure, other than being a privilege as the great Billie Jean King said, is that you can make it work in your favor. Treat it as your friend instead of the enemy."

I frowned. "How so?"

"Think about why the pressure exists in the first place. You're part of this amazing crew, one of an elite band of professional athletes, a rarefied position. Every move on that ice has the potential to make your team, your family, your city happy, sad, and everything in between. Every time you step out there, you're taking them on a journey. The highs, the lows, the agony, the ecstasy. Pressure produces diamonds, son. If you think about the benefits, after a while, you start to want it. You find you can't thread that puck through the five-hole without it. It becomes the thing that spurs you on and makes you better every game."

I inhaled a breath. I should have listened to Summer and talked to him sooner.

"Dad, are you sure about leaving?"

"Yes, I am. I've won the Cup four times, got to play on the same team as my son, and ensured that the legacy continues. If there is such a thing as the Kershaw cap, then my leaving will free up that spot."

"Conor will be thrilled. But I know he would have loved to play with you. Jason, too." That had been my privilege alone. I wish I had appreciated it more instead of whining about it affecting my play.

Because Dad was right. I was all caught up in Summer, and that probably blurred my focus more than anything.

CHAPTER THIRTY-EIGHT

ADELINE

Sorry, I can't do lunch today. But maybe we can talk tonight?

ME

Of course! But lips still zipped, okay?

ADELINE

Definitely!

AFTER DINNER with the Kershaws last night, I had returned home to an empty apartment. Addy was with Lars and Mabel while Rosie spent the night with her mom's family. So many times, I was tempted to text Hatch, call him, even go over to his place. I wanted to know if he had talked to his dad.

I wanted to be his person.

But I also worried about giving him the wrong idea.

Rather than show weakness, I worked on a couple of reports and sent them to Lauren.

Just after lunchtime, I walked into the living room to find Rosie and Franky sitting on the sofa with a bowl of Pirate's Booty and a bottle of wine.

"Oh, sorry, looks like you guys want some sister time."

Franky waved me in. "As someone who has recently undergone a dramatic life change, I would appreciate your take."

I shot a quick look at Rosie, who raised an eyebrow. "Want a glass of wine?"

"I have to work this afternoon, so no, thanks. How are you, Franky?"

"As you're probably aware, Sean has turned me down. Which is surprising because I made it clear I expected nothing from him but his genetic material."

"Right, but fathering a child isn't something that everyone can take with a grain of salt. He might want to be more involved. Look at how Lars stepped up."

"Only because it was forced upon him by the biological mother. All I want is a spoonful of spunk. It's hardly too much to ask."

"Why not use an anonymous donor?" Rosie asked.

"They all lie. Sure, there are questionnaires, but I'd prefer to be able to run my own background checks, so knowing the identity of the donor is key. Sean and I have no feelings for each other, but it appears he's more emotional about this than I thought."

"Surely there are other candidates," I said. "You have a list—did no one else make the grade? Even one who might be temperamentally unsuitable?"

She narrowed her gaze. "You're referring to Jason Isner?"

I shared a glance with Rosie who picked up the baton. "He's the only one on the list you struck through. Yet you had him on the list in the first place."

"Purely from a scientific method standpoint, to ensure an absence of bias and that the choice wasn't pre-determined. I listed all the ostensibly eligible men of my acquaintance. He's one of them—excellent physical pedigree, family history known, and not anyone I would ever expect to feel obligated to me."

"Sounds like a winner, so what's the problem?" I wondered if Franky's self-esteem precluded her from going for a hunk like Jason. The guy might only be half-brother to Theo, but he definitely had more than fifty percent of the Kershaw charm. Muscles, too. "What did you mean by 'temperamentally unsuitable'?"

"He once called me ..." She took a sip of wine. "A name."

"What name?" Rosie barked, ready to go to battle.

"It doesn't matter. While he might otherwise meet my requirements, that exhibited a cruel streak that I would not like to be part of my child's genetic make-up."

Something about this sounded off. "When did this happen?"

"When I was seventeen."

"Twenty-one years ago!" Rosie yelped. "When Jason was ... *thirteen*?"

"Correct." She sat up straighter. "It's set the tone. Any time we meet, he makes it clear he finds me to be a weird egghead type. I once overheard him tell Sean he doesn't understand how we're friends. Suffice it to say, I wouldn't take his genetic material if he begged me. And I certainly won't be begging him."

Okay, then. A couple of minutes later, Franky excused herself to go to the bathroom. (A snail-free space, I hoped.)

"Poor Franky," I murmured. "Maybe it's good Sean said no? Give her time to think if this is really how she wants to do it."

Rosie shook her head in wonder. "That Jason business is wild, isn't it? I wonder what he said, though he probably doesn't even remember ... because he was thirteen!"

I giggled and covered my mouth. "Sorry, but it's kind of funny-sad to still have a beef with someone from childhood."

"I know!" Rosie laughed, too. "I'll have to ask Hatch if his uncle even remembers this shocking name-calling."

The mention of Hatch provided the perfect opening. "So, I hope you don't mind, but Addy mentioned that you had a thing for her brother."

"Conor?"

"No, Hatch." Weird that Conor was her first thought, though.

"Oh, that's old news. I've known him all my life—we were born a week apart—and people used to joke that we were the Rebels' arranged marriage. Hatch and I were always, *eww, no*. We hated the teasing. But then a while back I started to ... not hate it?" She shook her head. "I'd see him with other girls and wonder what it might be like. To be honest, getting away for a year of world travel really helped."

"Well, you had no shortage of man adventures on that trip."

"A woman in her prime has needs!" She cackled. "I can't be waiting around for Hatch Kershaw to notice me. Also this last year, he's been kind of moody and withdrawn.

I thought maybe he had some girl he wasn't telling anyone about, but if he had, he's not fessed up."

Maybe that business with Ava had hurt him more than he let on.

Rosie continued. "Anyway, I realized that we wouldn't be compatible. At all. I need a guy with a more outgoing vibe."

"Hmm, like you?"

"Right. Don't get me wrong. Hatch is one of my closest friends and I want only the best for him, but frankly, I don't think he could handle me."

Rosie exhibited main character energy, for sure. "Not sure any guy could."

"I am *a lot* of woman." She leveled a hard-nosed gaze at me. "So, are you doing a sisters-before-misters check-in before you go for it with Hatch?"

"What? No! We're not—I mean, we haven't—" I sighed. "Oh fuck it."

"Knew it!"

I covered my face in my hands. "I don't know how it happened."

Oh, don't you, Summer?

Argh, Shelby Mae!

"I saw how he looked at you over dinner. And he's always acted so weird around you." She pulled my hands away. "That's you in the photo that's doing the rounds, isn't it?"

"You've seen that?"

"Yeah, but honestly it's not obvious. And the Motors cap? That shit's as good as Clark Kent's glasses." She added a knowing wink that had me giggling. It really was absurd that more people hadn't seen that photo and caught on to the facts.

Franky came back in and assessed the situation like we were slugs in her lab. "Everything okay?"

Rosie looked at me, seeking permission. I nodded.

"Summer's got a thing for Little Lord Hatchling."

"Little Lord Hatchling?" I *loved* it.

"When he was a kid, we used to call him the golden child and the puck prince, but I liked Little Lord Hatchling." She looked positively gleeful. "So you were in Saugatuck? How did that happen?"

I filled them both in on my church getaway and lakeside bolthole, skimming over the more salacious details. Not that I could get away with that.

"So, was it good?" Rosie asked. "The sex, that is."

"It doesn't matter." My cheeks were on fire.

Rosie turned her thumb down. "Boo!"

Franky retook her seat. "I'd rather not know about the sexual prowess of a boy I used to babysit. Also, I can see this causing problems with Dash and the team dynamics."

"It won't. Hatch and I will not be taking it any further."

Rosie looked aghast. "Why not?"

"There's no future in it. I vowed not to get involved with any more hockey players. I'm choosing my career first."

Franky squinted. "The delivery career? Because that doesn't seem incompatible with a professional athlete."

"No, I want to work as an analyst or a scout for a franchise. Those jobs are team-specific, so I won't be following any guy if he's traded."

Rosie looked skeptical. "And does Hatch know this?"

"Of course he does."

Hatch might claim I was his end game, but even he couldn't fight the forward momentum of Project Summer.

"HEY, Ken, it's Summer. So, I'm calling to verify my afternoon schedule."

Kennedy hummed. "Didn't I send it to you?"

"Yes, you did. So I need to do a grocery run for Hatch Kershaw. And when I've delivered that, I need to pick up his dry cleaning but not before five p.m. It's only two p.m. now, so I don't have anything on the schedule in between?"

"Yep, that's it! You can take it easy in the break, grab a coffee, run some of your own errands. Whatever you want. It would be easier if you could pick it up earlier, but Hatch was steadfast about the timing."

"Okay, thanks. Just wanted to be sure. Oh, one more thing. Did Hatch request me?"

"He did. Said you did a great job the last time, and he wondered if you were available. Is that okay?"

"It's fine! Just curious." I clicked off and considered Hatch's grocery list.

- *Triple crème brie cheese*
- *Maple syrup*
- *Salt n' vinegar chips*

We could have ourselves a real party.

Armed with my small batch of groceries, I found Hatch waiting outside his door, looking every inch as delicious as the man of my dreams. His Rebels tee bunched at the sleeves, and the outline of his pecs made my fingers itch. He smiled as I approached, and a pure giddiness overtook me.

"M'lord."

"Wench." His lips curved. "Do you have a minute?"

How about a lifetime?

Really, Shelby Mae?

"I—what's that smell?" Something fragrant and delicious wafted from his apartment.

"Care to see for yourself?"

"Sure, Granny, what big cooking smells you have."

He grinned and ushered me inside. I went easy. But then I was a weak, weak woman where this man was concerned.

Hatch startled beside me because I'd just let out an ear-piercing shriek.

"What's wrong?"

"Lord, this is beautiful!" I grabbed his arm, needing something to keep me upright. "It's like something in a fancy hotel."

He had set a table with a pretty floral runner and full flatware settings, then added a pitcher of orange juice, a fruit plate, and a vase of flowers. Pale pink roses, my favorites. That should have bothered me because they were part of my wedding bouquet, but it didn't. I liked the idea of that bad memory being attached to something new.

"Thought you might like to eat in a nice setting. As Conor would say, 'chicks dig that shit.' It's a French toast bake, kind of a Kershaw tradition." He looked a little embarrassed, probably at my OTT reaction. "This is what I wanted to feed you for breakfast before you fled Saugatuck."

I couldn't believe he had gone to all this trouble. But then I remembered the schedule timing for this afternoon.

"Is this why I can't pick up your dry cleaning until five p.m.? Have you actually booked me for the whole afternoon?"

"I figured it's the only way to get on Summer Landry's busy schedule."

"I-I can't do this. It's not ... professional."

"Violates the client-delivery person relationship, does it?"

I thumped his arm for his cheekiness. To be fair, this example was probably the least egregious of our sins. It was only breakfast at two in the afternoon in the home of someone who employed me vis-a-vis an independent contractor. Barely a blip on the ethics radar.

We spent a couple of minutes getting situated: juice poured, fruit side plated, napkins unfurled (cloths ones with pewter rings. I was in heaven.). He had even made me English Breakfast tea in a teapot! I took a bite of the eggy bread and closed my eyes.

"So. Good. I love French toast, but this is out of this world. What's that flavor?"

"Flavors. Cinnamon, vanilla, and orange zest."

I licked my lips. His gaze dipped to my mouth turned smoky.

"And?"

"A dollop of love. Or that's what my mom would say."

I grinned. "That's it. Made with love."

"It's the first meal my dad made for my mom."

"Really? Was that after they'd spent the infamous one night together?"

"Before, actually."

My eyes went wide. "Sounds like a good story."

"You've probably heard some of it. Dad in his dinosaur-themed underwear and a Santa hat."

"I knew you were nicknamed Dino Boy, but I never got all the details. Dash said it was locker room talk, and I wasn't allowed to ask."

Hatch arched an eyebrow. "It's rather tame for the locker room. My mom used to be in the military with Levi Hunt—"

"The league's oldest rookie?"

"That's the one." Hunt had been famous back in the day for giving up his spot in the draft so he could serve his country. By the time his stint in the Green Berets was done and he was ready to join the league, he was considered old by hockey standards. "Anyway, my mom had completed her service, and she came to stay with her old army buddy, Levi Hunt. My dad was living across the hall, and he was interested. But Mom wouldn't give him the time of day. In public, anyway."

"Oh, I like where this is going. Secret crush, huh?"

"The way my dad tells it, Mom was stalking him online. He had a zillion followers on Insta and he was doing daily lives that she'd be watching with her finsta. Dad was always busting into Hunt's place to raid the fridge, so one morning, after he'd locked himself out of his own apartment wearing just a towel—"

"Classic."

"Right? He snuck in with a sack of groceries to replenish the fridge."

I started giggling. "That's what we're calling it? 'Replenish the fridge'?"

He took a sip of tea, clearly trying not to laugh himself. "Not a euphemism. Anyway, long story short, he made her French toast for breakfast, chicken parm for lunch, and they watched Hallmark holiday movies while my dad sat around shirtless in his Dino-themed boxer briefs."

"Parmed, armed, and charmed. Your old man had moves." *And so do you, Hatch Kershaw.*

"Mom was a goner, and when she got pregnant, he immediately stepped up. He never had a doubt about where he was meant to be. His own dad had abandoned his mom—

my grandmother, Aurora's daughter—and he was determined to not be like him."

"Oh, that must have been tough. Does he know his dad now?"

"Yeah. Grandpa Nick isn't the easiest guy. But Dad got Jason and Sean as new brothers, and their mom Jenny is awesome, so he figures the pros outweigh the cons."

I liked his attitude about it. "I didn't know my dad either."

He grasped my hand. "No?"

"He left when I was little, and my mom brought me up by herself." With an assist from Smirnoff vodka and Kraft Mac 'n' Cheese.

"Is she still around?"

"As far as I know. We fell out. Sometimes I think about getting in touch, but it feels like backsliding to this part of me I tried to leave behind. Shelby Mae is supposed to be history."

He looked thoughtful. "So, don't take this the wrong way. But when you were with Carter and working in the front office, you always came across as this sunny, wide-eyed, friend-to-woodland-creatures kind of gal. And I thought it was an act."

"An act?"

"I didn't doubt that you were a nice person. A kind person. But sometimes I'd get this snarky vibe from you ... but only with me."

I barked a laugh. "Because you deserved some snark. You were such a jerk to me!"

"True. And when you landed on me outside that window and we went on our fun journey to Saugatuck, you seemed a little sharper, more honest. In a good way, like you weren't holding your breath anymore and were more your-self. Maybe more like ... Shelby Mae."

Oh. "I was a bit wilder back in Thunder Creek. My rough edges needed to be smoothed so I could succeed."

"Ever think that you might be a little hard on that version of yourself? She's the one who got you out of a bad situation, who gave you the grit and determination to succeed. She got that tattoo, came up with the syllabus for Project Summer. She might even have prodded you to jump out that church window. Maybe she's not so far in the past after all."

I had always seen her as my nemesis, the wild swamp girl I needed to expunge. In breaking free of the Shelby Mae cocoon, I would become that beautiful butterfly, the person I was destined to be. How could that girl exist at the same time as Summer?

How could she not?

Maybe Hatch was right. I should be more forgiving of her.

Why, thank you, Summer!

Still with the snark, Shelby Mae?

After that detour, Hatch brought the conversation back to the main road.

"Carter said you didn't have any family at all. That's why Addy made sure all the team sat on your side."

In a way, the Rebels were my family, so it made sense even if they didn't quite understand how much it meant to me.

I swallowed. "I must seem like a strange duck to you. So alone I need the seat-filling services of an entire hockey franchise."

"I'm lucky I have a big family, and the way my dad has connected with players and more over the years, it feels like this huge network I can rely on. I can't imagine not having them. With that said, there's plenty of love and support to go around, Summer. It's not a finite resource."

Tears thickened my throat. "I do love being a part of this org. I wasn't close with my mom. She drank a lot and treated me like her property. She hooked up with this guy ..."

Hatch looked alarmed.

I placed a hand on his arm. "No, it wasn't like that. But he arranged for me to marry someone, an older man who was a pastor in Thunder Creek."

A muscle twitched in his jaw. "But you were sixteen."

"You can marry with parental consent at that age. Or you can be forced to marry because most kids are owned by their parents. I knew if I ended up trapped like that, I'd never leave. Next would be babies and a life I couldn't escape."

"You ran."

"My special skill, right? I'm obviously not destined to be a bride. I thought I was making my own choices with Dash, but apparently, I was just sleepwalking into another cage, one of my own making. I think hearing Mrs. C talking about these future kids of ours was the trigger to wake me up, right after I'd quit my job. I was about to lose all autonomy, like a Stepford Wife, and Dash was completely on board."

His thumb rubbed my wrist, its stroke incredibly soothing. "But you figured it out. And now you can do anything you want, Sunshine."

But I wouldn't marry. I wouldn't cede my independence ever again. What that meant for my future with Hatch ... well, I couldn't think of that now.

Anxious to turn my mind in a more positive direction, I changed the subject. "I have something to show you."

He gifted me a wicked grin.

"Behave, Dino Boy. Last night, I ran a couple of reports for Lauren and sent them to her."

"Very cool."

"It is. I love getting into the weeds of analyzing stuff, which made me think about your stats from last season."

His face fell. "Not so cool."

I shook my head. "Actually, it kind of is. It would be easier to demonstrate on a laptop. Do you mind?"

"Not at all."

We moved to the sofa, and I used the guest login he had given me in Saugatuck to access my profile on his laptop, which meant I could pop right into my Box account and open the files. Hatch sat close, but not close enough, giving me the space I'd asked for, though in truth, space was the last thing I wanted from this man.

I was so gone for him.

I refocused on the task at hand. "I ran an analysis on your playing stats from last season, looking for patterns based on who you were playing with."

"Other teams?"

"Other Rebels players. Analysts will do this to ascertain which players might be more compatible, which lines work best, that kind of thing. First off, I was interested in the times you and your dad played together versus when you didn't. And funnily enough you played much the same regardless of whether you were on the same roster or not."

He frowned. "Okay. So you're saying I still sucked even if my dad was on the same ice."

I chuckled. "No, I'm saying there didn't appear to be any significant pressure on you because you were on the same ice as him. You played better than you might think. It's odd how outside influences like the media and inside ones like your brain can make things seem worse than they truly are. What was more interesting was when I compared your stats with and without Dash."

"Carter?"

I nodded. "Often when you're both dressed, you're on the same line as him. And you two on the same line don't work that well. A lot of incomplete passes, lower possession percentages overall. But see here?" I pointed to a line in a graph that trended up. "This was the month Dash had a groin pull"—*still didn't stop him from wanting sex, though*—"and your stats were solid. Better than solid, pretty great. You were more likely to be paired with Peyton Bell, Francois Gaultier, or Dex O'Malley on the second or third line, and over thirty-two percent of your season's points came from this stretch alone. Then once Dash comes back, one, you're not put in as much, and two, when you are, you're usually on the same line as him—and that's not a good combo."

He looked stunned. Finally, he said, "Fuck."

"Yeah. Fuck."

He rubbed his mouth. "So I'm ... allergic to Carter?"

"Are you?"

He stood and paced, hands on hips. After a few torturous seconds, he stopped and faced me.

"I hashed it out with my dad last night. He's retiring after all."

"Oh wow!"

"It's still hush-hush, but in talking to him, I realized that I've been blaming my poor game on the wrong reason. I thought it was because I hated to suffer comparisons to him, and while that's true, the real reason is because I didn't want to be in Chicago. Near you and Carter."

"Oh." I moved the laptop to the coffee table. I wasn't sure how to feel about that. I was happy to blame my ex for

Hatch's poor form, but not so thrilled to take the credit myself.

"I especially didn't want to be on the same team as him. What you're saying with these stats confirms this. It's not that we're incompatible on the ice, though that might also be it. Really, it's that I was so fucking jealous that the sight of him screwed with my brain. And I'm seeing now that it might also have screwed with my game."

My heart thundered hard. "Are you saying … what are you saying?"

He stared at me, willing me to understand. I tried to piece together everything I knew from my time in the Rebels front office.

"You were in talks to join the Rebels three years ago, but it didn't happen."

"It didn't happen because I didn't want to see you and Carter together. You were another guy's girl, and that didn't look like it was going to change, so for my mental health I stayed away. But this past year, with it likely being Dad's final season, I bit the bullet. I refused to admit it to myself for the longest time. I wanted what Carter had. I hated him for being with you, and I—I hated you, too. Because I saw how he treated you and you stayed. I told myself that made it easier. If you could crash off the pedestal I'd placed you on, then I might not want you so much."

My heart keened for him. "Oh, Hatch, I can't believe you felt this way. You barely knew me."

"I knew enough. I knew that the sun couldn't hold a candle to you. That when you walked in the room, the air felt thick and heavy and I could barely breathe. That those gold flecks in your eyes sparked when someone pissed you off, usually Carter. I knew that I wanted and couldn't have you and that spending any time in your orbit would be hard for me. But I thought I could control it. I *needed* to, for my dad. For my family because they wanted this too, and I would do anything for them. So I signed with the Rebels, was celebrating my new team in the Net, and then—"

"Dash and I got engaged."

He nodded, and his shoulders—the ones that had borne a weight I had known nothing about—sagged. "I left for Saugatuck and all that stuff with Ava happened. I thought I was over you but ..." He trailed off, the emotion of the moment too much for him.

I had assumed Hatch just didn't like me because he had notions about my suitability as WAG material. I was so wrong. Rosie had said he was moody and withdrawn this past year, and I put it down to what happened with Ava. It never occurred to me that he might have had feelings for me all this time.

"When did this start?"

Another tortured look.

No. Impossible. "Not when we first met?"

"Hook, line, and Summer."

The night of the Rebels Christmas party, five years ago.

It was an infatuation, of course, because he had little to go on beyond that first, almost wordless meeting. But that didn't mean his feelings weren't real and important.

I had to let him know that wanting me so badly and for so long was the most amazing gift. Jumping up, I closed the gap between us and cupped his jaw. In searching those deep green eyes, I saw everything reflected back at me. Pain, torment, regret.

Love.

This man was in love with me. Had been for ... *years.*

I had never seen this in Dash's gaze. I had never seen it in anyone's.

So much of Hatch's behavior since I'd met him made sense now. It had hurt him to see me with Dash, so he stayed away. Any interaction between us was fraught with tension because he wanted me and couldn't have me. He had even made a huge career decision so as not to spend any time in my presence. Until circumstances forced his hand and he finally came on board during his father's swan song year.

I didn't believe in love at first sight. I had been attracted to Hatch when I met him, even considered what it might be like if he made a play for me. How I would have dropped Dash like a hot potato if Hatch had shown the slightest interest.

Because you knew there was something there.

But I wasn't a romantic. Not like this man before me.

If only he had said something.

If only I had realized Dash was a bad bet sooner.

If only.

And now, Hatch and I were caught up in this drama. I had also fallen for him, but I meant what I said: I wouldn't choose a man, especially a hockey player, over my career.

Of course, I had to have a career to choose first.

But Hatch was here now, his expression filled with such longing. All the obstacles crashed in the face of that look.

I touched my lips to his.

He moaned, like I was the water to his thirst.

Before I had a chance to react, he scooped me up and wrapped me around his body. Hard thighs, hard chest, hard … everything.

He must have been reining himself in before.

No more.

This was Hatch Kershaw unleashed.

CHAPTER THIRTY-NINE

Hatch

THE FLIP from misery to joy was instantaneous. She was finally here in my arms, where she was meant to be.

I was in love with this woman, and I wanted everyone to know it.

But first, I would tell her. With my mouth, my hands, my body. I would tell her with every kiss, every touch, every moment between us.

Lifting her up, I headed to the bedroom, needing room to work. Quickly we stripped, each moment we weren't touching a torture. My mouth found hers, moved to her neck, her shoulder, her throat. Repeat. Not an inch of her went untouched.

"I love your body," she said. "I love how well it fits mine."

Said just as I entered her, finding that perfect fit, loving how we just made sense. Our gazes locked and held as I moved inside her. She had never been shy with me, but there had been a reticence before, a reluctance to acknowledge the growing connection between us.

Not anymore. This was Summer in full bloom.

"You feel so good," I murmured against her mouth. "You feel fucking perfect."

She squeezed her muscles, testing my mettle. "Think you can hold on?"

"You'll never let me forget it, will you?"

"Not a chance, Flash Man."

"Better than Dino Boy. Or Boat Boy. Or St. Hatch of the Blue Balls."

I kissed her laughing mouth. How strange to feel such happiness in her presence when for so long I'd felt nothing but misery. I kept the thrusts slow and deep because that was how she liked it. And I loved anything that kept my woman happy and our bodies and souls connected.

I grasped her hand, laced my fingers through hers, and whispered, "I love you."

I didn't need to hear it back. The freedom of being finally able to tell her, to say it aloud while we were joined as one, was about as much as my pea-sized brain could take right now.

Her body told me everything I wanted to hear. That slick slap of our flesh, the breathy moans as each stroke found new points of pleasure, that final sob as she came. The sounds of Summer, the woman I adored.

And when I finally found release, I roared her name loud enough for the gods to hear and be put on notice. She was mine, and I was hers.

A while later, we lay wrapped in each other as I traced patterns with my finger on her shoulder. A perfect peace surrounded us.

"By the way, your sister knows," she said.

So long harmony.

"Apparently your seduction-by-cheese tipped her off. I can't believe you were so careless."

I squeezed her tighter and burrowed my nose in her neck. "I don't care who knows."

"*You're* not going to be a social pariah if people find out. That'll be me. Dash is going to think something was going on all along."

If people find out? More like *when*.

"I'll handle Carter. You won't have to even speak to him. And if he says another word against you, he'll regret it."

She didn't respond to that. So she was worried, but if this was going to work, we had to push through walls. No way was I letting her go now that we had finally figured this out. I had stumbled before when I should have steamrolled over the situation and taken my shot. Now no obstacle would stand in my way.

A phone buzzed.

"That's mine." Summer reached over to grab it. "It's a text from Ryder. He wants to talk to me."

Watching her face light up at the prospect gave me such a thrill.

"Better call him back then."

"Okay."

She pushed back the sheet and gave me a glorious view of her curves as she bent over, looking for her underwear.

"Cheese has treated you well," I said as I smoothed my hand over that peach of an ass.

She smiled over her shoulder. "Not just cheese."

WITH SUMMER on the phone in the other room—she had dressed before returning Ryder's call because she thought it would be odd to speak to her former boss naked—I took a moment to assess the current state of play.

Orgasms delivered and received. Check.

Feelings discussed and hearts flayed open. Check.

Sneaky plan in motion. Check.

I lay back, more than a little self-satisfied because finally everything was going my way.

Summer knew how I felt about her.

My dad and I had talked it out—damn, I wish I'd done that sooner.

And my mental block when it came to skating with Carter would soon be a thing of the past now that I knew the root cause. Summer and her amazing analysis had opened a whole new world to me.

This next year was going to be fucking awesome.

She appeared at the door, looking far more somber than the situation warranted.

"Everything okay?"

"You asked Ryder to offer me a job?"

I had asked him to keep my part in this under the radar. But Summer was no fool. She would wonder what had changed to flip Ryder's thinking.

"It's an internship with the Rebels. What you wanted. You get to do this thing that's your dream."

You get to stay with me.

"I don't want your help. I don't *need* your help."

"We all need help, Summer."

She threw up a hand. "And I've accepted about as much as I can. I'm accepting help from people every day."

"How is that a problem?"

"Because there comes a time when I need to stand on

my own two feet. Make my own way. I can't be relying on you like I did with Dash."

"I'm not him."

She looked exasperated. "I know that! But you're a professional athlete with a big career that will always come first."

I shook my head. "Who says? If you prove yourself with Ryder and the Rebels brass, you can get a job anywhere."

"Oh, is that what you're going to do? Make every franchise hire me when you're traded?"

"If I have to!"

She stared at me. "Hatch—"

"I can't always be the good guy. Sometimes, I have to take what I want." I threw back the covers and stood upright. Let her see what I was offering. The whole fucking package. "And I want you."

She held my gaze, and I would have kissed her—I needed to kiss her—but she had to make the move here. She was the one with doubts.

For the first time in my life, I had none.

She remained still. "This 'can't always be the good guy' thing? Are you saying that because you came on board the Rebels for your dad?"

"Right. I didn't want to disappoint him, so I made that move for him. Now I'd like to make a move for me. I waited a long time for you, Summer. Are you telling me you're going to invent some other reason for us not to be together?"

She took a step back, in the completely wrong direction. A weird look came over her face.

"Maybe you should have made a move five years ago before Dash and I were truly a thing. Maybe everything happened this way for a reason. As a warning to me *not* to get involved with an athlete. I'm no man's trophy. I'm not some prize to be won because you think you deserve it after you've suffered for so long. Suffering you brought on yourself, I might add, because you decided it was better to be a jerk to me instead of getting to know me."

This was going all wrong. I had obviously hit a nerve.

"That's not what I meant." I cupped her jaw and drew her close. "I've never thought I deserved you. But I do think you're a prize, and I'm prepared to work like hell to win you. Is that so bad?"

Her eyelids fluttered. "No, it's not."

"Tell me you don't care for me, Summer."

"I can't do that. You know I can't. But ..." She trailed off.

Fuck, that hurt. She cared, but not enough to make this work. "I see."

"I'm not sure you do. Of course I care about you, but I've already said I can't jump into something so soon. Now you're finding me a job and deciding how my life should be arranged. I just jilted my fiancé less than six weeks ago! This is happening way too fast."

Not fast enough for me. Summer was right about one thing, though: I should have fought for her back when I had the chance. Now the window was closing, and my fingers were about to get slammed.

"So we keep it under the radar for a while. We've done a good job so far."

"Oh sure! Conor knows, as do Addy, Rosie, and Franky. Jason, too, no doubt. Probably your parents, Aurora, and even Tilly! We've done *such* a great job. Are you seriously telling me I should be announcing a new relationship to the world and look, he got me a job, too?"

"These are just details. Try to look at the bigger picture."

She snatched a quick breath. "I am. I turned down the internship."

"What?"

"I had to, Hatch. The only reason Ryder gave that to me was because you asked him. And of course, the Kershaws always get what they want."

"Not always," I said morosely.

"I couldn't take something I didn't earn, but I did ask him about the internship program with the affiliate. It's less competitive, and he said I could apply for a spot there. He's confident that with the work I did for Scott and his recommendation, I should be able to get it."

My heart leaped. This was more like it. "The Rockford Royals? That's great. A long commute, but we can make that work."

She pulled away. "The internship is two months, and I need to live close by the offices. I have enough savings if I live on ramen."

I understood that she needed to do this, but it didn't mean we were over. Did it?

"I could come visit. Or you could come here."

She placed a hand on my chest. "No, Hatch. We need to call a halt to this madness."

Not now. Not when we were so close to the finish line.

"Summer runs again, huh?"

She jerked back, like I'd slapped her. Well, Sunshine, the truth often felt like a blow.

"This time, I'm running toward something. There's a difference. After Dash, I said I would put myself first. I meant my career—and now I have a chance to work in the field I love. To learn on the job." She sniffed. "You were never supposed to be part of that equation. Falling for you was not part of the plan."

Plans changed. People fell in love. Surely she was flexible enough to go with the flow.

She reached up, cupped my jaw, and kissed me, soft and perfect. I tried to hold onto that sweetness, but she pulled back before I could drag her in deep.

"Let's part as friends, Hatch."

Friends? My heart was fucking breaking here. I had opened a vein and she was supposed to be the suture.

"After all we've been through, 'friends' is the last thing I thought we'd be."

She peered up at me. "Is it so bad?"

"No, Sunshine," I lied. "It's not so bad."

CHAPTER FORTY

SEPTEMBER

Dash Carter has a New Love!

The Rebels forward was spotted frolicking at his family's private beach in St. Bart's with Sports Illustrated Swimwear Issue model, Sienna Colson. The curvaceous beauty couldn't be more different to Dash's former fiancée Summer. And she already has an invite to one of the Carters' many vacation homes. It took at least three years for Summer to claw her way into Mama Carter's good graces. Well done, Sienna!
-@HotGoss

Chicago Rebels training camp starts tomorrow, and all eyes are on Jason Isner, who has been brought on board to shore up a defensive bench made weaker with the retirement of Isner's brother, Rebels legend Theo Kershaw. Can the new Rebels' defenseman help as the team moves into a rebuilding phase? And while Hatch Kershaw didn't play to his full potential last year, it seems the Rebels are betting on the Kershaw genes to come through with a three-year contract worth 14.5 million. Will Kershaw Junior play better now that his father is on the sidelines? -@RebelsInsider

---

Summer

ROSIE

So Dash Carter is taken. How sad for the bunnies!

ADDY

She seems like a good fit for him.

ROSIE

Diplomatic as always.

ME

I'm very pleased to see him frolicking with a curvaceous beauty. Definitely more Dash's speed!

ROSIE

Lets you off the hook, I'd say. Though you're plenty curvaceous. At least you should be after the care package we sent.

ME

What care package?

JK, it's only crumbs now. But we do have cupcakes in Rockford so no need to go to all that trouble.

ADDY

Do you have Sweet Mandy B's? No, you do not. And nothing contributes better to the curves than a Sweet Mandy B vanilla cupcake.

ROSIE

Or chocolate! Oh, how did the presentation go?

ME

Great! The assistant GM marveled at my breakdown of our talent options. They even made a decision based on one of my recs!

ROSIE

Isn't that the point of you doing all the analysis? So they make decisions?

ME

Sure, but before, it seemed like I was creating reports for theoretical purposes. Now, I'm having an actual impact. It's a dream come true.

ADDY

Any hot hockey players?

ME

No idea. I no longer see muscles. How's living with Lars and Mabel?

ADDY

So good. I love seeing them all the time, and I know I'm going to love being home when Lars gets in from an away game once the season starts.

ROSIE

Instant delivery of the D! Gotta love the
live-in sitch, though I miss you, roomie. I
miss you both.

ADDY

Well, Summer can have my room if she
comes back to Chicago.

A FEW MINUTES after the text conversation wound down, a call came in from Addy. I answered immediately, knowing what was on her mind. It was the same subject she'd covered in every other call since I left Chicago.

She launched right into it. "You know this is good news, right? About Dash."

I didn't pretend to misunderstand. Reading the news about Dash's new girlfriend should have lightened my load and made me feel less guilty about what had happened with Hatch.

"It doesn't change anything, Addy. Dash would still be hurt if he knew about your brother, and it would cause major drama with the team. It's better that we leave things the way they are."

Addy made a noise of discontent. "Listen, I spent months last season worried about the team's dynamics if my dad found out about Lars. That shouldn't be a factor."

Easy for her to say now that her love life was sorted. "You know it's not the primary problem here."

"Sure, but don't you want to know how he is?"

Of course I did. I craved every last morsel of information about him. "If you want to tell me."

"How about 'I don't have a freakin' clue!'? He's spent the last six weeks traveling and has barely checked in. Because he's nursing a broken heart."

"He hardly knows me well enough to be in love with

me. I think he fell for a version of me that didn't exist. The woman he couldn't have. And yes, we connected while we hid away in Saugatuck, but it wasn't real."

Addy sighed. "And when you came back to Chicago? You were working for Kennedy and he was running the hockey camp. Those are real things. That was real life. Are you telling me you weren't still drawn to each other? Because I saw how he looked at you at dinner, Summer. How he made up that cheese plate! All this time, he's had it bad for you. Don't you want to see where it goes?"

I already knew where it went. To hurt and heartbreak. I was thrilled to see him renew his contract, and I expected he would have a great season. Maybe an even better one without the distraction of me.

"I let my life become smothered by Dash's. I can't do that again with another man, especially one whose career always takes precedence. I want a job that uses these skills I have, and that requires me to be tied to an organization."

I could hear her smile. "You really love what you're doing, don't you?"

"I do. And even if I was lucky enough to get a similar gig with the Rebels, what happens if Hatch is traded? Do I up sticks and follow him around? After Dash, I vowed I'd put myself first."

She hummed. "My brother's pretty miserable without you, though."

Believe me, I could relate. "I hate hearing that."

"Well, you should! Stop running and give him a chance. So you don't want to be the second banana, but surely in this day and age, you can figure out how to make this work. Long-distance, phone sex, remote work. There are solutions for everything, but you guys have to talk. Let's face it, the lack of talking is what got you into trouble with Dash in the first place. Now you're going to *not*-talk your way out of something that could be amazing?"

Was that what I was doing? Falling back on my usual patterns? Finding excuses to not be with Hatch because I was scared of being hurt? As each hurdle fell, I seemed determined to find another to take its place.

Summer runs again. That's what Hatch had said, and part of me agreed.

The problem was I couldn't trust my instincts. Scrappy little Shelby Mae would know what to do, but Summer was too much of a coward.

CHAPTER FORTY-ONE

Hatch

I HAD SPENT the last six weeks of the summer following in my sister's wanderlust footsteps: Split, Brasov, Helsinki, Edinburgh. I left Summer alone, except for a couple of cheese deliveries, but Addy kept me informed. She was smashing it in her internship as I knew she would.

By the time training camp was ready to start, I was determined to put my best skate forward. New season, new teammates, new attitude. I was even feeling magnanimous toward Carter who had moved on in a public way. Summer had to have known that—it was all over the tabloids—and the fact she didn't reach out to me hurt. I understood the obstacles, but that didn't make being apart from her any easier.

On day one of training camp, Carter blew into the locker room like he'd just landed in his family's private jet, high-fiving everyone in his path. "Hey KJ, how was your summer?"

"Not as good as yours."

"Yeah, you saw that? Definitely leveling up."

"Glad to see you're back in the game, man."

"Fuck, yeah. Now let's skate!"

So, we did, and I wondered if what had happened between Summer and me in Saugatuck was merely some hazy dream. I wanted to hold on to everything: that first kiss, parking at the lake, cheese nights and summer breezes. But the longer we stayed apart, the more those memories faded and the dimmer my hopes became.

Training camp provided a semi-decent distraction. It was nice not to feel like a Rebels rookie anymore, and hanging with the guys made me realize how much I'd missed people, especially goofs like Boden and Dingaling. I also missed my dad's energy in the locker room. He was finally taking a well-earned rest while he contemplated next steps. But it was great to be playing on the same team as my uncle. Jason was so solid in the back third and having him in my life on a more regular basis was going to do great things for my mental health.

Because, fuck, I needed it.

I needed my support system. My family. My people. Most of all, I needed Summer.

I wondered who had her back. Was she getting what she needed in Rockford? She didn't know anybody there but maybe that was how she liked it. Lone-wolfing it to prove she could. At least she had Rosie and Addy checking in.

On the last day of camp, we had just finished up a hard session. I had felt really good out there, like things were connecting. Someone must have run some analysis because

Coach didn't put me on the same line as Carter. (Did I dare hope that Summer had provided her reports about me to the coaching staff? You bet I did.)

Instead of Carter, I ran with Gaultier and a new kid called Asher, which sounded like a name you gave a supermodel. As for C-Dog himself, he might have been enthusiastic at the beginning of training camp, but there was only so far that would take him. It looked like he'd drunk a bit too much tequila and eaten a few too many of his personal chef's French meals over the break. He came out slow and never really skated his way into form. Sixty guys were fighting for a place on the roster, and I had to wonder if Carter would make the cut.

While the team player in me worried about that, the lovelorn idiot in me didn't mind at all.

Back in the locker room, I took a seat on the bench ready to untie my skates. My head was down and the only reason I looked up was because a shadow fell over me.

The punch, when it came, hurt like a mother.

I held my jaw and took a good look at a wild-eyed Carter, who loomed over me with his fist clenched and cocked, ready for another. Slow on the ice didn't translate to slow in the locker room, evidently.

"You fucking asshole. Did you really think I wouldn't find out?"

I had no idea what exactly he knew or how he knew it. I wasn't going to deny it, though. If anything, it was a relief.

"This isn't about you, Carter."

"Oh, really? You've been screwing my girl for fuck knows how long and it's not about me?"

"Could we talk about this in private?"

"No, we cannot." He lunged at me, only to be restrained by Jason.

"Let's not, Carter," Jason said. "You want the world to know your business?"

The world already did—or at least had a heads-up. The rest of the team was watching us, double-fisting metaphorical buckets of popcorn.

"How long?" Carter bit out. "How long have you been fucking my fiancée?"

"Nothing happened …" I caught my uncle's eye. "Until after the wedding."

Jason winced.

Carter's mouth fell open. "Don't believe you, dude! Do. Not. Believe."

"It's the truth." Maybe Summer had told him? I had to admit the punch would be worth it if that was the case. It might mean she was ready to move forward.

Ready for us.

"You took her to your secret little love nest? Acted like a couple mere freakin' hours after she left me? What kind of teammate does that?"

I had no defense, but I tried all the same. "It was over between you before anything started. I might not have behaved well, but I can assure you of that, Carter."

His expression shifted from anger to disgust. "You want my sloppy seconds, Kershaw. Have at it."

This prick. "You know what? I feel sorry for you. You had this amazing, loyal, incredibly special person in your life and you couldn't see it. But let's be clear here. If you say one more harsh word about Summer or so much as breathe in her direction, make no mistake, I will fucking annihilate you."

His eyes widened, and his mouth moved wordlessly. Finally, he yelled, "Asshole!" and broke a stick against a bench before crashing out of the locker room.

"Holy shit," New Kid Asher said.

Gaultier muttered something in French that didn't sound all that complimentary.

"How do you think he found out?" Jason asked.

NoBo held up his phone. "Tabloids, dude. Someone saw you in Saugatuck."

I retrieved my phone from my cubby. The screen flashed several missed calls from Special Agent Lauren, along with a text notification from her.

> 💀 Urgent. What the FUCK is this?

A link blared ominously from the message bubble. I clicked into an article from everyone's favorite tabloid, *Hot Goss*:

Dash Carter's Ex in "Summer" Hideaway Shocker!

It looks like Summer Landry, ex-fiancée of Rebels player Dash Carter, has found comfort in the arms of his teammate, Hatch Kershaw, son of Rebels legend, Theo. We all wondered where she had run to after her wedding day escape—and it looks like it wasn't very far. The new couple were spotted in a coffee shop in Saugatuck, Michigan, where the Kershaws have a vacation home, the day after the wedding that never happened. While Summer was wearing a Detroit Motors ball cap pulled low to hide her pretty features, there was no doubt that this was the blonde beauty who threw the entire wedding day congregation into turmoil when she jilted Dash at the altar. And just in case you have any doubts, Hot Goss spoke with various townsfolk who confirmed that Summer stayed at the Kershaws' lake house and was even spotted with Hatch at dinner and on a boat outing during her stay there.

Neither Hatch nor Summer have been seen together since. We do know that, until recently, Summer had been rooming with Hatch's sister, Adeline. Sounds like they've had plenty of opportunities to build on their acquaintance, though we have to wonder if they knew each other better than everyone thought prior to the abandoned wedding? And what impact will this have on the Rebels team dynamics this season? Now that Theo Kershaw is no longer around to shield his son from criticism, Hatch will have to skate solo on this one—or call on his uncle Jason Isner's defense skills to come to the rescue.

A hush had fallen over the locker room as everyone read the article. What a joy for us all to have this united experience. Team building par excellence.

"Someone gave them the photo," Jason said, referring to the one in the article.

"Coffee Shop Gemma sent it to Mom, and she sent it around." I stared at Jason. "You don't think someone in the fam leaked it?"

He gave me a look of *how dare*. "More likely they got a tip-off that Summer was seen in the Tuck, and they headed down there and started showing her picture around. Once they got to the coffee shop, I'll bet the woman who runs it handed over the goods. End of the summer season, probably looking to juice her sales." He leveled a serious gaze at me. "Better out than in, H."

"Is it? Summer doesn't even want to see me. She told me to stop sending her cheese."

"Cheese?" NoBo, who had been pretending not to listen, weighed in.

Before I could respond, my phone rang with a call from Lauren.

"I'd better get this." I stood and headed outside. "Yeah?"

"Don't 'yeah' me, you asshole! Is this true?"

"It might be."

"Might be? Don't fucking mess with me, Kershaw. I will end you!"

I believed she would. "I helped her leave the wedding. Not planned or anything, I just happened to be there. She needed a place, so I kept her hidden for a bit."

"Well, obviously not well enough! Wait until Carter hears."

"Yeah, about that." I filled her in on the latest episode in the Hatch-Summer-Carter psychodrama.

That earned me another profanity-laced tirade. Finally, she calmed down enough to come up with a plan. "I'll put a call into Natalie in Rebels PR and try to get ahead of it. As for you? Go home and do *not* show your face until I tell you."

AS WAS my habit in times of stress, I headed to my parents' house. I walked downstairs into the den to find Dad kneeling in front of the media cabinet.

"If it isn't scandal in the flesh!"

"Oh, shut it. I've already heard about it from Mom and Lauren. Aurora thinks it's great though."

"That woman does love the drama. You can sell naming

rights for her next martini. Rebels Love Triangle has a certain ring to it."

I took a seat on the sofa. "What's up?"

"I'm looking for the DVD from the first time I won the Cup."

"That's in the cloud, Dad. Addy digitized them all."

"I know. I just like watching it on the old media—there it is!" He popped the disc in the player and sat beside me. It was Game 7 against LA, a game I'd watched a million times as a kid.

"This is one of your best."

"Yep, I was on fire that game." We watched for a couple of minutes, long enough for my dad to get whatever he needed from a twenty-five-year-old hockey game. Retirement was hard for him, and I expected he would be reliving the glory days for a while.

He turned to me and assessed my bruised jaw. "Carter?"

"Yep."

"Within his rights, for sure. But now that it's out in the open, you and Summer can finally figure this out."

I groaned.

"No?"

"She doesn't want to be second-best in any relationship."

My dad nodded his understanding. "Listen, I know all about waiting out a woman. Your mother tried my patience to the extreme before you were born. She was spooked, and I was fucking perfect."

I rolled my eyes. "Can't say I've been perfect. But I have been all in. Once I knew she was truly free from Carter, I pursued her. I knew she wanted a job in this business, and I made that happen. But it was the wrong move."

A grimace this time. "Did you really think that taking away her agency was the way to go? She wants you to sympathize, empathize, listen. Not throw your weight and wealth around."

"Sounds like you're speaking from personal experience."

My dad gave me a wry smile. "So, you know a lot about how your mom and I got together."

"'A lot' is putting it mildly."

His grin was wry. "I only tell you so you can learn from my mistakes. Well, not only was your mom determined to handle her pregnancy with you as independently as possible, we also had the problem of your grandparents."

My mom's parents were once grifters, meaning they bilked people out of their savings and used their daughters, my mom and my aunt Amy, to help them with their scams. Mom was well out of their schemes by the time she met Dad, but she kept her past a secret because she was worried he would think she was out to swindle him.

The woman didn't know Theo Kershaw at all.

But I did. I knew exactly what my dad would have done. "You tried to deal with them?"

"Uh huh. I paid them off. In my defense, I felt that this was the best way to keep your mom stress-free in the final months of the pregnancy. She didn't quite see it that way. According to her, I was patriarchal and infantilizing and a whole bunch of other big words I can't remember. So I hear what Summer's saying. She gave up her job because someone she thought she loved or she thought loved her told her she didn't need it. That job meant a lot to her, right?"

I nodded. "And I thought getting it back for her or something like it would make her happy."

"But were you thinking of her happiness or were you

thinking of your own? And I know we like to assume that they're one and the same. But not always. When I paid off George Butler, I convinced myself this was for Elle's benefit, but really it was so she would see me as her protector. Her savior. I had ulterior motives that aligned with my preferred self-view."

This sounded a little too familiar.

"I want Summer to be happy. I thought the job would make her happy. I also thought it would keep her in Chicago. With me."

He raised an eyebrow.

"Is it so selfish to want her with me? To want to carve my own path?"

So we weren't just talking about Summer.

"No, son, it's not. But she needs to figure out what she wants first, without pressure from you."

"But what if she figures out this job is all she wants? Or that she doesn't love me like I love her?"

My father looked at me, more serious than I'd ever seen him. "That's always possible."

So *not* what I wanted to hear. "She said that I fell for someone I didn't even know. That I couldn't possibly be in love with her because that person didn't exist. She was just some princess I put on a pedestal. And maybe that was true, once. But not now. I got to know her, Dad, the real her. That's the Summer I fell for."

She had never told me she loved me, though, and for the last two months, I'd sat with the knowledge that the debacle with the job was just an excuse to cut me loose.

"You've given her time to think on it. You have a couple of days after training camp ends and the pre-season games begin." My dad leveled his gaze at me. "Time to make your play, Dino Boy."

CHAPTER FORTY-TWO

Summer

MY PHONE WAS BLOWING up with notifications, as if I needed anyone to tell me what was wrong. I had fucked around, and boy was I finding out.

I needed to handle this in person.

So here I was, adulting the hell out of it, yet still feeling like a fraud as I stood before Victor in my old apartment building. With cupcakes.

"You didn't have to do that, Miss Landry."

"It's Summer. And I never thanked you properly for saving my belongings. I hope that didn't get you into trouble."

"It was a pleasure. And no trouble. A couple of days after Mr. Nyquist picked up your stuff, I got a visit from Mr. Kershaw who told me not to worry. Gave me his number and said to call if"—he lowered his voice—"Mr. Carter tried to punish me for going against his wishes. Said he could get the team's lawyer to assist with any employment issues. Luckily, Mr. Carter didn't retaliate except to act a little cold to me, but it was nice to know a guy like Mr. Kershaw would think of a guy like me."

Yes, it was. "Theo is one of the best."

"Not Theo. Hatch, Kershaw the Younger."

Hatch had done that for Victor? And he hadn't breathed a word about it. That was so sweet, but then everything about Hatch Kershaw was.

The phone on Victor's desk rang. "Yes, Mr. Carter. Right away." He turned to me and said, "You can go up now, Miss Landry."

"It's Summer," I muttered.

My internship had ended yesterday in Rockford, and this morning I drove to Chicago to see Dash. He'd unblocked my number and was apparently receptive to the idea that I would visit in person and apologize for how much I'd hurt him.

Again.

But first he needed to exert another power play. For fifteen minutes, I had been forced to wait in the lobby.

I was to squirm.

I was to grovel.

I was to crawl to him on my knees.

That's when it struck me.

Shelby Mae would never.

What was I doing here when the one person I truly wanted to see was less than a mile away? I had messed up with Dash, and I had apologized for doing so. I wasn't going to apologize for the circumstances of my getaway, or the fact I felt free for the first time in years, or that Hatch was the man who made all that possible.

Was the man I loved.

And I *did* love him. So fucking much.

I took a step back from the lobby desk.

"Miss Landry?" Victor frowned as I backed up even further.

"I won't be seeing Mr. Carter today." Or any day. I refused to give him any more of my power.

"You won't?" Still baffled.

"No need for you to do a thing, Victor. Enjoy the cupcakes!"

THE FIREPIT'S FLAMES FLICKERED, casting shadows on the various plants and flagged stones around the patio. I pulled the fleece blanket tighter around my shoulders, hoping to fight off the chill of the night as well as my doubts.

He wasn't here.

After abandoning my visit to Dash, I had tried to surprise Hatch at his condo. When he didn't answer, I called Addy, who said he'd gone to Saugatuck. So here I was, aiming to surprise him with a grand romantic gesture.

The only one surprised was me. The house was shuttered, the rooms dark. I had retrieved the key from under the stone frog, and now I was sitting outside because I felt closer to him here than anywhere else.

Sending him a text after going dark for so long seemed weird. But I needed him to know I was trying.

> Funny story …

> I came to the lake to find you. Kalamazoo, not the other one.

> You're not here.

Then I waited. Each moment that passed without a response was absolute torture. Distancing myself from him had seemed like the best option, but once our secret became common knowledge, a new clarity overtook me. I had an idea about how to make things work, but first I needed to talk to Hatch. See if he felt the same, if he had felt the void of separation as deeply as I did.

If he could see his way to forgiving me for pushing him away.

I checked my phone again, its silence damning. The night air edged cooler, the flames started to dim, and with them my hopes of—

Was that a footstep?

A figure appeared at the end of the path leading to the not-pool house. Hatch emerged from the shadows, looking seriously grumpy.

"Why aren't you in Rockford?"

"My internship ended yesterday. I drove to Chicago to see you today."

"Well, I drove to Rockford to see *you*."

"You did?"

"I wanted to surprise you. Then Addy called me and said you were here."

"She told me *you* had come here."

He smirked. "Well, I didn't want anyone to know I was going to see you, so I told everyone I was heading to Saugatuck for a little pre-season R&R. I'm tired of everyone knowing my business."

He came closer, and just the sight of him in the firelight had my heart clattering wildly. His face was tan, his hair a little long, his eyes—sparkling, if somewhat irked that I couldn't for the life of me make it easy on him. Typical Summer.

"You're here," I breathed.

"I am." He held out his hand. "Let's go for a drive."

As my palm curled around his, I wanted to squee, but I was also too nervous. I shouldn't have been. After all, we'd taken decisive steps toward this moment. Both of us moving toward our destinies, another chance at redemption.

He opened the passenger side door of the SUV and helped me inside. On the road, neither of us spoke. I knew where we were going: a place that had history for us, where we had come together in explosive fireworks. Once parked, it was second nature to allow him to hoist me on the hood. He climbed up and wrapped the blanket around my shoulders.

"Still beautiful," I said, gazing at the lake.

"Sure is."

I turned to find him looking at me with that trademark Hatch intensity. "Still corny."

"Hey, it's a romance classic."

We were here, where it all started, and I hoped, not where it would end.

"How did your internship go?"

"I learned so much. I felt like my work really made a difference."

He smiled. "I'm happy for you. You deserve to have your hard work recognized."

I reached for his bruised jaw. "Dash hit you." Addy had told me and I couldn't resist touching the evidence.

"I had it coming."

"I didn't talk to him after the article came out. I thought I should but then ... I realized I can't keep apologizing. I can only do what will make me happy."

He turned to me, his eyes shining with so much hope it almost broke me.

"Your career—that makes you happy. I get that, and I'm sorry I tried to fix it my way."

"No, please. You were trying to do right by me. It might not have been the best method, but the intention was lovely. I overreacted. Lauren told me about your contract. How you made signing it contingent on getting me into the internship." I shook my head. "She was not pleased."

His lips curved. "I signed anyway. Ryder had made a good faith effort to honor my request. And I wanted to stay in Chicago."

This guy. "But you did that. For me."

"I would do anything for you, Summer. Tell me you came to see me because you want to make it work. We can do long-distance, I'll fly to wherever you are, I'll fucking clone myself. Whatever it takes."

I couldn't help my smile. "More than one of you? Not sure the world could handle that."

But he didn't smile back. He was hurting. I had hurt him, and he wasn't ready to joke about it, clone offers notwithstanding.

"Tell me why you're here," he whispered, his voice laced with pain.

"To see you. To talk to you. To ask you about what comes next."

"Ball's in your court, Sunshine. You tell me."

I bit my lip. "I've found a job."

"Already?"

"I've been working toward it for a while now, but I couldn't tell anyone until some things were settled. Have you heard about Lauren's plans?"

"She's leaving Mallinson to create her own boutique sports management agency." A long pause while his mind made the connections. "You're going to work with Lauren?"

"She asked me to come on board to do research and analytics with a view to becoming an agent."

His eyes lit up. "Based in Chicago."

"Right. And if anything was to happen, such as my boyfriend being traded to another city, I can work from anywhere. There'll be a lot of travel, and our schedules might be crazy but—"

He drew me close. "Ball's in my court now."

And then he kissed me.

The relief at his lips touching mine flowed through me like a sensuous wave. I had missed him so much, and this closeness, in the dark where it all began, was filling my heart to overflowing.

"I can't believe you're here," he murmured against my lips. "So many times over the last couple of months, I've looked up at that moon and wondered if you were watching it, too."

"In all those strange countries? I want to hear everything about your travels."

"Sad in Split, heartbroken in Helsinki, miserable in Marseille?"

"I'm so sorry."

He shook his head. "It's okay. I needed to be all those things. I needed to miss you like hell because while I was doing that, you were on your own journey. One I hoped would lead you back to me."

I touched my forehead to his. "This journey of mine didn't just start the day we said goodbye. It started the day I jumped out of that church bathroom. You broke my fall, Hatch, in more ways than one. You caught me, rescued me, held me close. I needed that. I needed you. Then I needed you to let me go."

"Which I did. Reluctantly."

"Yes. But you still did it. You tried to shield me and keep me safe, but ultimately you recognized that I needed to rescue myself. That I had to make my own way, at least for part of the journey."

He released a sigh. "I get that. I do. Only you've been making your own way for so long, Summer. I think you thought Shelby Mae was gone, replaced by this new, improved you. But she's still with you. She's the one who had the guts to claw her way out. To fight. I want Shelby Mae and Summer. I want all the parts of you."

I swiped at a tear. "Thank you."

See? I'm not such a bad bitch to have on your side.

No, Shelby Mae, I guess you're not.

Hatch smiled at me. "Also, I want to travel that road with you, not because I think you can't manage by yourself, but because I think the path sometimes has potholes and rocks. I want to fill those gaps and kick those rocks out of the way for you. I also happen to think the view from the path looks better when two people are traveling it, looking out for each other." He shook his head. "Damn, that's one tortured analogy. What I'm trying to say is that I don't want to be the boss of you. How could I be when you've owned my heart for so long?"

More tears welled. "I've made you suffer, haven't I?"

"It's been good for me. The Golden Child shouldn't get everything too easy."

I laughed softly. "You mean you're glad you didn't shoot your shot all those years ago?"

"Fuck no. We've missed out on five years, and frankly these last two months have probably taken another five years off my life, so you owe me. Big time."

I smiled. "Ten years?"

"Forever."

I liked the sound of that. I leaned my head against his shoulder.

"I love you."

"Thank Christ, because I love you, too."

"I think I've been falling for you since you made me a sandwich that first day, since you put taking care of me above your heartache. I realize now how hard that was for you, but you were still there for me. No hesitation. No reservation."

Hook, line, and Summer.

"I'll always be there for you." He gentled me back on the hood. The moonlight caught the copper tones in his hair, the perfect chisel of his jaw and cheekbones, giving him that dark angel energy I loved. My man had never looked more beautiful.

Or more focused.

I pulled at his belt buckle. "Think you can last this time?"

Those moss-green eyes shone back at me, more than up to the challenge. "With you, Sunshine, I can last as long as you need me."

EPILOGUE
JANUARY

Theo Kershaw Says Goodbye

It's expected to be a glittering event tonight as Rebels, old and new, gather to send off legendary defenseman, Theo Kershaw, into his golden retirement years. Though some of us here in the Hot Goss bullpen doubt the Empty Net, a seen-better-days sports bar in downtown Riverbrook, can really do "glittering," insider sources tell us that the place holds special meaning for Theo and his wife of over twenty-five years, Elle Butler Kershaw. A trawl through the Hot Goss archives reveals that the Net, as the locals have nicknamed it, was once the site of a physical altercation between Theo and then Rebels teammate, Levi Hunt. (Will former player Hunt appear at the party? Or does this ancient beef still cast a pall over their once-tight friendship?) One source, who insisted on anonymity, informed us that Elle told Theo about his impending fatherhood in this very bar. Or the owner's office, to be precise, where apparently all the good stuff related to the Rebels happens.

I don't know about you, but I feel like I know <u>way</u> too much about Hatch Kershaw's conception, gestation, and birth! Those rumors about Theo Kershaw's dinosaur-themed underwear on the night the eldest Kershaw was conceived were confirmed by Hatch himself during an ESPN interview at the start of the season. Kershaw Junior was much more cagey about his relationship with his teammate's former fiancé, replying with "no comment" when pressed. But as long as the readers crave it, we'll keep reporting on the Rebels royals and their R-drama.
-@HotGoss

Hatch

"SO I DON'T KNOW about you, but I feel like I know *way* too much about Hatch Kershaw's—"

"Yeah, yeah." I cut Jason off, then glared at him to shut him up. I'd like to say that *Hot Goss* had gone too far this time, but I'm sure they'd pissed me off even more at some point in the past.

Let them gossip all they want about my personal life because my professional one was on fire. No one could argue with my results so far this season. Three months in, I currently led the league in goals and was second in points. I'd finally found my groove. (And Jason didn't have to screw up any passes to make me look like "the good Kershaw," either.)

Another reason to celebrate was the exit of Carter, who had decided to take some time off after a couple of wobbly games and healthy scratches. The truth was that after saying he "didn't need this shit" one too many times within the earshot of Coach, he was encouraged to take a break to see if it resulted in an attitude adjustment.

It did not. Carter was out.

I was confident I could have survived the rest of the season with a griping Carter shooting stabby eyes at me during every practice, shift, and post-game celly. But Summer didn't enjoy seeing him around, and my woman's mental well-being and happiness were all that mattered. So what if I wouldn't get the chance to rub his face in it as he'd unknowingly done to me for five years? I could be the bigger man here because I had won.

And my prize was coming toward me, violet-blue eyes glittering, a sultry sway to her hips, or maybe it was those thigh-high boots that gave her all that sexy swagger. Tonight, they would definitely be staying on when I went down on her.

"Sunshine, you're late."

She wrapped her curvy body around me and peeked up. "I had to finish a report for the boss lady."

"Figuring out which hotshots will one day replace me?"

She grinned. "Better watch your back, Dino Boy."

Lauren had barely waited six weeks before promoting Summer to junior agent at her brand-new boutique agency. My Summer had a knack for it. Knew the game, the people, the players inside out. Could turn on the charm when she needed it, too. Sometimes I'd hear her on the phone with a potential client or wavering team owner, and that Southern twang got more pronounced as Shelby Mae stepped up to the plate.

Damn, I loved that scrappy girl from Mississippi. She had brought Summer home to me.

"How's your dad doing?"

I looked over at him, yukking it up at the bar with Levi Hunt, Gunnar Bond, and Cal Foreman, just a few of his former teammates and closest friends. Everyone had come out to see him—the Durand brothers, the Chase sisters, Rosie's dads, his old coaches, all the players who had mentored him, and the ones who learned how to be good teammates and better men just by spending a moment in his presence.

"I think he's going to miss being a Rebel."

"Once one, always one, right?"

I kissed her forehead. "It's a pretty special club. Even front office alums and Rebel WAGs get member jackets."

She smiled up at me. "I like the Kershaw club better, even if I don't officially carry the name."

She was still skittish about the idea of marriage. Each day, the trust between us grew stronger, and I hoped that there would come a time when she'd trust herself enough and agree to be my wife. Until then, I'd regularly pat my pocket to check on the ring Aurora had given me, the one I carried with me at all times, just waiting for that sign. And in the meantime, I'd hold my girl close and never let her go.

"You're one of us, Sunshine. Don't you forget it."

I looked over her head at Jason, who I had happily ignored as soon as Summer arrived. His attention was elsewhere, but before I could track his target, Conor bounded up, blocking my sightline.

"Hey, lovahs! What's shakin'?"

My brother was home for a flying visit to attend Dad's

retirement party. He'd had a great start with Detroit and was already being talked about for the Calder, the trophy they gave to rookies at the end of their maiden season.

He kissed Summer on the cheek, high-fived me, and turned to Jason.

Then turned right back with a typically Conor-cryptic, "Interesting."

"What is?"

"Just something I know."

I rolled my eyes. "Are we in for a night of vague-booking and veiled references to your favorite hot beverage?"

"That would be Shelby Mae's fave." Conor had loved learning that tidbit about my girl's past. "You still digging that teapot I gave you?"

She squeezed his arm. "It was my favorite birthday present, Connie."

"Ahem," I coughed.

"After my man's gift subscription to the Cheese of the Month club. I mean, duh!"

I brushed my lips across the top of her head. Damn, I shouldn't have been this happy.

Conor nudged Jason. "I see your sworn enemy is here."

Jason frowned, and his cheeks flushed slightly. I followed his gaze to Rosie and Franky, who were on their way over to greet us.

"Don't you mean yours?" I asked. Conor and Rosie liked to snipe at each other like a couple of fishwives.

Rosie hugged Summer, then kissed me and Jason on the cheek. She made a point of ignoring Conor. "Hey, girl, I found one of your bras stuffed between the sofa cushions!"

Color painted a watercolor bloom over Summer's cheeks. "Not sure how that got there."

I had an idea. Fun times while the roomie was away.

"Must have been left behind when you moved in with your hockey player boyfriend before the holidays." Rosie rummaged in her purse. "I have it here—"

"Later, Ro. Sheesh!"

"I dunno." I squeezed her waist. "I think we'd all like to see it now."

"Hatch!" Said like *Haa-itch*.

I loved when her country came out. But I didn't have time to appreciate it because just then, Franky took off her coat.

And turned.

Summer gasped. Rosie grinned. My mouth fell open.

Because Franky St. James was sporting a baby bump.

Conor raised his eyebrows in my direction. "Yep."

Somehow, this fucker already knew.

Franky pushed her glasses back up her nose. "As you can see, I'm pregnant. I was loath to steal focus from Theo's party, but Rosie insisted I come. I hope he doesn't mind."

She looked over to where my dad was busy shaking Dex O'Malley's shoulders. The man had no idea what was happening in this small corner, but as he was a lover of the drama, I suspected he would be thrilled. And then he would be curious.

Like us all.

"I'm sure you have questions," Franky said.

This statement was greeted with a chorus of "oh, no!" and "not at all!" followed by heartfelt congratulations. This was her dream, and I was thrilled to see it coming true for her.

Franky chewed on her lip. She was nervous, a look I didn't think I'd ever seen on her. "I should visit the bathroom before I ingest any liquid."

Summer and Rosie took her by the arm on either side. "We'll come, too."

My girl shot a quick look my way, assuring me she would get the goods. As the trio headed off, I couldn't help noticing Franky's searching glance over her shoulder.

With the women out of range, I turned to Conor. "Okay, spill."

"Remember that time you warned me to wrap it before I tap it because I said people were too attached to their sperm?"

My heart sank to the unvarnished floorboards. *Connie, what have you done?*

"Don't worry, bro, it's not me! Someone else we know decided that it was time to unwrap it and tap *his* swimmers for a very important mission." My brother gave a hammy chin jerk toward Jason, his expression one of barely restrained glee.

Summer didn't need to get the goods from Rosie after all. The tea was being poured right here.

Jason blew out a breath, rubbed his mouth, and said:

"Well, kids, let me tell you a story."

Summer

I ENDED the call and sent a prayer of gratitude up to the heavens.

"You get 'im?"

Turning, I was immediately distracted by the handsome and gloriously shirtless deck hand who had just dropped anchor over the side of the boat in Kalamazoo Lake.

"Hmm, what's that?"

"Eyes up here, Shelby Mae." Hatch ran a hand over his chest, slick from sunscreen. A rather evil move, I thought. And he wondered why my tongue was rubber and my bikini bottoms were damp? He looked like a Greek god who had decided to gift us mere mortals with an impromptu visit.

Reluctantly, I shook myself out of a Hatch-induced trance. "Yeah, I got him." Him, being Jean-Luc Toussaint, aka JLT. Rumors had swirled at the most recent All Star Game that he was in the market for new representation.

Landing a big fish like that was huge for me, and the look of pride on my man's face told me I'd done good.

"C'mere, Super Agent."

"I'm still Agent-in-Progress."

He wrapped his arms around me, squeezed my butt, and said, "After two years of making Lauren and your clients a shit-ton of money, I'd say we're past 'in progress.'"

"I know. Just trying not to jinx it."

Next week, I would sign the paperwork that made me a full-fledged partner in the agency. Two years of hard graft had produced this amazing result, but right now it was the last thing on my mind. I'd signed JLT, my big task of the month, and I felt like school was out for summer. On the boat, bobbing lazily on the lake, my guy holding me tight—only one thing could make it better.

I took a step back and shrugged out of my linen coverup.

Hatch blinked. "That's not my sister's bikini, is it?"

"No. I've put on so much weight that if I wore that, I'd be flashing every boater on this lake." But I *had* purchased a tiny red number that was about 10% more fabric than Addy's childhood swimwear. I gave a twirl, so the matching high-cut bottoms also got their due.

"Sunshine, I'm not sure I want anyone to see you in that."

"They can look, but only you get to touch." And touch he did, his hand cupping my butt cheek as his greedy gaze roved all over my body.

"Christ Almighty, how did I get so lucky?"

"Right place, right time," I murmured against his lovely, searching mouth. "Of all the church windows ..."

"It could have been NoBo. He was there a couple of minutes before you made your exit."

"But it wasn't." I squeezed his gorgeous ass in return

and rubbed against the hard evidence of his growing interest in me and my bikini. "It was you. It was always meant to be you."

I had given a lot of thought to the years we lost because we'd both been too foolish to recognize what we needed. But Hatch was right in that we had to see what was missing first. That we needed to fight for it. That's what had led us here.

Panting, I drew back. "We should eat before this gets out of hand."

"Eat, you said?"

"Cheese, Hatchling."

While he grabbed the pre-prepped cheese board, I poured us some sparkling water. As he set the board down on the table, I motioned to the cooler. "There's more cheese in there."

Curious, he opened the lid. "Triple crème brie? I have that one already."

"Not this variety."

He picked up the spare wheel of Brie, wrapped in wax paper, and peeled it open to reveal a standard round of cheese.

"What's going on?"

I took it from him, and with shaky fingers, separated the pre-sliced halves, pulling the top one back like I would a jewelry box. Ta da!

His gaze shot to mine. "I don't want to alarm you, but there's something embedded in that hunk of cheese."

I swallowed. "I wanted to—I didn't know how else to do it. Aurora's ring is in there—"

"I can see that."

Hatch had been carrying his great-grandmother's ring around with him for the last two years. Biding his time until

I gave him a hint that I was ready. The puck was in my zone, and he would never force my hand—or ask for it— until I was sure. Which meant it was up to me to make my move. To put aside the fear that I was giving up a part of me instead of making myself whole.

"I know you want this—or at least, I thought you did before I ruined a perfectly good round of Brie with a couple of hunks of metal."

Not just Aurora's ring. He pulled both rings out of the soft cheese and held them up to the light.

"You got me an engagement ring?"

"I did." Nervous as a virginal bride, I jumped up from the bench where I'd been sitting. "I'm getting this all wrong."

A slow, knock-me-dead smile curved his mouth. "No, you're not. Just tell me what's in your heart."

I inhaled. "If I did, we'd be out on this boat all summer because there's so much in there, so much feeling for you that I don't even know where to start, Hatch. I love you so much. Every part of me loves every part of you. You wanted me for so long, and I think I've been worried I couldn't live up to that. Because your love for me is so ... epic! I'm sorry I waited to take this extra step and make my promise to you."

"Baby, you have nothing to be sorry for. Nothing to live up to. Every moment with you is a blessing and a gift, ring or no ring. But I love that you're ready to do this. If you really are ready." His voice held a note of trepidation, like he couldn't trust me to go the distance.

Oh, I was going there. "Hatch Wayne Butler Kershaw, will you marry me?"

"Shelby Mae Summer Landry, it'd be my honor."

And then I burst into tears, but they were happy ones, an outpouring of relief and joy. Hatch hugged me close and kissed my forehead and told me how precious I was to him, and then he slipped his great-gran's ring, a classic oval-cut solitaire, on my finger though it still had some cheese attached. That seemed right, somehow.

"You don't have to wear the ring I bought," I said. "I just thought it would be strange to have nothing for you."

"Are you kidding? I want everyone to know I've finally managed to pin the quick-footed bride down. Wait until those *Hot Goss* hacks hear about this." He looked at it more closely. "There's something engraved on the inside."

"Yeah, crossed hockey sticks and a butterfly."

His lips curved as he slipped it onto his finger. "This is perfect." He held his hand next to mine, our rings side by side, the noon sun glinting off the precious metals.

I touched his chest, loving the *th-thunk* of his fast-beating heart. "Is it? Perfect? I know you want more."

By more, I meant children. I saw how Hatch acted around his little sister, his teammates' babies, and especially with Jason and Franky's little one. He was big brother and favorite uncle to all the ankle-biters.

"Hold up there, Shelby Mae. I'm barely engaged and you're already trying to railroad me into bein' a daddy?"

"Your accent needs work." I peered up at him. "Just sayin' I know your heart's desire, Hatch Kershaw."

He gathered me close. "Sure, I want all that. The woman of my dreams, a flock of kids, a long career, health and happiness for everyone I love. But I also know you're on a mission to establish yourself as the best sports agent in the country. We've got time. And when I get broody, I'll just tickle someone else's kid right under your nose and remind you of how great a dad I'm going to be one day." He dropped a kiss on my forehead, then traced his lips over my eyelids and cheekbones. My happiness was so bright it was liable to make my heart burst. "First, we have a wedding to plan. Have you heard? We're getting married, Sunshine."

"We are." I giggled as I landed a kiss on his sensual mouth. "It doesn't get cheddar than this."

Up next in the Chicago Players series: *Top Shelf Stud*

ACKNOWLEDGMENTS

Thank you to my editor, Kristi Yanta. Thanks also to proofreader Julia Griffis for your perfect attention to detail.

To the team at Qamber Designs, my gratitude knows no bounds for the beautiful illustrated covers you've created for this series.

All my thanks goes to Miranda for helping me stay on top of communication with my readers.

And thank you, Jimmie, for all your support these last few years as we adjusted to a nomadic life. Onward to the next adventure!

ABOUT THE AUTHOR

Originally from Ireland, *USA Today* bestselling author Kate Meader cut her romance reader teeth on Maeve Binchy and Jilly Cooper novels, with some Harlequins thrown in for variety. Give her tales about brooding mill owners, over-sexed equestrians, and men who can rock an apron, a fire hose, or a hockey stick, and she's there. Now traveling the world with her soulmate, she writes sexy contemporary, sports, and LGBTQ+ romance featuring strong heroes and amazing women and men who can match their guys quip for quip.

WRAPPED UP IN YOU

Hot in Chicago Rookies
COMING IN HOT
UP IN SMOKE
DOWN IN FLAMES
HOT TO THE TOUCH

Hot in Chicago
REKINDLE THE FLAME
FLIRTING WITH FIRE
MELTING POINT
PLAYING WITH FIRE
SPARKING THE FIRE
FOREVER IN FIRE

Laws of Attraction
DOWN WITH LOVE
ILLEGALLY YOURS
THEN CAME YOU

Hot in the Kitchen
FEEL THE HEAT
ALL FIRED UP
HOT AND BOTHERED

For updates, giveaways, and new release information,
sign up for Kate's newsletter at katemeader.com.

www.ingramcontent.com/pod-product-compliance
Lightning Source LLC
Chambersburg PA
CBHW051435190726
48289CB00001B/204